COMMUNITY LIBRARY
3 2301 00171292 0

D0531812

ALL THAT FOLLOWS

ALSO BY JIM CRACE

Continent
The Gift of Stones
Arcadia
Signals of Distress
Quarantine
Being Dead
The Devil's Larder
Genesis
The Pesthouse

NAN A. TALESE | DOUBLEDAY
New York London Toronto Sydney Auckland

JIM CRACE

ALL THAT FOLLOWS

a novel

This book is a work of fiction. Names, characters, businesses, organizations, places, events, and incidents either are the product of the author's imagination or are used fictitiously. Any resemblance to actual persons, living or dead, events, or locales is entirely coincidental.

 Published in the United States by Nan A. Talese / Doubleday, a division of Random House, Inc., New York.

www.nanatalese.com

Originally published in Great Britain by Picador, an imprint of Pan Macmillan Ltd., London.

LIBRARY OF CONGRESS CATALOGING-IN-PUBLICATION DATA
Crace, Jim.
All that follows / Jim Crace. — 1st ed. in the U.S. of America
p. cm.
"Originally published in Great Britain by Picador, London, in 2010."—T.p. verso.
1. Musicians—Fiction. 2. Hostages—Fiction. 3. English—Texas—Fiction. 4. Texas—Fiction. 5. England—Fiction. I. Title.
PR6053.R228A78 2010
823'.914—dc22
2009031130

ISBN 978-0-385-52076-8

PRINTED IN THE UNITED STATES OF AMERICA

10 9 8 7 6 5 4 3 2 1

FIRST UNITED STATES EDITION

The whole problem with the world is that fools and fanatics are always so certain of themselves, and wiser people so full of doubts.

—BERTRAND RUSSELL

ALL THAT FOLLOWS

1

THE HAIR IS UNMISTAKABLE: old-fashioned Russian hair, swept back from the forehead, thickly and unusually abundant. Leonard stands on the rug a meter from the television screen to see more closely. The video footage is grainy and unsteady, purposefully amateur. The man reading the prepared statement in the curtained room does not mean to be recognized. Indeed, he has masked his face to the bridge of the nose with what appears to be a child's scarf. His voice, crudely distorted on the sound track, is childlike too. He wears sunglasses, defiantly unfashionable E-clips, ten years old at least. The light beam from the camera is lasered at his chest and the lower half of his scarf, so that what little of the face can be seen—the ears, the eyebrows, and the forehead—is underlit and ghostly. But still the hair is unmistakable.

Leonard sits. He stands to find the remote console. Sits again. He is breathless, and it is with a shaking hand that he clicks open an on-screen toolbar, pastes a password, enters "Personal Briefcase," selects Menu, Archive, Album, Austin, and waits for the file of photographs to download. A hundred or so chattering thumbnails peel out of the icon and tile across the desktop. It is easy to spot the group of images he wants. They are indoor shots, flash bright, and the only ones without an intense sapphire sky. Those days in Texas were almost cloudless. He highlights a single photograph with an archive date of 10-27-06 and expands it. And there they are, the three of them, posing side by side in Gruber's Old Time BBQ, meat spread out across the table on butcher's paper, with polystyrene tubs of pinto beans and coleslaw, and a line of bottles—Shiner Bocks. The room is blue with smoke and, he remembers, blue with swearing. He zooms in on the man to the left in the photograph and drags the expanded image up the screen so that it is parked next to the newscast box. It is only a few minutes before the video segment is repeated, and only a few seconds after it begins Leonard is able to freeze an image of the masked face. Now he can compare. He cannot tell exactly what he hopes to find.

On the left, photographed without much care or interest eighteen years previously by the girl who cleared tables at Gruber's, is Maxie, the big-smiled American son of Russian immigrants. That much is certain. His black mustache and beard were sparse and adolescent in those days. His hair, long on top, parted slightly to the right, was swept back over his ears, with just a few loose strands. He looked like the teenage Stalin in that famous early photograph that became the poster for the biopic in the early 2020s, *Young Steel*, unfeasibly handsome and intense. And on the right, snatched from the newscast, is the masked man, guarding his identity and filmed by whom? A comrade, colleague, accomplice? Neither of the images is well defined—a frozen, hazy video clip and an overexpanded photo detail, a mosaic of pixels. The evidence is blurry at best. But Leonard is convinced. These two images, separated by almost eighteen years, are of the same man: the same swept-tundra look, the same wind-sculpted brow, the same off-center widow's peak. No sign of balding yet, or gray. It's Maxie, then. Maxie Lermon. Maxim Lermontov. On active service, evidently. His head at least has aged extremely well. His head has aged much better than Leonard's own. Leonard's hair is gray, a little prematurely. It is not abundant. As (almost) ever, Maxie has the edge on him.

Now Francine has come home. He hears her keys, the two sentinel notes of the house alarm, the impact of her bags on the hall floor, the clatter of her shoes, the squeak and whine of the lavatory door and the air extractor. He listens while she urinates, flushes, rinses her hands, squeaks the door once more. Should he say anything about his disquieting discovery? he wonders, deciding no. But her not kissing him when she comes into the room, her not even pretending a smile, and him so disappointed, seeing her so pretty, makes him speak.

"See this," he says.

"See what?"

Again he banks the images and places Maxie-masked and Maxie-young next to each other on the screen. "What do you think? Are they the same man?"

"Probably." She chin-tucks. Her Chinese teacup face, he calls it. The corners of her mouth are down. It means she is impatient, wants to get to bed. "Who is he, anyway?"

"This is the one"—he points—"who's got those hostages. You haven't seen the news?" She doesn't even shake her head. What does he think a teacher does all day? "This one . . . well, he's someone I used to know. In America." Again he chatters thumbnails across the screen. "See, look, that's me. In Austin. Almost twenty years ago."

"You eating meat?"

"Pretending to."

"Boy, I should say. What is that place, an abattoir?"

Maxie is still talking to the camera, though after Francine has gone upstairs to bed the telescreen is muted to a whisper. He is repeating his demands and suggesting a way—some government concessions, some troop withdrawals, safe transit to an airport, a flight to somewhere he won't specify—for "finishing this without *mishap*," a word so much more menacing than *bloodshed*, say, or *death*, especially when spoken behind a mask and dark glasses, especially when deliberately mispronounced and with the slightly comic Yiddish inflection that Maxie is using to disguise his voice. Leonard shapes his hands ten centimeters from his stomach, miming his saxophone, and blows a pair of notes, three times, at the screen: *Misch-app. Misch-app. Blood-sched.*

The same reporter, accumulating coats and scarves as the evening gets chillier, updates every half hour, standing in the street fifty meters from the house of hostages. The "suspects," who took refuge "randomly" when fleeing through the gardens after what the police are calling "a bungled incident," have at least one handgun that has already been "discharged at officers." They might have more, she says. The broadcast helicopter shows a suburb darkening, the whirring siren lights of police, ambulance, and fire brigade, and the orange glow of curtained houses. The garden trees and sheds and greenhouses become more formless as the night wears on. The hostages—no details for the moment—are being baby-sat by Maxie Lermon, as yet unrecognized, as yet unnamed.

Leonard flattens the futon and fetches the guest duvet from the cupboard. He will not go upstairs tonight. Francine will already be asleep. Any noise he might—he's bound to—make (he's a slightly lumbering left-hander) will irritate her: the light switches, the bathroom taps, the floorboards and the mattress, the intricate percussion of getting into bed in a modern wooden house with its muttering, living materials. She needs more sleep than he does because she's never quite asleep. She's waiting for the phone to go, waiting to be woken by the phone, dreaming of it so persuasively that many times she has sat up abruptly in bed and reached out for the handset in an almost silent room. She lifts it, even, and only hears the dial tone and her own somersaulting heart.

Leonard could pick up the telephone at any time to offer information to the police. He knows he should. Identify the unidentified. Supply a name. Provide intelligence. But it is already late and Leonard is still trembling. It has been a tense and shocking day, and he is too tired and troubled for anything except retreat. It has gone midnight. Everybody will be sleeping now, or trying to. The police, the comrades, the hostages. Leonard will be sleeping soon, still dressed, on his futon, so frequently his bed these days, the television flickering, Francine unreachable upstairs. Tomorrow he should phone. He will phone. He will never phone. He does his best to sleep.

2

LEONARD LESSING DOES NOT DREAM of Gruber's BBQ or Maxim Lermontov. His dreams belong to Francine yet again—not her in person exactly, not as far as he can recall, but her in mood. His has been an apprehensive night, and when he wakes too early, disturbed by the muted, active telescreen, its erratic light hoisting and flattening into the tightly blinded room, and by the closed community of garden birds crying off a jay without success, he knows that if he does not rise at once, get on, attend to Francine's current and persistent misery, do what he needs to do, then he will steep like unattended tea, growing darker by the moment. Leonard has been a morning man for many years. It is not difficult, once he is standing, to feel genuinely . . . well, not elated. Optimistically agitated, perhaps. Every dawn renews his hope and courage, briefly, he has found. This is the day, is what he always thinks. He will not disappoint himself today. He will not fail again today.

For once he does his morning exercises, not just the stretches to improve what elasticity remains in his right shoulder, but also the routine of bends and sit-ups that he observed fairly regularly before his illness or injury or accident or whatever it was that caused his rotator cuff to lock and hurt in the first place. He has been lazy recently. Pain is his excuse, and boredom. He cannot work if simple acts like putting on a shirt and tying his laces cause such lasting discomfort. How can he lift a music stand or put his back into a saxophone? On his doctor's advice, he has awarded himself a sabbatical, an unsolicited but welcome break from studios and concerts, and even—imprudently—from practicing. He is less thrilled by music and performance than he used to be; he has fallen out of love with gigging, not only the bragging company of musicians, their often self-destructive lives, but mostly the endless tours, the exhausting and precarious nights away from Francine. He has become a man who seeks the tranquillity and shelter of home. His current well-being is dependent on having the house, with its modern, regulated lack of clutter and its old-style reclusion, to himself for much of the week, especially during the day, when the natural light is at its most flattering and consoling and every room and landing is nuanced with blocks of tapered radiance and shadow that can seem as physical as furniture. He'd rather be at home than anywhere. "You've turned into a dormouse. Or do I mean a tortoise?" Francine says. Either way, it is not flattering. But Leonard does not doubt he deserves this prescribed hiatus, this chance to hibernate. His patrons and audiences can wait six months or so. Likewise the bank. Likewise the garden. Likewise the household maintenance and repairs. Likewise his social life. His knotty frozen joint postpones everything. He hoped to celebrate his fiftieth birthday feeling youthful, fit, and heroic. Instead, with only two days of his forties left, he has become gimpy and irascible. Today his right arm will not reach in front of him much farther than the elbow of his left. With effort, he can touch his waist. He cannot reach his back with it at all. But still he perseveres with his routine. It gives him time to plan his journey. A short trip away from home will do him good, he thinks. To drive is better than to phone.

He washes at the downstairs sink and, naked in their long, wedge-shaped kitchen (or the trapezium, as the architect has called it), turns on the panel television and lays a tray for Francine's breakfast. An autumn-term weekday, with an early start for her, and so it's coffee, muesli, yogurt, fruit. He makes a thermos for himself—green tea, lime juice, and honey. He's trying to stay young and fit through diet. Nevertheless, he has put on weight; he has a drummer's paunch. His muscles are becoming spongy.

The *Rise-Time* television show on the little kitchen screen has no new angle on the hostage house. The same reporter as last evening, this time wrapped in a green shawl, her hair tied back, says that she has nothing fresh to say. The night was quiet and uneventful. The police are happy to be patient. The hostages have been identified by relatives and neighbors: an unnamed family of five. Three generations, evidently. Leonard listens for their street vicinity and writes it down: Alderbeech. Two trees where probably no woods or orchards have survived. He knows at once what kind of upright suburb it will be. He can get there in an hour or so if he uses Routeway points and takes the motorway. Then what? He can't be sure what he might do, or should. Being there, he thinks, will help him to decide.

Francine is not sleeping. Her reading light is on. Leonard hesitates outside, holding her tray unsteadily in his good hand. He can't settle on what lie to tell. He'll keep it simple, he decides: tell her that he's going walking. She won't be pleased to hear that. She'll be working, after all, plagued by toddlers and curriculums, while she imagines he is having fun on what promises—incorrectly, as it turns out—to be a dry and pretty day. October at its best.

"I wish you wouldn't do that," she says, when finally he backs open the door and steps round the bed to place the breakfast tray across her lap.

"Do what?"

"Walk about with nothing on. Before breakfast."

"You used to like it once. More than once, even."

"Well, that was then." She's smiling, though.

"Curtains?"

"Please."

He has his back to her as he pulls aside the heavy Spanish prints until the sunlight slants and corrugates across the bed. "I might go up into the forests today. See some trees. Some autumn color. I need the exercise. I'm getting portly." He pinches the flesh at his waist and stretches it out a few centimeters. She cannot see his face, though he can see her in the window glass, sitting up in bed and staring squarely at the skelfwood cupboards opposite.

"Yes, go," she says. "Enjoy yourself"—not meaning it but wanting to.

HE DRIVES THE GIGMOBILE, his aged liquid-fuel camper van, taking his time. He has all day. He is not even sure if he will complete the journey. He does not take the motorway after all. Making it circuitous and slow, on minor routes, not only saves him Routeway points but allows him greater opportunity to change his mind and flee back home. At first he does his best to concentrate on Maxie Lermon, listening to rolling news on the radio, playing out the conversation he might have with the police officers, and even rehearsing an interview on television with the woman in the shawl: "Yes, we were friends." But Francine's odd remark troubles him. "Well, that was then." What does she mean by *then*? Before what? Before he became the tortoise with the paunch? He shakes his head. He's worrying too much, as usual. But certainly he felt foolish and disappointed when she said, "Well, that was then." He hoped to be attractive to her, naked, one-armed, with the tray. Once, many years ago, when they first met, she called him "Waiter" as he walked round the room with nothing on, and the breakfast he brought her went cold while they made love.

So music, then. To cheer himself, he will listen to himself. Most of his own recordings as well as cover versions of his compositions are stored on the van's system. He does not like to play them at home. He is by nature both modest and secretive. But when he is alone and driving, who is there to care? He scrolls through the menu and selects *Live at the Factory*. This session, which was broadcast on the radio to hardly anyone as part of the "Approaching Midnight" series of new work, was judged too obdurate and odd at the time (a raging winter evening, almost ten years ago) to be issued by his recording company. This is Leonard's own download. It is not perfect. But he is fond of it. He truly stretched himself that night—and was rewarded for the stretching in life-changing ways. "In an unexpected adjustment to this evening's jazz recital," the announcer explains, as the van heads south through suburbs and doughnut estates into the managed countryside and its network of preservation highways, "composer and saxophonist Lennie Less will play unaccompanied. Owing to the severe weather, his quartet has not been able to reach Brighton." There is laughter and applause, and someone shouts out "Less is more," as someone nearly always does when Leonard's in the lineup. Then the concert host, reduced to cliché by the pressure of live radio and the panic of a green on-air light, overloads the microphone with "Ladies and gentlemen, let's welcome to the Factory tonight . . . on tenor" and then steps a pace too far away, reproved by his own feedback, to offer, not audibly enough, "Mister. Lennie. Less." ("It rhymes with penniless, as befits a jazzman," his agent said when they agreed on this stage name instead of plain, unexciting Leonard Lessing.)

LEONARD STILL REMEMBERS—and relives—the panic he felt that evening. His colleagues, turned back by blizzards, abandoned vehicles, and debris on the motorway just ten kilometers out of London, warn him only twenty minutes before the gig that he will be alone. All those fresh pieces they rehearsed and that are promised in the program will have to wait for the next night's venue, Birmingham's New Drum, weather permitting. The lead sheets and pages of chord patterns in his music case are useless now. Leonard will have no sidemen, then, to share the blame; no rhythm section to provide depth and camouflage, or any stout string bass to anchor the bottom line for him; no call and response from familiar colleagues, feeding him their hooks and cues; no points of rest; no nodding in another soloist at the end of a progression and stepping out, side-stage, to rest his mouth and hands for sixteen measures or so, or to empty his spit valve, adjust his reed, or sip a little water. Here he will be the solitary player, the nightlong soloist, the only face onstage. There can be no hiding place. What to play? When he first hears the news about the snowbound quartet, he thinks that unless someone at the Factory can magic up a *Real Book* full of comforting standards within the next few minutes, he has no choice but to offer a program of lollipops and show tunes—undemanding numbers he can reproduce entirely from memory.

But by the time the sound engineer appears at the door of the eerily empty green room to finger-five that the concert is about to start, Leonard has accepted the inevitable: for this radio concert he must not take the easy option. Everybody is expecting more. Lennie Less does not play show tunes or unembellished standards, no matter what. Lennie Less plays only taxing jazz. He'll start cautiously, he decides finally, with his tenor version of a Coltrane classic solo, "My Favorite Things." He's played it, duplicated its patterns and glissandos, many times before—as an encore, something obvious that even the shallowest of aficionados can recognize. He knows it is a bit of a hot lick, begging for predictable but unwarranted applause—the enthusiasts will be clapping themselves, their own tuned ears—but applause is always a welcome boost at the start of any show. It is an agitating prospect, though, and frightening. Live audience, live radio, no band—and some evidence, from what he's spotted through the stage curtains, that the concert hall is papered with free tickets. Every seat is taken, and that is suspicious for a contemporary music event. There are more frocks and ties than usual, and many more women. He'll be playing not only for the usual pack of devotees, in other words, but for jazz virgins and jazz innocents as well. They could be restless, wary, bored, and certainly irritated. And the venue itself is off-putting: unraked plastic seating, poor sight lines, overhead industrial plumbing, and deadening acoustics—curtains, for heaven's sake! The Factory is devoid of what jazzmen call *the climate.* Even now Leonard sweats at the memory: the trembling apprehension of that long wait before the Brighton broadcast begins, how shakily he adjusts his mouthpiece and the tuning slide, how he runs the keys and rods of his tenor so anxiously that his knuckles begin to clack, how he fusses over his jacket sleeves and his belt, unable to get comfortable or stay cool, how he practices his embouchure and lolly-sucks the reed until his lips are tense and dry.

But that applause, that darkened stage, the flustered concert host, the sense that at least some in that full, damp audience have battled through a storm to listen to his saxophone, the "live on radio," make him feel—almost at the moment that his lips close on the reed, almost too late—too playful for Coltrane's dark and modal meditation. But not too playful for some nursery rhymes. His entry still thrills him, the walk from backstage, playing, out of sight for the first few bars, a distant sobbing animal, the legato opening—the cheek of it—of "Three Blind Mice." In the key of C. Four slow bars: three notes / three notes / four notes / four notes. Simplicity itself. See how they run. And then he finds the spotlight, his semicircle of sound boxes, microphones, and water bottles, his comfort zone where he can bend his knees, fold his shoulders, lean into the saxophone, and blow. See how they bleed, he says to Brighton with his horn on that appalling night of early snow and wind. Listen to the cutting of the carving knife.

However, as Leonard remembers all too well when those first slow but risky bars fill up the van once more, there is no grand design as yet. There's certainly no cunning. He is simply taking what he has and stretching it, making phrases from those few root notes, subdued at first, using vibrato sparingly and attacking most notes on pitch, like a beginner. He is not ready to decorate or bend them or embark on any doodling with fillers and motifs. He knows he needs to make it sparse and stable, until he's settled in. He's just pub crawling, heading for the next bar, not rushing the notes but waiting to catch them as they pass. Keep it tidy till the sixteenth. That's the rule. But then, too soon, he makes his first mistake, and has to dare. It is a misjudged voicing that, even as he listens to it now, ten winters on, causes him to shake his head and suck his cheeks, as if to take the notes back from the air.

Yet this is where the concert finds itself. The best of jazz is provisional. It often emerges in panic from an error. He hears himself attempt to rescue the mistake by restating it until the error is validated by repetition and seems to be deliberate and purposeful. He listens to the audience, both the virgins and the devotees, applaud his juicing of the blunder. They've all been fooled. They think he has planned every note of it. Do they imagine that he planned the snow, that high gusts from his saxophone have blocked the motorways with trees?

Leonard's band has not been fooled, of course. They are never far from his thoughts, even as he busks his way toward the final bars of this first tune, if tune it is, even as he syncopates the singing rhyme, cheekily matching every grace note with a note denied. He can sense them laughing as he plays. Trapped inside their car, hard up against their instrument cases and overnight bags, listening to him on the radio, they will not have mistaken his misjudged voicing as anything but wide of the mark, a blaring gaffe. And they will not have missed his nervousness and inhibition, the loss of pitch caused by a tight throat and tense mouth. He knows they will be chuckling as they hear him "digging his way out of jail," as Bradley, the percussionist, calls it. So he plays for them as well, and even though they cannot comment on a single note, he hears their contributions in some auxiliary chamber of his ear. No improvising jazzman will deny that there is telepathy. Indeed, the group's most recent release is titled *ESP*. So Leonard measures every note he plays against each chord—each sweetness or each dissidence—that they might have offered had they been onstage with him. He sends his absent rhythm section clues, invites them to add accents to his saxophone, to harmonize with him, to influence the color of his play. He imagines how a single furry and hypnotic note that he holds for the full length of a bar might be accessorized if there were comrades on the stage. Thus he perseveres, extravagantly, a soloist in imagined company, murmuring, then sharpening his edge, more shaman now than showman—until that eerie modest rodent tune, as familiar as heartbeats, becomes both pulsing anthem and lament.

LEONARD LISTENS AND TAPS his fingers on the steering wheel in half-time, happy with himself, happy now to have been so happy then. He sees Lennie Less—as Francine has so many times recounted seeing him that evening—from the third row of the gallery: the spotlight at the center of the stage, his casual and expensive suit, blue-black, the brass-gold glinting saxophone extemporizing its one-night-only bars. *"Did you ever see / Such a sight in your life / As three blind mice?"* The van replays it back to him through her.

Francine says she was attracted to him "not quite straight-away—but soon." Disarmed by music she has not expected to enjoy—she's come reluctantly, at the last moment, and only to oblige her sister, who's been given several tickets—and by the flattering stage lights, which make Leonard seem complex and shadowy, she has begun to think of him, despite the grotesqueries of his bulging throat and cheeks, as someone she might like to kiss. And she's had fun, she says. At times his playing has become knotty, shrill, and edgy, just as she's feared. On occasions he is more blacksmith than tunesmith. It is witty, though. And it has helped, of course, that she has rushed a few drinks in the pub beforehand and that she, and every other virgin there, has quickly recognized the common language of each tune, the program of nursery rhymes that on an impulse he has decided to play once his "Three Blind Mice" has struck such chords. "Baa, Baa, Black Sheep" follows, to more laughter and applause—initially, at least. The less sophisticated and less sober concertgoers, Francine included, have actually sung along with "Yes sir, yes sir, three bags full," until Leonard's tenor deprives the singers of their tune and embarks on eight measures of bare but oddly poignant bleats, loosely pitched at first, then joyously unruly.

These are the moments—the blacksmithing, the bleats—that most please and terrify Leonard, the moments of abandonment when he can sense the audience shifting and disbanding. He fancies he can see the flash of watches being checked. Certainly he can see how many in the audience are on the edges of their seats and how many more are slumped, looking at their fingernails or fidgeting. He knows he is offending many pairs of ears. They've come for those *cool* and moodily bluesy countermelodies that have made the quartet celebrated, not for these restless, heated, cranked-up overloads. But still he has to carry on, he has to nag at them, because he won't be satisfied until he has lost and possibly offended himself. So that night, *this* night, at Brighton's Factory, this night of radio and storms, this night of musical soliloquies, is one he cherishes because he has not backed away. The watches and the slumpers spur him on. As soon as he's dispatched the mice and sheep, he's taking further liberties, he's giving Francine and two hundred others in the audience, plus any late-night listeners who've not switched off their radios, "Ding, Dong, Bell," sending pussy down the well into musical deep space with a tumbling crescendo, followed by some risky trickery, not blowing on his saxophone at all but drumming with his fingers on the body and the keys close to the microphone so that it seems a lost and distant cat is scratching frantically at bricks.

However testing this might be, however intractable, no one there can say that Lennie Less does not love or does not suit his instrument, his perfect southpaw tenor, a costly Selmer paid for by *Mister Sinister*, his unexpectedly successful first collection. From the sardonic extra curve of the crook where the body meets the mouthpiece and the lips to the great flared bell that, depending on the slope and stoop of his back, can just as readily swing priapically between his legs as fit snugly against his abdomen or thigh, this saxophone has become a visceral appendix to the man. Flesh and brass seem unified. It is as if his fingertips and the flat tops of the keys are made from one material, as if breath and metal share substance and weight. So he is mesmerizing. Even for those who are impatient with his gimmickry or antagonized by his excesses or dislocated by his syncopation, there is plenty to wonder at and watch. This man who has come onstage in a dark suit with a shiny patch on the right trouser leg, at pocket level, where the bore and bell of his Selmer have worn the cloth, this man so evidently beset by nervousness that he at first can hardly lift his head to face the audience, this musician who has opened so carefully and timidly with "Three Blind Mice," has started to transmogrify—there is no better word—before their eyes. It's theater. You could be deaf and it would still be theater.

Leonard feels it too. He's on the tightrope, balancing. It's technique and abandonment. He is elated, yes, but he is also terrified. Usually when he is stepping in to improvise he can expect to play what he hears: all his daily practices, those hours spent running through arpeggios or exploring patterns, accents, sequences, and articulations in his song repertoire, provide him with a soundscape of tried and tested options; he merely has to choose and follow. He has exhaustively prepared in order to seem daringly unprepared. But here, tonight, he is not playing what he hears; he is hearing what he plays, hearing it for the first time, and only at the moment he—his lips—impart it to his reed. Each note is imminent with failure. But there is no retreat. Nor does he want to find a safer place, "a comfort groove," as it is called. This is the moment he's been waiting for, the moment when the wind picks up the kite and lets it soar. Some of the greatest improvisers claim, at rare times such as this, that when the music tumbles out unaided, as it were, it seems as if the notes are physical, fat shapes that dance, or colors pulsing, currents, swirls. For Leonard, because he always taps a foot, playing is more commonly like walking, corporal and muscular, walking tightropes, walking gangplanks, walking over coals, also walking on thin air, on ice, in darkness, on rock, on glass, but always walking blindfolded. Tonight, though, he is walking through a landscape forested in notes toward a clearing sky. The wind is at his back. The path ahead is widening. Statement, repetition, contrast, and return. Another sixteen bars and he'll be there.

Recognize when you have done enough, he tells himself. Head home. He's hardly moving now, no showboating. He doesn't even tap his feet or rock his body. Apart from fingertips just lifting and the bulging of his throat, he is a statue voicing nursery rhymes, the final measure, ding dong bell.

The music's ended for the moment—but this rare night in Brighton has an unrecorded track, an afternote, a human lollipop. Leonard has finished signing a handful of booklets and programs with a shaking hand, his autograph a mess. Euphoric and consumed, wanting more but not expecting anything except a hotel room, he heads out of the auditorium onto the snow and toward his taxi. A small group of intimate strangers in the mostly deserted lobby smile at him and shake his hand. They call out, "That was beautiful." And "That was fun." And "That was truly weird." All men. All hardcore fans. Then, yes, then Francine speaks to him. She has delayed him at the taxi door. Her hand is on his arm. "Truly valiant," she says, blowing smoke, still a little tipsy and not quite knowing why she's chosen the word, a word that even now has resonance for both of them. Leonard sees a woman just a little younger but a good deal shorter than himself, large-featured in a girlish way, her hair unkempt, her red coat still damp from the storm and smelling slightly wintry. "Valiant?" he repeats. "Does that mean rash?" Rash as in reckless? Foolhardy? He hopes it does. "No, I mean valiant," she says. "You know . . . valiant, taking risks. Yes, it was pure valiance." Embarrassed by her loss of eloquence, her tipsy failure to summon the simple word *valor* when she needs it, she laughs. Such a pealing, mezzo laugh. The evening's most melodic note, he thinks. And that becomes the start of it, his great romance.

NOW, WITH THE WORST of the country roads and the best of that day's weather behind him and with fresh suburbs gathering, their snouts pressed up against the fields, Leonard listens to himself again, listens to the music of everybody's childhood, spontaneously reshaped, listens to the retrieved mistakes that masquerade as wit and bravery, the risk-taking, the nerve, the *valiance*, almost unaware of traffic, the dimming sky, or the windscreen wipers, and certainly without much thought of Maxim Lermontov. He presses the track button and returns to the beginning of the broadcast. "In an unexpected adjustment . . ." And then again. And then again. Announcements and applause, with Francine in the audience—but that was then—admiring him.

3

BY THE TIME LEONARD has been navved to Alderbeech and parked the van outside the makeshift village of personnel buses, television trucks, portable lavatories, and police catering units on designated waste ground near the hostage street and the inevitable crowd of spectators, the gunman in the mask has been identified, or almost. He is, the radio announcer misinforms, "Maxie Lemon, a U.S. national." Renamed, he sounds more like an end-of-pier comedian than a criminal or a terrorist. He has, they say, two accomplices, of whom no details are available, though one is possibly a female. Leonard wonders briefly if she might also be somebody he could identify but will not. He is at first a little disappointed that Maxie has been named already—but above all he is relieved. His knowledge hardly matters anymore. No decision that he takes will make a difference. When has it ever? If he chooses, he can stay dry—it is still raining despite the assurances of that morning's forecast; the pavements are slippery with leaves—and drive home straightaway, with an almost easy conscience. He has not betrayed his Texan, despite his greater duty. He should feel more pleased than he does. He calls up Francine on the van's speakerphone, but her handset is turned off. He can picture her in class, sitting with the children at her feet, singing nursery rhymes, her voice unburdening. Three blind mice. He hesitates for a moment when her answer service picks up his call. He wants to say that he has lied to her, and then explain it all. But it would take too long. Instead, he records, "It's Leonard. Soaking day. I'll be home before you are. Give yourself a hug."

He needs a break from driving, though, and he is keen to get closer to events, to step into the news, to be at least an eyewitness. How can he come this far and not commit those extra meters? That would be perverse. He has not brought wet-weather wear, although there is a beach cap in the glove compartment: yellow linen with the logo QUEUE HERE across its peak. He turns up his collar, pulls the cap low, protecting his thin hair, and walks across the waste ground toward the street. It is a windy day as well as wet. The best of it is sorbus leaves, brick-red and orange, snapping free with every gust. The worst of it is beating rain. That morning's blue has been misleading. It has been *mischleading*. He says the word out loud. Then, "Soaking day. Hugs, hugs . . ." He's talking nonsense to himself. He's walking through the wasteland mud in his beach cap, unprepared for anything but summer, and talking to himself.

Leonard has imagined on the journey down that he will be able to walk past the house as closely and as innocently as someone exercising a dog, that he will stand outside and stare into the rooms. And then, will Maxie Lemon / Lermon / Lermontov be peering out, behind his mask and E-clips, and see him there? The female too. He dreams up recognition on that veiled face, an eyebrow lifting possibly, a hand half raised, a gun held out at shoulder height and pointed playfully at Leonard in the street. *Kapow. You're scathed. Kapow. You're dead!* But of course the streets around the hostage house are sealed and Leonard must, like everybody else, like all the curious and nosy, find a place behind a barrier and try to glimpse—beyond the fire engines and ambulances, beyond the little group of armed officers in flak jackets and armor coats, beyond the row of freshly naked rowan trees (no alder here, or beech), the cars, the city furniture—a skinny view of the house's gable and its chimney pots, little more than silhouettes on this dusklike morning. When Leonard arrives, the know-alls in the crowd are pointing at an upper window where a landing light has been turned on and there is a shadow, briefly. Everybody watches for a while, until a helicopter catches their attention, and then a running man in uniform (but running only to escape the rain), and then some other movement at the curtains in another room.

It's tedious to stand and stare. Such scenes-of-crime are always more dramatic on a telescreen, when they're well framed and mediated by a journalist. Here there's very little to observe, and nothing to experience except the waiting. Leonard checks the time. It's almost noon. He'll stay till noon, six minutes more, and then decide on how to waste the afternoon. But finally and just in time there is a fresh development. Not in the street but on the television news, of course. Leonard's neighbor at the barrier unfolds the screen and turns up the volume on his palm set for a headline summary. Maxie Lemon was identified, it claims, by an "estranged British relative. No more details at this time."

One of the curbside experts has the information, though: "It's the daughter. That's her, see?" How can he be sure? "I overheard." He says it boastfully, as if overhearing is a talent. "She's just a kid." He points toward a group of officers and there, not blending in, a spot of uncamouflaged color among the khakis, blues, and blacks, is an adolescent girl in a red beret, her face made indistinct by the weather and distance, her back turned to the hostage house, either speaking closely to her cell phone or crying.

She's not a kid, thinks Leonard. She's not a kid if she is who he thinks she is. He works it out. Austin in October 2006, and then some months. She would have been born in the summer of 2007, the summer of no sun. So that would make her not a kid and not a woman yet but seventeen. "Brave kid," he says out loud. Yes, brave. Yes, valiant. While he hesitated by the phone last night—he will phone; he will never phone; he sleeps—Maxie's daughter determined to put on her hat and go out in the rain to do what Leonard should have done at once. Name names. Again there is a reason to be disgruntled with himself, not quite ashamed but downcast, rather. He's fumbled his opportunity. But still, as he knows well, an error can be retrieved and embellished in its retelling, and he is tempted to share his own information at once with this crowd of onlookers. I know him. I knew her, the girl, before she was even born. I can guess who the woman is. I thought I loved her once. But again he hesitates and the moment is lost.

He considers that possibly, no, *probably*, later in the evening, when he confesses to Francine what he has really done that day, not walking in the forest, he'll add the detail—almost true—that he (an "estranged British friend") has offered information to the police. Surely she will applaud him for it, and to be deserving of her approval, if only briefly, is what he most desires, her approval and her happiness. He envisages an evening like they used to have, before Celandine went missing, went silent, became estranged, whatever she has done, and his wife's depression set in, an evening when he prepares the meal and they sit side by side with it on trays, their thighs and elbows bumping, watching television, and just for once not fretting for the phone to ring with news, good news or any news, of Francine's daughter. Drive home, he thinks. Enough of this. There's nothing to be done for Maxim Lermontov. That's history. He's history. But Francine needs you home.

It is the beret that he notices as he drives past on the first kilometer of his return to Francine. The "kid" isn't wearing it but holds it in her hand. The wind is strengthening, but the rain has almost cleared. There are even a few blue shreds hoisting up from the west and enough sharp light for fitful shadows to spread across the road. Her hair, he sees, though bunched, is thick and sinewy like her father's, but she has her mother's squarish build and sun-shy English coloring. She is walking to the tram station, he thinks. On impulse he whirs down his side window and accelerates to draw alongside her on the pavement. But a teenager like her will know not to talk to cruising men in old-style vans with QUEUE HERE on their caps, and so he drops back and parks, despite the single yellow lines and PERMIT HOLDERS ONLY signs, and hurries after her on foot. He cannot call her name. He does not know her name and never has. He only knew her parents briefly. But there is one good reason to feel intimate. He was present in that Texan loft when they discussed aborting her. He thought but did not say—it was not his business, after all—that in his view, in his analysis, based on his older sister's suicide aged twenty-two, terminations rarely terminate for the mother. His sister's cut-short child, a boy, haunted her, a kind of toddler ghost, until she gave up the ghost herself. In a kinder universe, Leonard would be an uncle now. Instead, he has no sister and no nephew, no children of his own, and just one stepdaughter, Celandine, one missing stepdaughter. He is an orphan without heirs, he often thinks. And thinks it right now—how could he not?—as he pursues this teenage girl. His walking shadow clips her heels.

"I knew your father," he says, too softly, to her back. He says it again, and takes his beach cap off, more embarrassment than formality, before she has a chance to turn round.

Although it's damp and cold, they sit outside in the Woodsman's yard, on a short timber bench, their shoulders touching or their elbows clashing when they lift their drinks: his prudent "regular" measure of wine and the defiantly large, liter glass of beer that Leonard has reluctantly bought her without challenge from the barman, even though she looks, and is, underage. Despite the tobacco ordinances, she smokes, an edgy and unbroken chain of roll-ups from a tin, as she justifies that morning's "snitching" on her father: "What am I supposed to do? Sit back and watch it happen on the television? There're hostages. He's taken hostages . . ."

"There're guns!" adds Leonard, and he is unexpectedly roused by the effortless drama of the phrase. He's keen for her to know he's on her side, that (as he says, striving for effect) she has been "a mensch rather than a snitch." Emboldened by alcohol and being far from home, he is airing for both their benefits a more truly daring version of himself. What is there to stop him? As far as this young stranger is concerned, he is an unmarked canvas that he can color in any way he wants. "Guns," he says again, and then adds a line that, even as he says it, seems lifted from the tritest gangster movie: "He's armed. He's desperate. He could do anything . . . so we should do something. Yes?"

"Well, yeah. That's what I said to Mum . . ." (Here she imitates her mother's evidently apprehensive voice.) "She said, 'Be sensible. Don't get involved.' Well, let's be honest, that's never on the toolbar, is it? That isn't me. I always get involved. Feet first. *She* always got involved when she was my age. So she says."

"She *was* an activist."

"My mum, the activist? Not nowadays she's not. She's . . . what's the opposite?"

"A dormouse," Leonard suggests.

The teenager laughs. "Just a pinch more lively and opinionated than a dormouse."

"A rightist, then?"

"No, not that. She hasn't changed her mind. She's more, you know . . . a smolderer. All smoke and no fire? She's shouting at the TV news all day but doesn't even vote."

"A sofa socialist." It's Francine's nickname for her husband nowadays.

"A sofa socialist. That's it. Pass the velvet cushions, please." She mimes a yawn onto the back of her hand.

"She was a firebrand, actually," Leonard says. "She really was. We both were. Once upon a time. Red Nadia." In fact, for a moment, earlier, he expected to discover that her mother was Maxie's female comrade in the hostage house.

"Is that you now, a sofa socialist? Or are you still the activist?"

"I'm still ready," Leonard says. Not quite a lie. Ever since his teenage years he has been ready for the fray—politically, at least. Where other boys had sports or girls or evening jobs, little Lennie immersed himself in his music, or in protest groups, his meetings and his high hopes for the world. "One has to throw one's pebble at the wall," he adds, a modest phrase he's always liked.

"So let's get ready with the pebbles, then." She high-fives him, and Leonard responds a little clumsily, sending wincing pain into his shoulder. Then they sit awkwardly and silently for just a shade too long. Too long for Leonard, anyway. He has to speak. "I hope I haven't lost the fire." He is rewarded by an entirely unguarded smile that can mean anything: that she finds him laughable, admirable, embarrassing, dishonest. But he is charmed by it, and by her openness. Again they sit in silence, staring at the back wall of the pub. This silence is no longer cumbersome. The teenager is thinking, even nodding to herself.

"Yeah, what you said is right," she says finally. "He's armed. We should do something because he could do *anything*. That's great, you know? Do it, do it, do it now." She drums her knees and sings. "*Yup, Davey Davey, do it now.* You know that Jo Bond song? *I've reached the beating heart of you / But I won't fall apart for you / Unless you do it now, ba-dum ba-dum ba-dum.* That's almost how it goes. I'll send it to your cell if you like. Great track." She drums on her knees again. "Want one of these?"

Leonard used to smoke, and to validate himself a bit with her—and with anybody watching from the rear windows of the busy bar; they must seem an ill-matched pair—he takes a cigarette, his first since both he and Francine gave up three years ago, despite the assurances printed on low-risk brands that nicotine in moderation might protect the smoker from dementia. He feels self-conscious in her company. She's noisy, odd, and unpredictable. And she is the curl-up-and-nestle sort who sits too close and touches people when she talks to them, a hand spread lightly on his arm, to show support or sympathy, a finger prod to acknowledge a joke that does not quite deserve a laugh. She's still unfledged and gullible, blurtingly self-confident, both at ease and twitchy. Uncalculating, actually. Only a kid after all, and behaving, physically, as a teenager might behave, perching at a tram stop with her mates.

Leonard is not blurtingly self-confident, except on rare nights with the saxophone. But he is old enough to be her father. He could have been her father, if things had worked out differently in Austin. He was besotted, briefly, with her mother, after all. Anyway, he'd rather be mistaken for her father than for—his current apprehension—an older and inappropriately attentive man sitting far too near to this too trusting, this underage girl. Her groper boss, perhaps. Her ancient grooming predator. So it might appear to anybody catching them wrapped together in a veil of smoke. She certainly is close to him. The bench is short, of course, but it's too late to move to another bench and his own elbow room. That would seem standoffish—*sit*offish, actually—and shy, both of which are timid attributes and not consistent with the man who has just promised that none of his fire has been lost. He'll stay. The cigarette, the much-missed fellowship of nicotine, he thinks, provides an alibi. He'll try to let the roll-up burn down between his fingers, not put it to his mouth. Still, he can't prevent the cough. Her smoke and his are overpowering. She puts her hand on his, as if to stay his cigarette. "Don't finish it," she says. He is infantilized by her. He lifts his cigarette, inhales. He clears a strand of tobacco from his lips with his tongue. He is determined not to cough again.

Sitting next to Maxie's daughter on the bench is the closest Leonard's got to intimacy of any kind, carnal or otherwise, for many weeks. Of late, his life has shrunk by stages. Age, routine, and common sense plus the adhesions in his rotator cuff have combined to frustrate most fleshly pleasures, not just sex. He has been drug-free and loosely vegetarian since his thirties, but now he is a dieter as well, a resister of alcohol, chocolate, dairy, modified foods, and whatever produce is currently targeted as unsafe or unsound. In his household, shopping is a morally burdened expedition; cooking is a series of ethical quandaries. Dietary self-defense has turned every meal into a combat zone. He does his best to be a "naught percenter," as health-conscious citizens are called. Naught percent sugar. Naught percent salt. Naught percent saturated fats. Cholesterol has become for him a grave and present enemy. Certainly he does more these days to combat sticky deposits in his own bloodstream than any failings in the body politic. He is more regularly engaged by the struggle to keep below seventy-five kilos in weight than by any dogma or belief. And while it has become a simple matter to exile his aspirations for the world to the back of his mind, his ambitions for a trimmer waist or a lower pulse are never far from the front of it.

So naught percent passion, then, naught percent fire, naught percent tossing pebbles at the wall, but he can at least take comfort from his evident personal control, his lifestyle sacrifices and restraints. He still has public political principles, of course, but he has been able to persuade himself that fighting for these principles on the street, as he tried to do when he was younger and has only affected to do more recently, is far too facile, especially given his safe distance from the problems themselves. How hard is it to wear a badge? Or sign a sheet? Or send a check? It's living by his private principles that's hard. Yet he cannot help but reply, "Why ever not?" when she drains her glass, stands up, says, "Gluggedy-glug," half roguish child and half stage drunk, and asks, "Another one?" And he cannot help but stare at her back and legs as she walks toward the rear door of the pub and judge how physically attractive she must be for men, well, kids, of her own age. She's fiercely lovely on the eye, he thinks—stocky, strong-featured, and theatrical—and her voice is teenage-husky, sore-throated and seductive. She smells of something smoky, woody, something freshly sawn, not food or soap, not perfume either, he decides, but toothpaste probably. Eucalyptus toothpaste, yes. She smells of trees. And adolescence. She also smells of fire and nicotine. Apart from the beret, a vivid scarf and gloves, and her thick loganberry tights, she is wearing only black. Black coat, black top, a scalloped black skirt, black hiking boots. She is arresting, certainly. And just a little mad.

Leonard spreads across the bench while she is at the bar. He beats a rhythm on his own old knees, *ba-dum ba-dum ba-dum.* He's wildly happy for a change. Yes, do it, do it, do it now. Can he be a little tipsy, even, after just one "regular" glass? Perhaps it is the nicotine that has made him feel so light-headed and defenseless. He cannot stop himself from smiling with satisfaction and some arousal, possibly, when she returns from the bar with packets of bacon snacks—he's not eaten bacon for at least ten years—and more drinks.

Leonard actually is not generally attracted to younger women, not sexually. He likes them as an uncle should, admiring youth but not desiring it. He has been the least menacing of stepfathers. He and Francine have not seen or spoken to their absent Celandine for very nearly eighteen months. But when they did speak, when they lived together, she trusted him like flesh and blood, even though she was never able to call him Dad (or Leonard, come to that). She called him Unk, for Uncle, a fitting title for a stepfather, both fond and distancing. Especially fitting, given Leonard's sister's suicide and his lost nephew. So he's tempted—when he and Maxie's daughter finally exchange names—to tell her that he is called Unk, to keep himself unspecified. He has never been keen on his own name. Leonard—it sounds so undramatic and timid. It is, as a disagreeable and far too clever former girlfriend once commented, sending Leonard to a dictionary, "a *pavid* name." And Len or even Lennie sounds too breezy and too immature, though no less unremarkable. But nonetheless, he accurately names himself in full, identifies the unidentified for her, provides his information, perhaps because he wonders if she might possibly have heard his name before, from her mother or from his recordings. He has been shortlisted for a Mercury, after all, he's played with all the dinosaurs, and his sound track for *Cup Half Full* went platinum and still keeps him relatively wealthy. It finances his current sabbatical. But no, she clearly does not recognize his name.

Her name, she says, is Lucy, not Lucy Lermon / Lermontov but Lucy Emmerson, her mother's family name. "Why would I have my father's name?" she says. Again, another child who won't say Dad. "I'm the 'estranged British relative,' remember?"

"How long were you estranged?"

"Since forever. Year Zero, actually. I was only about six months old when they kicked Mum out."

Leonard has his fingers crossed. "You never knew your father, then?"

"Not physically. By reputation, yes. The Texan headbanger. The handsome lunatic. Until about two months ago, when he turned up at home with the big paternal doorstep scene—though Mum was never going to let him in. He beat her up. Did you know that?—all he's ever meant to me is one phone call—yeah, that's the lot—when I was about six. And he sent a couple of birthday cards, well, *three* maximum, and a photograph. Big hair."

"Your hair." Old-fashioned Russian hair, he thinks.

"I hate my hair. I think I'm going to get a badger cut. That long." She makes a tiny gap between a finger and her thumb.

"No, don't do that," he says, remembering Maxie doing something similar an age ago.

Leonard has a print of the Gruber's photograph in his wallet. For the police. Had he ever spoken to the police. He unfolds it now for Lucy. "He's hardly changed," she says. "My God! That's quite a meal." She folds the photograph and hands it back. "That's him. The hair. That was the giveaway on last night's news. He's far too vain about his hair to wear a hat. How clever's that?"

"That's what you told the police?"

"I told the police as little as I could. His name, that's all. Well, I didn't spell his name quite right. I didn't want to stitch him up entirely. Girl Judas, understand? It's up to them, the police, what happens now. It's up to us as well, I guess. It's up to us a bit."

"It is a bit, I guess." Leonard doesn't like to add, *Not me.*

"We must do something, like you said. I've got a genius idea. I mean, we can't just leave it there. You know, just say, 'That man's my father,' give his name, then split and run. That's gutless, isn't it? We have to think of what to do, like something more than just . . . well, just betraying him."

"Like what? There's nothing I can do. I haven't seen your father in almost twenty years. Before you were even born. He never liked me, actually. So."

"No, but then . . . this is an opportunity, our meeting up like this. Mum won't do anything. You're right. She's such a sofa socialist. You nailed her there. But suddenly there's you. That's kismet, isn't it? It's like we've got no choice. You said you're ready, didn't you? You can't have come down here just to stand and watch. We're sort of comrades now. So if anybody dies and we've not even tried, we'll not forgive ourselves. Will you forgive yourself if someone dies? Will you forgive yourself even if it's *only* my newly discovered father who gets shot up by the police?"

Most probably, he thinks. He says, "I couldn't live with that. But then we mustn't overdramatize. This isn't television—"

"Yes, it is."

It must be the lunchtime wine that traps him, makes him drift beyond himself, because when she says, "We're sort of *comrades* now," reclaiming that sweet, outdated term, Leonard feels it could be true. He has to swallow a half sob, he is so gratified and touched. Caught out, as well. It's a winning remark, naive and generous and undeserved. She thinks he's better than he is. He's Comrade Leonard now. For the moment, more than anything he does not want to let her down, not while she's here. "Okay, then, you're the chief. Let's hear your genius idea."

"I can trust you, can't I?"

"All the way."

"You're on my side?"

"I'm listening," he says, a little guardedly. "Go on."

She shakes her head. "I can't. You first. You talk."

"Just talk?"

"I want to know the story. I don't get anything about you lot, my mum, my father, Mr. Lemon and his gun. You firebrand sofa-hating activists."

Leonard laughs out loud at this. If only it were true. "*No pasarán,*" he says, raising his right fist, enchanted by any description that includes him among the activists.

"What's that?"

"*No pasarán?* You know the Spanish Civil War?"

She shakes her head. "Were you in that?"

Leonard throws his head back again, not laughing at Lucy's innocence but delighted by it. Why should a girl of seventeen know about the Spanish Civil War or, come to that, the compulsive part it has played for so many years in his imaginative life? "No, that was way before any of us were born. More's the pity, possibly. I might have gone and done my bit." And he embarks on telling her—his captive audience, who at least is pretending not to find him tedious—about his political epiphany. "Let's see, I was twelve years old, so 1987." He was, he explains, "a fervent and precocious little boy, a bit too earnest for my age perhaps," and one that was as keen to take part in politics as others at the time were to play in football games or form a gang. "It was all *Maggie, Maggie, Maggie, Out! Out! Out!* in those days. Thrilling times." Lucy nods as if she knows who Maggie Thatcher was, from her mother, possibly. "I remember . . ."

Leonard stops to check her expression. Celandine always grimaced or held her hands up in mock horror whenever her stepfather said *I remember*. "Try to remember wordlessly, Unk," she once suggested, spitefully. But Lucy has tilted her face in interest. Her shoulders are still rubbing his.

". . . there was this older man, one of the organizers. *Mr.* Perkiss," Leonard continues, failing to recall the Christian name and then fleetingly recognizing that he is now the older man and one who also hopes to be inspiring. "He had only one hand, the left. The right was missing from the elbow. He always had the empty sleeve of his jacket turned up and safety-pinned to his shoulder. Walked a bit crablike. He must have been getting on for seventy. But he was still the fastest leafleteer among us. He'd been a milkman." Leonard smiles to himself; he's never forgotten Mr. Perkiss's oddly sideways bearing, nor his unhesitant agility—even though he was not a southpaw by birth—at gates where others fumbled, and his confidence with growling dogs and hostile residents. This, to a lad of only twelve, looked like political heroism. Leonard wanted nothing more than to earn this man's approval.

"Did you find out about his arm?" prompts Lucy, as dutifully as a TV host, rescuing Leonard from his short silence.

"I didn't like to ask at first. It was a bit too personal, I thought. But I did ask him, finally. I said, 'What happened to the other one?' Not exactly subtle. I can still remember Mr. Perkiss lowering his voice, as if he thought it all too small a matter to discuss, and telling me, 'I left my arm in Catalonia.'"

"Hey, that would make a mighty lyric for a song."

"He'd been a volunteer, you see? In 1937. The Spanish Civil War. That's why I mentioned it before. *No pasarán*. 'They shall not pass.' He was a member of the International Brigade, when he could hardly have been out of his teens. Maybe just a year or two older than you are now, Lucy."

"Boys are not like that these days. Not at my college. They go to Spain to get a tan. And to get wrecked."

"My Mr. Perkiss, he got wrecked—in the old sense." Leonard begins to tell her about the battle of the Ebro, in which Perkiss was a stretcher-bearer. "Nineteen of his troop were killed that day. Can you imagine it? Frenchmen, Russians, Americans, Italians. The *International* Brigade. Good mates of his, Lucy. He's doing what he can to save some lives and then this Fascist soldier lobs a grenade at him. He takes full blast." Leonard slaps and detonates his chest, a brass player's concert trick. "He takes full blast of it. Got shrapnel in his face and legs and chest. They had to pick the pieces out with kitchen tongs!"

"Did my father know this man?"

"Of course not, no." Her question puzzles him. But then he understands why she was so thoroughly attentive at first but is now fidgeting. Maxie is the one she wants to hear about. That is what she thought all this was leading to. Leonard would rather tell her about the pivotal and inspiring day that Mr. Perkiss let him see and touch his "war damage," the shiny scar, six centimeters long, below his knee, the other scar along his underjaw and down to his Adam's apple, a hairless and pitted length of tight and damaged skin. He could never grow a beard, thanks to General Franco. "The worst luck was that the detonator hit Mr. Perkiss just below the elbow," Leonard continues, speaking more quickly. "Can you imagine,

Lucy, what a chunk of steel the size of a pigeon's egg can do if it hits flesh at speeds like that?" Lucy starts to roll a cigarette. "It punched a hole in his arm. It sliced the artery and then passed through and only missed the comrade behind him by a whisker. Half a centimeter closer and that man would've lost his face. Mr. Perkiss's arm was hanging from a thread. Snip, snip, and that was it. Neat job. They left it where it fell. In Catalonia. Didn't even save his watch. Didn't stop him doing this, though. One arm's enough." Leonard raises his clenched fist, feeling foolish, finally. "The Socialist salute. That's who I got it from."

By now it's obvious Lucy is not truly interested in Leonard's hero of the left or the fact that Leonard himself, when he was Lucy's age, still dreamed of emulating this man and hoped, when he was older, in his gap year possibly, to make a sacrifice, though not of a limb, for something he believed in.

"I'm only telling you all this," he says, hoping to regain lost ground, "because the one other man I've met who's come close to Mr. Perkiss is your father. You know, prepared to lay down his life for a cause. He was always lost in one cause or another." He doesn't add out loud what he is thinking: that unlike Mr. Perkiss, Maxie Lermon could be brutal and stone-hearted, that his high-sounding principles were only a smokescreen for his transgressions, that her father was fanatical, preoccupied with action, careless of effect.

"That's why we have to stop him, isn't it?" she says. "Because he's not the sort to stop himself."

What she proposes is a mirror kidnapping. "You kidnap me, or seem to anyway," she says, too sweetly passionate to warrant opposition. "You threaten tit for tat. It's quite a neat idea. It's biblical. It's eyes and teeth. No one's going to guess what's really going on."

"So what is really going on?" Leonard hasn't understood. The drink has made him sluggish.

"Not a lot, in fact. And that's the joy of it. I only disappear into your spare room for however long it takes. A week at most . . . Come on!" She slaps his hand. "I bet three days. I just hang out, read books and stuff. I'll be your cook! And you send ransom notes and make phone calls. You say, 'We've got the headbanger's darling girl here. She won't get free until the hostages get free. And if he hurts the hostages, then she's hurt too. If they go hungry, she goes hungry. Shout at them, and she gets shouted at. Simplissimo as that. But when you free them, the family, we free her, the long-lost daughter. It's your call, Mr. Lemon.' No, this is really genius." And it does seem genius. It seems the sort of intervention that is both honorable and risk-free and, with red wine on its side, might even be mistaken for daring.

"What do you reckon?" Lucy asks. Her hand is on his arm again.

"I reckon, let's have another drink and talk it through," Leonard says, managing to sound both hesitant and roguish. "See if it's okay."

"What's not okay?"

" 'See if,' I said."

"It's so okay that Dad"—her first use of the word—"is going to be totally disarmed. You know, *disarmed*, like doesn't have a choice. Not unless he is a complete monster." Lucy is becoming more excited with everything she says.

"Well, that's a possibility."

"It's not. It's truly not."

"Maxie's not predictable. Maxie can be"—Leonard has to say it carefully—"too passionate." He means *unhinged*. Thuggish and unhinged.

"I think he is predictable. I've met him for myself. We've talked—"

"For twenty minutes at the most. Three birthday cards and a photograph, you said."

"No, more than that. Not only on the doorstep when he came in August, just suddenly. But since." She lowers her voice and leans in toward Leonard, as if to trust him with an intimate disclosure. "He's phoned. We've met. We've been on walks. We've been in pubs. Don't say. My mum'd have a stroke if she found out."

"Well, mum's the word. Trust me." Her eyes are wet, he sees.

"But it's for me, not Mum. I had to talk with him. Why wouldn't I? Aren't I entitled to? And now I know he sort of loves me. In a way. I asked him and he said he did. Or would. Give him the chance, at least." She sits up suddenly, a fresh bright girl engaging with the world, a practiced catchphrase from *FBH*, the television show, on her lips: "It's Flesh and Blood and *History* . . . and common sense. They're on our side."

"That's quite a lineup, Lucy."

"Yes, it is. It means he'll never let me come to any harm. Admit it now, this is how it works." In her scenario, her father dares not tie his victims up for fear of ropes around his own girl's wrists. He dares not use his fists or fire his gun at anyone, the family or a policeman, anyone, or let his comrades do it either, for if he does, then Lucy will be beaten up or shot as well. A wound to match a wound. A death to match a death. A love to be rewarded with a love.

"Equivalence," says Leonard.

"And if he wants a ransom," Lucy adds, "or makes demands, you know, a helicopter or a wad of notes, all you do is ask the same for me. It's only words. And if he tries to kill himself, he can do it knowing you'll kill me as well. Don't laugh. I see you couldn't hurt a fly. But only we know that. How sweet is my idea? He'll have no choice. He'll have to . . . what's the word? Resign?"

"Surrender, do you mean? Admit defeat? Capitulate?" Leonard smiles; the thought is satisfying. "You know what, then? Just think it through. If he backs down, if he caves in"—sweet phrase—"is that the end of it?" He shakes his head. She does the same and waits, biting her lower lip. "No? Exactly. Your newfound father will be dragged away in front of all the cameras and then locked up for one very long time. Don't kid yourself. How will you live with that?"

"I'll visit him in prison every week. I'm doing him a favor. There's no defeat. I'm saving him." This is where her argument is won.

She loves her father, Leonard thinks. Or at least she loves the idea of her father. Well, no surprise. Unquestionably, Maxie is a man who's easy to be beguiled and inveigled by, on first encounters. Lucy will not have had the chance to feel his rage or spot the thug in him, as Leonard has. She will have found him handsome, charismatic, and mythically romantic. Overpowering, in fact. Of course she doesn't want to lose a man like that for seventeen more years—forever, probably. She needs to know exactly where he is, even if that is in a cell. She wants him within reach. And more than that, she's offering him the chance, his first and only chance, to prove he loves her. Yes, that's her genius. What she proposes is a test of love. Leonard lifts his chin and offers Lucy Emmerson a loving smile of his own. She's overpowering as well. He is the one who has capitulated. He has become Lucy Emmerson's slavish comrade. Her only help. There's no one else. He daren't say no. At least, he daren't say no to her face.

Lucy, like an excitable adolescent, wants to baptize the plot and their confederacy by pricking their fingertips with a brooch and shaking bloody hands, but Leonard will not stab himself. He says he is too old for punctures and perforations. But he agrees "in principle" to her grand plan. Overnight, he'll square the idea with his wife ("No problem there," he boasts) while Lucy collects her few "unsuspicious" things from home. "Nothing that looks too planned," she promises. "I mean, I'll leave my toothbrush in its usual place, and my BaxPax, stuff like that. It has to seem like I've just been grabbed. Right off the street. Like a genuine kidnapping. No witnesses." She kisses Leonard's cheek. "You're really nice," she says, delighted with the caper she has planned and now can share. Rather than return her kiss, as she seems to expect, Leonard raises his good hand for her, the painless one, and clenches it again.

"*No pastarán,*" she says. "We're going to get on fine. I'm going to be the perfect guest. Three days maximum. Radiant! Tomorrow, then. High noon." They arrange to rendezvous in the car park of the Zone superstores near the airport's Charles III terminus. "Just sit and wait. I'll find you," she says. "There's no mistaking that creepy van of yours." Now she tilts her face again and smiles. "Let's see that Texas photograph." She leans across, her hair in his face. His hand is on her arm. Good mates, no more than that. They talk and smoke until the lights come on, this naught percenter and this child that might have been his own. They seem unlikely comrades, sitting damply with their drinks, more drinks than he can manage, their two hats on their laps providing the beer yard with its only vividness: red beret, yellow cap.

4

LEONARD IS NOT SORRY to get back to the van and be himself again. Those hours spent behind the Woodsman, so thrilling and so promising at first, have left him cornered rather than resolved. He is relieved, though, to find that his van has been neither clamped nor towed. Throughout his meeting with Lucy Emmerson he has never quite forgotten the single yellow restricted parking line running under its nearside tires and has worried what ingenious excuses he might have to offer Francine to explain why he is so unexpectedly late home. He cannot tell her he has ended up, expensively, at a City Highways car pound after an afternoon of drinking and smoking with a pretty teenage girl. A more likely delay, given his white lies of that morning, would be having the vehicle locked in by careless rangers at some unattended forest clearing. But, thankfully, the van is untouched. He can save his inventions for some other occasion. For a moment only, his spirits lift. This trip has not proved to be an entire disaster. Not yet, at least. Not if he can go back on his promise. He knows he will, he knows he must. Leonard flushes hot and cold at the prospect. What folly has he promised Lucy Emmerson? Pressed up close together on that wooden bench, conspirators, he has abandoned his good sense. On the journey back, he can concoct the most convincing reasons for his change of heart, something that will satisfy both the girl and himself, though nothing he does now—including speeding or taking risks, as he has just done, pulling out too carelessly into lively traffic—will get him home before his wife as he has promised.

Leonard knows the law. He should not be driving at all: 25 centiliters of wine is the limit and he has drunk three times that volume. And on an empty stomach. He's risking a suspension. But it is only early evening, not quite dark yet. Random checks are not usually deployed until much later. He will avoid the motorways, however, where there are robot eyes to monitor the vehicles, and return the way he came, on rural routes. First, though, he turns the van round, drives back toward the hostage house, and parks again on the fringes of the mobile village with its circle of incident and rescue vehicles. Something pulls him there, something that he hopes is more than prurience. He is only idling, in both senses. He does not even turn the engine off or get out of the van. Instead, he reaches for his thermos under the passenger seat, where it has rolled and been forgotten during the jazz-fueled journey down. The lime-and-honey-flavored green tea is tepid and cloudy. It is reviving, though, and, he imagines, sobering. If he is stopped and questioned by the police (or Francine, come to that) because his driving or behavior is erratic, his grape-and-tobacco breath will have been partly cleansed and sweetened and might not betray him. Everything he does from now on until the lights go out tonight must help erase the day.

The parking ground is no less busy than it was this morning. Groups of officers come back off shifts, expressionless. Young men and women in uniform swipe their ID fobs at the catering van for their free drinks and sandwiches. Techies in hi-viz jackets fuss and tinker with their aerials and armories, issuing and taking back the beam guns or laser tasers that frontline officers from the National

Security Forces are authorized to carry and far too ready to use. The army and police forces do not mix with the rescue services, Leonard notices. Taking lives and saving lives are worlds apart. And they all despise the television crews. They are like playground gangs, keeping to their own kind and unhurriedly sharing their boredom with familiars. So the siege continues. Nothing new has happened this afternoon, he thinks, and is disappointed. Now Leonard understands what has pulled him back onto this open ground, something worse than prurience: it is the hope that the hostage-taking has been ended quickly while he's been in the pub, not only for the victims' sake, and not at all for Maxie Lermon's sake, but for his own well-being.

LEONARD SETS OFF ON THE JOURNEY home in a media-silent van. He needs to stay calm and unruffled, and he has to think. He's overreached himself, that much is obvious, and he suspects that getting back to safe and level ground will not be trouble-free. This is a tangle from which he knows he has to extricate himself at once. He imagines the conversation he will need to have with Francine, proving something she already knows: that he is foolish and suggestible, that thanks to him Celandine's old room is being given up to a missing young woman, but not the one his wife is praying for. Kidnapping of any kind is an offense, he tells himself, no matter that the victim is a coconspirator and more accountable than she might seem. The newspapers, the police, will know the truth: here is a "teenage child" who should expect good counsel and a restraining hand from her elders, not help and encouragement. Threatening violence is also an offense, even if the threat is little more than theater and could never produce anything other than blanks. And then there is the lesser crime of wasting police time. No one would blame Lucy for that. She's too immature, they'd say, to be the ringleader, to be the instigator of such a devious venture. Seventeen-year-olds have limited judgment, and less experience. But a man of almost fifty? How could a man of almost fifty, wittingly and willingly, go along with such a plan and give no thought to any of the consequences? *Leonard Lessing... Mister. Lennie. Less... On tenor... You are charged with willful mistreatment of a minor. And conspiracy. How do you plead?* No, this is not a good idea at all.

He flicks on the drive-time news and, hoping for too much, waits for an update on the hostages. But he has to listen first to the main items of the day, the forthcoming Reconciliation Summit and the many protests planned, and then a report from Los Angeles predicting a majority yes vote in California's unofficial Proposition 101, nicknamed Montezuma's Revenge, calling for the Latino state's secession from the union. "It is feared," the correspondent says, "that should these polls prove accurate and the majority embark on forced implementation, then many non-Latino Californians might resist with violence." Leonard imagines himself and Maxie holed up among the redwoods, comrades in arms, an International Brigade of two. It's *For Whom the Bell Tolls* filmed at Big Sur, though whether they would be fighting for or fighting against the rule of the WASPs of America is not clear. Am I the only one, he wonders, the only adult anyway, who has such childish, self-deluding fantasies? Is everyone a reckless hero in their dreams? Is everyone a Mr. Perkiss in their dreams?

Maxie himself is the third item in the newscast. It has been a quiet day for him and everyone involved, the presenter says. Pizzas and fresh fruit have been delivered by "elderly representatives" of the St. John Ambulance Brigade, and police, predicting "a long negotiation," have established telephone contact with "the group." Nothing promising. So Leonard turns to music once again: this time some classic Lester Young to fuff and schmooze him back to Francine. But he is too agitated to concentrate on music. And in pain. His frozen shoulder, which he has virtually forgotten while sitting in the pub yard with Lucy, has started to trouble him again. Driving stiffens it, he finds.

It is already eight in the evening when he gets back. It's too late to eat a meal together, so he has stopped in the district shop near home and bought, as he often does, a box of carob Florentines for his wife. There are no lights on in the house, and this is surprising and a little worrying, though a relief as well. But Francine's little car is parked in its usual place, charging at the domestic fuel box, and when Leonard steps into the moonlit gloaming of their glass-roofed hall, he can smell cooking and the beat of broadcast music. She's watching the Maestro channel in the dark, a Verdi opera, but as the telescreen pitches light into the room he can see that her eyes are closed and she is napping, worn out. Her legs are up on a stool, and only one of her slip-on shoes is still hanging from her toes. She has loosened the top buttons of her trousers. And as ever she has taken off her watch—"unwinding," she calls it—and put it on the arm of the futon, next to a used cup and plate. He lifts the surviving shoe off her foot, carries the crockery into the kitchen, washes it, and then returns to find her sitting up, awake and flushed. He sits down next to her and puts the Florentines on her lap.

"That's nice," she says. "Have I been sleeping?"

"Dead to the world."

"What time is it? When did you get back?"

"I've been back quite a while. I let you sleep." He leans across and kisses her behind the ear.

"You smell of cigarettes."

"I can't think why."

"Well, nor can I. Where did you go?"

"Into the forests, like I said. Pepper's Holt and up into the birch hursts. They were burning off the bracken. Maybe that's it."

"It doesn't smell like bracken."

She shakes her head at him and smiles, then takes his hand and wraps her fingers through his, something that she hasn't done unbidden for far too long. "It's nice to have you home. I hated coming back and no one here. Kiss-kiss." She pulls the hair back from her face and turns her head from him, offering the same ear that he kissed before. "I realize we're having bumpy times," she says, not facing him, "but . . . you know I love you more than all the buts. This morning, with the breakfast tray. I didn't mean to upset you . . ."

Leonard does not kiss her, though. He can smell the cigarettes as well. He knows that here he has a chance to recount the truth about his day, just to get it off his chest and have her agree with him that he must extricate himself. For a moment he even considers arguing that she should phone Lucy herself, with some excuse. It's tempting. But who can tell what Francine might think or what she might advise? He suspects she could be more angry that he has deceived her than with the scheme he and Lucy have dreamed up. It's possible that she could even like the prospect of a guest in the house, a bright young woman sleeping in a once-bright young woman's room. But, no, he will say nothing, because he understands from experience that once Francine has committed herself to something, she will be lost to it. He has married a woman with a wild stripe. She will be deaf to any warnings or any fears he might offer about willful mistreatment of a minor. "Oh, Leonard, do grow up," she'll say, as she has said more than once before. "I know what they'll put on your gravestone. It'll say 'Scared to Death.'"

So he pulls his hand away from hers and goes again into the kitchen. As he has feared while she's been holding him, his fingers do stink of tobacco. He plunges them into the suds left from the washing-up and wipes them roughly with the pan scourer. He swills his mouth with grapefruit juice and rubs his teeth. When he goes back in the room, sucking surreptitiously on a mint tablet, he is relieved to find that Francine is dozing again. He presses her earlobe until she half opens an eye. "Come on, go up, you need to get a good night's sleep."

"Carry me upstairs," she says, putting her hands around his neck and putting on her Helpless Hannah face. She loves it when he carries her. She's small enough.

"I can't. My shoulder's killing me."

"Well, don't be too long. Come up soon."

Leonard doesn't go up soon. It's cruel to have to stay downstairs. Life is playing tricks on him. Francine has made it clear—isn't it so?—that she does not want him to pull out and flatten the futon tonight, that he will be more than welcome on her side of the bed.

Everything she has done since his return is telling him she is ready, hoping even, to make love. It's what he's wanted for the past few weeks but has not dared to initiate. At last a window opens in their life. But Leonard cannot attend to his wife or even satisfy himself just yet. His mind is fixed elsewhere.

Leonard has to hunt to find the remote console pushed into the folds of the futon. It's behind the still-warm cushions where Francine has been sitting. His hand is shaking even more than when he loaded Maxie's photograph the previous evening. He has been aroused by Francine's attention, the warmth and smell of her, his love for her too infrequently expressed. That's cause enough to make him shake. But he is shaken by the lies he's told as well. And by the stupid criminality he's felt, the guilt, of coming back to his wife stinking of Lucy's roll-ups. But most of all he's shaken by the phone call he must make. He'll do it now and go upstairs for his reward. *Do it, do it, do it now, ba-dum ba-dum ba-dum.* He'll phone. Yes, he will phone.

Leonard clicks an on-screen toolbar and, half watching for updates in the headlines window that is minimized in the corner of the screen, opens Utilities and scrolls through the options until his arrow locates TelecomUK. He specifies Domestic and Residential, types in Lucy's full name, and identifies her hometown, not expecting any luck and not getting any. Cell phone numbers are always hard to find with so little information. He presumes her mother will have a registered home address, though. What isn't registered these days? He tries again, with "Emmerson, Nadia." But gets nothing other than "This person could not be found. Check your data." Maybe she has changed her name, he thinks. Or has a married name. Or has adopted a more exciting title: Red Nadia, Nadia Firebrand, Ms. Sofa Emmerson. He simplifies his search, her surname only. The engine offers seventy results, only four of which have *N* as their opening initial. He highlights and strikes out the rest, and then strikes out "Nigel Emmerson." He's narrowed it to three. He writes the numbers and addresses next to the initials N. H., N., and N. T. T. on a scrap of card torn from the cover of Francine's Florentine box. He'll have to try them all until he strikes lucky. But Leonard cannot risk calling the numbers from the house—there is an extension next to the bed that always Morses its own erratic commentary when the terrestrial line is in use—and so he puts his shoes back on and, hoping that Francine is too fast asleep by now to hear the chime of the front door, goes out into the street and to the parking bay to try these numbers from the van, even though he knows it's almost ten o'clock and late in the day to be calling strangers.

N. H. Emmerson, or at least the person who answers the phone, is female and not quite British. Canadian, perhaps. She sounds anxious, not used to evening calls.

"Is Lucy there?" he asks.

"Lucy who?"

"Lucy Emmerson."

"We are Emmersons, but we haven't got a Lucy here."

"Do you have a Lucy in your family?"

"Who is this speaking, please?"

Leonard ends the call rather than answer, rather than be ill-mannered and not reply. He knows he has mishandled it. This time, with N. T. T., he'll be more subtle. But there is no need. "Lucy's living with her mum these days," an older man volunteers at once.

"Is that with Nadia?"

"Correct."

"Can I check her phone number with you?" Leonard reads out the last remaining number on his list.

"Correct," the man says again. "Is it Lucy that you want? Say hi from Grandpa Norman, will you, when you speak? Do you take messages?"

"I can."

"You can tell her that I'm sorry about her bicycle. Some people'll help themselves to anything these days."

"Somebody stole her bicycle?"

"Correct."

Leonard cannot phone at once. His heart is beating and his

mouth is dry. He drains the last few drops of now cold tea from the neck of his flask and clears his throat. If it weren't for Francine, perhaps awake indoors, and maybe even calling out his name to no reply before coming downstairs in her bare feet, hoping to find her husband safe and deaf to the world between his iPod earphones rather than dead on the carpet, he'd leave this final call for fifteen minutes or so. Enough time for a fortifying shot of rum, if they still have any rum. Enough time for deep breaths and embouchures. He dares not risk the fifteen minutes, though. He keys the number at once and lets it ring. He will allow ten tones and then give up. A second and maybe better possibility would be showing up tomorrow at the Zone as agreed and talking then and there to Lucy, explaining to her face to face why her genius is flawed. Yes, that would be less cowardly and less immediate. But Nadia Emmerson answers her house phone at once. Her voice is still familiar and unnervingly attractive, though any trace of adopted Texan has gone.

"Has anybody at this number lost a bike?" Leonard asks, unable to stop himself from disguising his own voice.

"Good heavens, yes. My daughter has. Who's talking, please?"

Leonard can hear a background voice, the television possibly, except that Nadia is shushing it. "It's a man about your bike," she says, off-mike, and to the phone, "Hold on. She's coming now." And here is Lucy on the line, teenage-husky and familiar. "Hey," she says.

"Lucy, listen to me, this is Leonard Lessing," he whispers. "Pretend to Nadia that someone's found your bike, okay? Then redial me on this number in the morning, at nine o'clock. Exactly nine o'clock. We have to talk. Tomorrow morning, then. Don't let me down."

Leonard lets himself again into a lightless house and undresses in the hall, wincing off his sweater and his shirt. He stows his shoes on the shelf and carries his used clothes upstairs with him for the laundry pile. The floorboards wheeze beneath his feet. It is the second time today that he has stepped naked into the bedroom. Now that his troubles seem at least partially resolved, he is in a celebratory mood.

Francine will leave for work tomorrow by half past eight, and by half past nine Leonard will have rescued himself from the madness that has trapped him briefly. He has been tired—the driving and the stress, the alcohol, the lies—but unexpectedly he now feels wide awake and optimistic rather than defeated. Francine has offered him an olive leaf. She's coiled her fingers round his fingers. She has said "Kiss-kiss." Perhaps she's surfacing at last from the hollow of her missing girl, he thinks. I'm here to help, I'm here to cherish her. So he does not put on his snooza shorts but slides under the duvet undressed. He puts his hand on Francine's hip. She's not asleep. "Too late," she says.

5

THERE'S TIME TO KILL. It's Friday morning, hardly light, and Francine is already out of bed and showered. Leonard, woken by the jerk and flap of her towels and then the bluster of a hair dryer, watches her get dressed, side-lit through the gap in the partly drawn curtains. She's always businesslike and practical on working days: her dyed auburn hair gathered at the nape of her neck in a grip, uncomplicated makeup, and what she calls her regimentals—trousers, cardigan, flat shoes, fabrics and colors that will not show dirt or mark too noticeably with scuffs from children's shoes or paintbrushes. His wife of nine years now is at her most striking when she isn't trying, in Leonard's view. The less trouble she takes, the more beguiling she seems. He recognizes her daughter, Celandine, in her, in the girlish part: the unguardedly expressive wide mouth and the forward chin now lifted for the mirror—which, though Francine is forty-eight years old, suggest a dauntless spirit and an adolescent impudence and temper.

"You're so alike, you two," he often said, usually when they were forging truces after arguments. It was an observation neither welcomed. What young woman wants to be the mirror of her mother? What mature woman wants to be considered petulant? But the comparison was inescapable, especially in Celandine's final months at home, at the beginning of last year. Then, during increasingly merciless and molten rows, their matching chins and mouths leading the assaults, Celandine's face and voice became alarmingly adult and indistinguishable from her mother's. They used to call him Cyrus, the Bringer of Peace (though more specifically the bringer of tea), on those occasions, allowing him eventually to broker a ceasefire by putting his arms round both of them and turning them to face each other until they would consent to hug. He suspected they despised him for it. Nevertheless, on occasion Francine would call out theatrically, "Cyrus, Cyrus, can we borrow you for a minute? Come here . . ." if a quarrel was brewing or if they needed arbitration. It is a pity, everyone agrees, that Cyrus was not on call that weekend when Francine's and Celandine's feet and fists took over from their mouths. There might not have been an argument at all, let alone a shocking catfight followed inevitably—given the two women's stubbornness—by this interminable cold war. He could have stood between the squabbling pair and blocked the blows: Francine's parental and reproving slap that drew blood (her wedding ring caught her daughter's cheek), and Celandine's excessive and intemperate response, followed by her midnight flight and spiteful, shamefaced silence ever since.

Nevertheless, it's gratifying for Leonard now, as he sits naked in the bed in this half-light watching Francine pull her knee-highs on, to bring to mind again the corresponding figures and smells of the two women in his pacifying embraces. He even attempts to extend his arms, almost involuntarily acting out a reconciliation that now is possible only in a fantasy, though maybe not even then, before being reminded how painful extending his arms can be. His right shoulder is usually at its worst in his waking hours. He can stretch out his good left arm until it's level with his shoulder, and higher even. But he can hardly lift the damaged one. Cyrus wouldn't be much good for making peace between Francine and Celandine these days; he could embrace them only one at a time. Leonard reaches out again, tries to make a *T*. His damaged arm sticks and stutters like the hand on a jammed clock. The best time he can semaphore into the mirrors at the bed's end, with his straight left arm marking the hour and his crooked right straining for the minutes, is 5:45, 5:55. His hour hand is stuck. The pain's demanding that he stop.

"You okay?" asks Francine, catching him in a mirror.

"Still killing me." She must be growing bored with his continual aches and pains. "The sound of one hand clapping," he adds pointlessly, and then, hoping to make light of his condition, demonstrates how clownishly hard it is for him even to put his fingertips together behind his head. "The one-armed man is king."

"You need more exercise."

AT LAST LEONARD HAS THE HOUSE to himself. He has already, from the pillow, made his resolutions for the day. More exercise, indeed. But first, and shamingly, he has to escape from Lucy Emmerson. He has to free himself from her and revoke his promise. He can, of course—he has considered it—not take her call at all, even though he has demanded it himself. He can just sit and watch the set vibrate. Then, when he does not show up at the airport rendezvous either, she'll be bound to figure out that Leonard isn't kismet after all. That should be the end of it. But she might persevere. She is the sort and age to persevere. She'll not be shaken off so easily. He quantifies the risks: she has his cell phone number but not his unlisted home address. She might make a nuisance of herself by phoning constantly, but surely not by knocking at his door. He has a sudden image of her trawling round the streets of his hometown, certain that she'll find and recognize his "creepy van." She daubs it thickly with black paint: LEONARD LESSING—SCARED TO DEATH. It is an improbable nightmare but a disconcerting one. No, there is no avoiding it. If Leonard wants to enjoy any peace of mind during the final day of his forties, he must put a stop to Lucy Emmerson at once. Their conversation might be thorny and embarrassing, humiliating even, but hardly as thorny and embarrassing as allowing her mad plot, this not-so-genius idea, to survive a moment more. He'll take the call. He will be rid of her. Then he can begin to mend his ways. No more bellyaching about his shoulder, he determines. No more frittering the best part of each day. No more wasting his sabbatical. He'll draw up a plan for the months ahead and for his sixth decade: the walks he'll take, the meals he'll cook, the worthy books he'll read, the music he'll try to write, the efforts and the sacrifices he'll make for Francine's happiness.

It is not yet 9 a.m. Leonard uses the remaining half hour before Lucy's promised call to shower properly and dress before sitting at the pivoted table in the kitchen with his *Times* online and breakfast plate. The *Rise-Time* show is drawing to a close. He listens to but does not watch the weathercast, some joshing, parting repartee among that morning's commentariat, and finally the rising headlines for the day: the Balkan Federation elects its president; another water crisis in Australia ("It's H_2Oz again!"); new treatment figures suggest that senile dementia has declined by almost 30 percent in the past decade; the death of the last Rolling Stone; Proposition 101. But not a word regarding Maxim Lermontov. Leonard checks the EuroFox channel and one or two of the more serious UK digitals, but discovers nothing. That's both surprising and suspicious. It has to signify a news blackout under the Home Defenses Act. Such "benign security obstructions" have become more frequent recently, especially with the fast-approaching summit and inevitable disruptions on the streets.

There is, however, a brief, dry summary in the home news columns of the *Times*, under the misspelled strapline "Seige Enters Third Day." Their correspondent writes: "The named suspect, an American national, is reported to have a record of criminal convictions including arson and motor vehicle theft as well as political ones, both in the United States and in Canada, where he sought and was granted protected residence in 2012 as a 'citizen by birth.'" Leonard can predict Maxie's irritation at such accurate reports, can almost hear him protesting in his stagy High Texan with that distinctive Yiddish edge, "I'm Russian, man! Russian out of U.S.A. So what, I wrecked a car or two? So what, I introduced some hellfire to a church 'n' cindered it? 'N' I hate to be picky, but it wasn't arson, it was firebombing! Y'all hear?" Then, in the closing paragraph, Leonard reads, "The armed group are thought to have been under police surveillance since entering the United Kingdom in early July, and although their purposes are unclear, it is not counted in security and intelligence circles as happenstance that their arrival coincides with the upcoming Reconciliation Summit."

Leonard would have preferred it if Maxie's apparent "purposes" had been less commendable: unambiguously criminal, perhaps, with psychopathic tendencies, brutally expressed. That would better befit a man who, in Leonard's opinion and experience, is "purposeless" and deserves little sympathy from liberals, a man who is more intent on turmoil for the sake of turmoil than on turmoil for the sake of change. But as ever, Maxie's immoderation of action is validated by latching on to a rational and sympathetic cause. No one vaguely progressive, Leonard included, could wish the Reconciliation Summit well. So long as nobody gets injured, any boisterous and dramatic disruption to the week of meetings—even this armed and desperate hostage-taking in Alderbeech—might almost be welcome, might even be counted proportionate, given what one campaign group has already labeled passionately, if not pithily, "the vile offenses of the summit's detestable guests." But with Maxie, as Leonard knows too well, there are always injuries. The day is not complete without a bloody nose.

There is, of course, Take to the Curb, a peaceful vigil Leonard can attend himself on Tuesday afternoon, if he's so concerned, with protesters lining the forty-kilometer route between the airport and the summit venue. It'll take more than eighty thousand people, standing shoulder to shoulder, if there are to be no gaps, or one third of that if they are prepared to stretch their arms and hang on by their fingertips. But no matter how hard he tries, Leonard cannot imagine himself in line these days. He means to play a part but rarely does. His shoulder isn't up to it, of course. It's shaming, actually, to be so disengaged. What will his contribution be, this fist-clenching man who only yesterday claimed he "hasn't lost the fire," when the summit and the demonstrations start? Not waving fists, for sure, except in private and at the telescreen. Not waving placards or leafleting. Not even standing silently in line. No, standing back, nursing his shoulder. He'll be standing back and watching it on-screen, at home, watching all the politics on-screen.

It's far too easy, though, in Leonard's current anxious and tormented mood—what will Lucy think of him?—to imagine Maxie at the demonstration, magically escaped from Alderbeech, just a couple of kilometers away from the route, and doing what he can to turn the vigil wild. Take to the Curb? It's not enough, he says. Take Up the Curb and throw those stone blocks against those limousines. Shoulder to shoulder? Hand in hand? Too tame, he says. Too fucking British. No, leave the line and put your shoulders up against the horses and the police and sweep those enemies away. Pit yourselves against their flesh. Tear into their flesh. Wrap your fingers round those bastards' throats. Then Maxie's at the summit gates. If there's a fracas, he is there, wielding the shaft of his placard like a truncheon. If only Maxie were less . . . no, *commendable* is not the word, Leonard thinks. *Resolute* is better. Wielding and unwavering. Now the pseudo-Texan leads the way into the summit grounds, into the summit hall, and stands with his handy placard shaft in the middle of the summit's "detestable guests." And sixteen gray-haired heads of state are knocked to the ground like scuttlepins, sixteen heads of state and one first lady of America. Blood is dripping from her nose onto the lapel of her pearl pantsuit. Leonard shakes his head, tries to drive the memory away. That final part is far too real, too near the truth, to contemplate again.

Lucy should be calling soon. He's almost eager for it now. Let's get it over with. He sits down on the futon with his cell phone resting on the arm. While he waits, prompted by his success with tracing the Emmersons last night, he idly enters "TelecomUK" and types in "Sickert," the name of Francine's dead first husband. It's something that for fear of finding nothing he hasn't dared to do, at least in any depth, since Celandine's original e-mail and phone accounts were canceled. Where should he start his search? He cannot specify a town or approximate a location code, a country even, but to satisfy the Web site's insistence, he narrows the field and offers the initial *C.* All he is offered in return is "Too many results found. Refine your search." This is not the way, Leonard thinks, closing the tab impatiently. He'll not secure a lead that easily. Instead, he Googles "UK Only, Celandine." It is the kind of given name a girl might either hate or love so much that she could never abandon it, no matter what. Francine's daughter never claimed to dislike her name, as far as he can recall, although she disliked many things, given half a chance. In fact, as a teenager she decorated the ceiling of her bedroom with suspended models of flying swallows, the bird from which her name (in Greek) was taken. They even had to call her Swallow for a while. More than fifty thousand results pile and tile onto the screen, twenty-five to the page. He shuffles through the openers as quickly as he can, but everything is horticultural—the greater celandine, the lesser celandine, the marsh celandine, the edible celandine—until the fourteenth page, where there are links to a Celandine Café in Bath and a sailboat called *Celandine* for hire in Falmouth Harbor. He does not reach the fifteenth page. His cell phone rings, and it is Lucy, button-bright and punctual.

"My God, that was so weird last night, about the bike," she says, before Leonard has a chance to speak. "How did you know about the bike? Did I say anything? What did I say? I told my mum I'd had it nicked. I'd flogged it, though. Now she thinks some bloke has found it. Wow, that's hilarious! Except it's put me in a fix."

"Listen," Leonard says.

"I'm listening."

"Today."

"Midday, I'll be there, yeah?"

"I won't be there. Sorry, Lucy, but I can't."

"Don't say you've changed your mind."

"I haven't changed my mind. Your idea's genius, it is—"

"But? But?"

But it's too risky, Leonard wants to say. It might be safe enough for you. You're just a lively kid who wants to rescue Dad. But I'm an adult and I have to be sensible, I have to be responsible. Except he dares not speak those words to her. *Sensible. Responsible.* Those are the words that teachers use on school reports for someone dull.

"Francine isn't up for it," he says, though he says it softly, just in case his lie can fly the nine kilometers to where his wife works.

"Oh, shit. Why not?"

"Well, number one, it's kidnapping a teenager, and that's against the law, big-time . . . she says."

"But I'm the one that's up for it. It's my idea."

"I told her that. She says you're just a child. I know, I know. She's anxious that she'll be held responsible. Even if it's not kidnapping exactly. She could be done for wasting police time."

"That is fucking useless, isn't it?"

"All right, calm down."

"I don't feel calm. I am pissed off."

"Well, don't blame me."

"I'm not pissed off with you." A pause. "So is she there?"

"Francine?"

"Yes."

"She's gone to work."

"Why all the whispering?"

"I promise you, she isn't here." He's frightened of this girl.

"Call her. Let me speak to her."

"There isn't any point."

"It's probably a woman thing."

"How can it be a woman thing? What sort of woman thing?"

"Because you want to bring a girl into your home, Leonard. And set her up in your spare room. Maybe Francine doesn't like the sound of that. I have to talk to her."

"Lucy, listen, I can promise you it isn't that . . ." He pauses, takes a different tack. He has to stop her even trying to speak to his wife. "But actually, you're not entirely wrong. Francine's own daughter ran away—she ran away from that spare room—about eighteen months ago. Spring last year. Okay? April the twenty-fourth. Just nineteen years of age. A girl like you—a girl who wanted to disappear."

"Where did she go?"

"That's what I'm telling you. They had a three-month quarrel, then a fight. Just fists. And feet. She packed a bag. She ran away. She disappeared. We know she's been in touch with some of her mates. So she's alive, at least. But Francine hasn't heard a word since then."

"That's bad."

"That's worse than bad, it's killing her. That empty bedroom with her daughter's stuff is all she's got to give her hope, to keep her sane." Leonard's straying into melodrama now. Still whispering. He has to bring it to an end. "You're right," he says, raising his voice. "No way she's going to take a lodger in that room, not even you, not even for a day. Now do you understand? It's difficult."

"Yeah, yeah, I'm getting it. She's squashed us flat."

"I'm sorry, Lucy. I did my best. But she went absolutely mad. We had a row about it. Quite a blazer, actually. There is no reasoning with her now. I'm just as disappointed as you are. I'm furious, in fact. It would have been, well, not exactly fun but . . ." He can't locate the word. But he thinks *valiant*.

"I think it might have made a difference. At least we would have given it a go," she says, dejected now.

"Yes, possibly. Let's talk again. I have to run. I hope we're going to stay in touch. You'll text me in a day or two, okay? Best not to phone."

"Don't worry, Comrade Leonard, Mr. Activist, *Mr.* Perkiss Number Two, I won't embarrass you." But now she has embarrassed him. Leonard flushes, head to toe. She adds, "I guess I should have known it was never going to happen when you wouldn't cut yourself yesterday, when you wouldn't shake on it with blood."

"Now, that's ridiculous—"

"What's her name?"

"Whose name?"

"The missing girl."

"Her name is Celandine Sickert."

"You're kidding me. I'd run away."

"What's that supposed to mean?"

"It means deed poll to me." She's being petulant, just for the hell of it.

"You'd change your name?" he asks, mostly glad that she has changed the subject.

"*Th*elandine *Th*ickert? That is terrible. Boy, yes, I'd dump that name. Anything with 'Sick' in it. And Celandine is pretty bad. It sounds like medicine. But Cel's okay. Yes, Cel is absolutely radiant."

"Sorry, Lucy," he says again. "Out of my hands."

"Hey, it's cool." A sigh of resignation now.

"So that's it, then? Hey, it's cool, and on our way?" Job done, thinks Leonard. Time to finish this conversation, before she wounds him any more.

"I guess it is."

"How do you feel?"

"Not happy. My little bag was packed. My father's still out there. I'm all fired up. Now what?"

And he can see her all fired up, tough and innocent, her great expanse of hair, her taming red beret, her little bag, waiting with a cigarette among the noonday vehicles parked outside the Zone superstores, the airline traffic deafening, a tough and stocky angel coming to the rescue of her dad.

"It's for the best," he says. But he's already talking to himself. She's gone. She really is a child.

IT IS ONLY 9:25 A.M. and Leonard has secured the rest of Friday for himself. He sits back on the futon, not certain whether he is feeling less burdened or more. His phone conversation with Lucy, or at least the outcome of it, has not been a mistake. He feels that in his bones. It certainly has simplified his day. He can breathe easy, knowing that there's nothing ill-advised ahead. This episode is finished with. He's got away unscathed again. He's made it back to shore. This is the day, he reminds himself, when he can take charge of his life. He will not fail again today. He will not disappoint himself again today. He lifts his one good fist and clenches it.

The Selmer has not been touched for several weeks. Its case has not even been opened. Leonard lifts the instrument out of its baize-lined mold. Taped inside the case lid is a timeworn gallery of memorabilia: a copy of his Mercury citation; a CD cover (*Less Plays Lester*) with a pleasing and convincing digital mock-up of Leonard sitting in a 1950s diner with Lester Young at his side; some small family photographs, his sister with his mother, happy days; shots of Francine and Celandine draped around each other at some music festival, more lost and happy days; and, on the flap of a torn cigarette packet, the fading, scribbled telephone number of Francine's old Brighton flat. She'd put it there herself, that windy and rewarding night of nursery rhymes. "But that was then," she said.

The saxophone feels heavy in his weakened arm. He has lost muscle tone. His frozen shoulder refers its pain across his back and down as far as the upper finger joints of his right hand. He clamps his jazz-soft Vandoren reed in place, ducks into the neck sling, checks that the spatulas and tone holes are still snugly sealed, and exercises the keys and rods with the usual practice set of unvoiced scales and melodic patterns before licking his lips and gums, lifting the horn to his mouth, and closing on that familiar, comforting rubber mouthpiece. But still he will not make a note. He takes deep breaths and pillows his diaphragm with enough air to support the sound, if and when it comes. He seals a tight, single-lip embouchure around the reed as carefully as a beginner might, judging how best to allow but still constrict a note, readying his tongue, his jaw, his pharynx, larynx, glottis, and his vocal cords, until these two vibrating tubes—the flesh, the brass—are ready to collaborate.

What to play? Not nursery rhymes. That day has passed and dimmed. He tests the sound. *Ba-dum. Ba-dum.* Four hurried notes.

He voices them again. *Do it, do it, Davey Davey, do it now.* But then he settles for something less agitated, something further from the bone: Simmy Sullivan's "Midnight at the Lavender." It's his graduation piece; it's his lollipop; he's played it round the houses, tired it out—on radio, at festivals, solo and in combos. Once—and this is not a happy memory—in Austin, Texas, even. Feel-good music. Schmooze. It ought to be unchallenging. But Leonard wants to test and exercise himself. It is a worry, always was a worry, that his musical daring might, like hearing, eyesight, concentration, sexual potency, continence, be a faculty that degenerates with age. Therefore he shifts up half a tone, toys with the opening four bars, and then returns to flatten it. An awkward sound. He starts again, jettisoning the basic chord progression and introducing vagrant notes. So he drifts away from key and stays away, lick after lick, until—almost out of the blue, though not exactly out of the blues—he finds a route from Sullivan's favorite Brooklyn bar to *Davey Davey, do it now* and finishes up with a piece he has arranged before, Shakespeare's greasy Joan. This is something—*Love's Labour's Lost* and agitated schmooze—that the world or at least the walls of this living room have never heard before—*ba-dum ba-dum, doo-wah doo-wah, tu-whit tu-whoo, a merry note*—and will never hear again, not quite like that, not quite so desperate and fine, not quite so raw. The tapered lights and shadows of the house seem, at moments such as this, architect-designed for jazz, chambers sloped and angled for the nuances of sound.

Leonard puts his horn down on the futon and stands at the window looking out across the Friday rooftops to a line of shedding trees. It's windy and the sky is pocked by autumn leaves, black against the gray. Loose notes on plain paper. He has settled something, something he has feared. Jazz has not deserted him. It's there. He hasn't lost a trick that practice won't bring back. His hearing's good—the top end's as crisp and clear as ever. He even smiles. No matter what the virgins and the innocents might say—our cat could make a better sound; why won't he leave the blessed tune alone; devil music; entertainment for the deaf and dead;

God's revenge on single men—he knows there's more to being a jazzman than sporting yellow socks and wearing shades. There's more to being a jazzman than just having a good-enough instrument and not too much supper. Good hands, good pipes, good chops are called for, yes, but a jazzman must be valiant too. A jazzman has to hold his nerve.

Enough. He boxes up and puts his saxophone away. Come Monday, when he's older, he'll reintroduce his old routines and practice every day. This brief workout hasn't done his shoulder any harm. In fact, while playing, he has forgotten all the pain. He has forgotten almost everything: the hostage house and Maxim Lermontov, Lucy and her genius idea, that morning's shaming conversation on the phone, Francine, Celandine. Even his fiftieth birthday, looming now (only fourteen hours left—of what? Being young?), promises advantage rather than loss. Unexpectedly, he's feeling bright. The weight has tumbled off him. That foolish escapade of yesterday, that skylarking, has left him virtually unmarked. A sore throat, possibly. An ego bruised. He wishes he had never taken the trip, of course, never promised anything to anyone, never thought that he could be the comrade of an almost-orphan teenager, never smoked her hand-rolled cigarettes, not told lies. But still, he's feeling happier than he has for weeks.

Leonard checks his watch. Francine will not finish work till late today—a staff meeting. He wants her home. Her unexpected—undeserved, in fact—kisses of last night, her fingers wrapped in his, her saying, "Carry me upstairs," have filled him with hope and expectation for this evening, despite her closing "Too late now" and the enduring "But that was then" of yesterday. As soon as she walks through that door, he thinks, before she has a chance to put her bags down in the hall, kick off her shoes, disappear into the loo, he'll make rapprochements of his own, he'll put an arm round her waist and press his embouchures on her to improvise his love. He'll carry her. He's energized. Can hardly wait. All he needs to do is survive the day without too much crushing introspection, and for that he needs to escape the news. He must not waste the day couch-surfing for bulletins from the hostage house. He has to step away from all of that.

It's raining resolutely, but nevertheless Leonard finds a raincoat and his wet-weather shoes and, setting the house to Alarm/Standby, steps into the leaf litter of the mews. The Celandines are still piled up across the screen.

6

THE PARK IS ALL BUT EMPTY. Only dog walkers and garden rangers labor through the rain and wind. A fast sky keeps on promising a break of light, but breaks its word. It hints at blue. It pulls its drapes aside to let a distant, better day grin through, but closes them again.

Leonard follows paved and surfaced paths, through copses of mazzard and mountain ash, skirting mud but not avoiding puddles. He's been this way many times before, though not recently. It used to be their regular stretch, especially when their terrier, Frazzle, was still alive and Celandine was young and biddable enough to tolerate and even like a walk with her parents and her pet. Now such family days are beyond reach, and would be even if Celandine were still at home, Leonard thinks, not unhappily. Kids grow up. You want them to. He's grateful, though, for the many satisfying afternoons they've spent together in this place, the three of them spread out across the path, hands linked, amused, bothered, and unified by their dog forever chasing geese and cyclists.

Leonard's smiling to himself as he recalls the afternoon when Frazzle, still an undisciplined and yapping puppy, came out of the undergrowth with a piece of wood like a sailor's corncob pipe in her mouth, and Celandine—she would have been about twelve—had the foresight and good luck, in the few seconds before the wood was crunched and dropped, to capture a hilarious, cartoonish photograph with her new Multifone.

"Popeye!" Francine said. "All she needs is the hat."

A passerby made almost exactly the same observation: "It's Popeye the sailor dog."

Celandine started chuckling, amused more by the unlikely repetition than by the joke. The man went off believing he was quite the wit. "All she needs is the hat," she called out after him, and then was lost to giggles.

"Show the photo to these people coming up," said Leonard, pointing at an elderly couple walking their own red setter farther down the path. "If you can make anybody else mention Popeye between here and the shops, I'll double your pocket money. I bet you can't." Celandine looked excited and determined, already plucking up courage to offer her photograph to strangers and wondering how she might prompt the winning and profitable words. But soon she and her mother were pressed against each other in a shaking hug, too drenched in laughter even to look at the approaching couple, let alone speak to them. The dog, the pipe, the photograph, the joke, the "Bet you can't," seemed then and still seem like a gift, a charm, a formula for happiness. He hears their laughter now. The park is hanging on to it, and so must he.

Leonard's feeling spirited again and boyishly adventurous. He takes the direct route out of the copses, striding off his stiffness and smiling to himself, until he reaches the bracelet of artificial lakes in the more formal part of the park, a few hundred meters from the shops where he has planned to treat himself to an early birthday indulgence—coffee and a pastry—and then book a bistro table for this evening. The ducks and geese draw in to him, like model boats on strings. Leonard shows them empty hands, a childish mime: no bread. They comprehend at once and drift away again, an aimless arc of coddled birds, as finally a more determined arc, of light, curves across the water, at the venting of the clouds, and resuscitates the day.

It's midday now. Leonard should be waiting at the Zone. His face is wet, as are his trouser legs, but now that the sun is strengthening he is no longer tempted by a coffee and a cake. He's bound to meet acquaintances or neighbors or some of Francine's many friends and have to answer queries. How's the shoulder? Any news of Celandine? How's Francine bearing up? Yet it's too promising—the weather, that is, and his mood—to spend the afternoon at home. Besides, this park has not provided the safe adventure he was hoping for. Too limited and tame, despite the vestiges of happy times among his family. Thirty minutes' walk is not enough. He wants to truly stretch and tire himself in grander and more vitalizing landscapes than a park.

Leonard drives the gigmobile along the ever-busy city loop and heads northward on the payroad. He travels in silence, not risking any radio and its invasive twitter for the moment. Not requiring any jazz. But he does instruct and activate the satnav and wait for its directive: *Take the next junction for the National Forest and Pepper's Holt.* This is not a bad idea, this little trip, this secret trip, he thinks. It will make good the lie. He'll do the walk he's claimed to have already done. Maybe in making good the lie he will also be making good the other embarrassments of yesterday, from hostage house to cigarettes. It will be like hitting the Restore button on a computer. By taking to the woods, he'll turn the clocks back to an Earlier Selected Date. He can imagine sitting opposite Francine this evening in whatever restaurant they end up in and being able to describe to her with brazen confidence his visit to Pepper's Holt. Thursday, Friday? What's the difference? And if she asks him what he did today, he'll say he played his saxophone, composed a tune called "Davey, Joan, and Lavender," then walked round the park but didn't feed the ducks. No actual fibbing there. He shakes his head, exasperated with himself. Why does he have to straighten out his life by complicating everything, by piling up, not lie on lie exactly, but secrecy on secrecy?

He pays his entry toll to a cheerily officious Natfo volunteer at the warden lodge and, following instructions, drives through disinfectant troughs and over wildlife grids into the woods and the cliff-shrouded clearings of the historic mine workings, where vehicles can park. Here the soil is still too impacted and toxic for any vegetable growth other than nettles, brambles, and knotweed. But beyond the barefaced cliffs, the light is high and bright, a fine day, at last, for walking. He will hike up into the birch hursts, where at this time of the year, with the trees half stripped of leaves, it should be easy to spot parties of deer and maybe even catch sight of this district's almost-native bustards or the families of escaped wallabies that the Natfo man has said are "a must" for any visitor.

Leonard reaches for his binoculars. As his hand frees them from the van's stowage box, he lets his knuckles brush against and nudge the radio alive. He can't resist. Before he sets off on the walk, he might as well discover (if the news blackout has lifted) that Maxie is all right. Or that Maxie is in custody. Or that Maxie has agreed to talk. For Lucy's sake, he doesn't quite want Maxie dead, but he would certainly be relieved to hear that her hopes of visiting her father behind bars are likely to be realized, and soon. He'll appreciate the hiking and the trees all the more, knowing that his caution and dishonesty this morning on the phone have been vindicated. No point pretending otherwise. But there is static on the set. The radio will only cough and clear its throat. He chooses another level of preselects, but these are no less bronchial. A couple more. With no success. And Retune fails to find any traction in the traffic of signals. The scanner shuffles through every single station and all the frequencies, chasing any signal strong enough to hold good. The numbers pelt across the screen; the stations briefly name themselves with their IDs, too fast to read, but nothing takes purchase. Then the names and numbers roll round again with little to delay them, not a note of music, not a human sound, not a word of news, just the woof and tweet of distant frequencies that sound like animals in undergrowth.

Neither the van's speakerphone nor Leonard's cell does any better. They offer only *No network provision. Try again later.* This clearing is not only toxic and impacted, it is information-dead as well, too buried in the countryside, too screened by cliffs and woods, too underused to merit contact. Whatever's happened in the hostage house, whatever shape the greater world is in, cannot insinuate itself into Pepper's Holt. Leonard is out of reach. He shrugs. He even says "So be it" to himself. Perhaps it's just as well, preferable even, to be beyond the bulletins. Where ignorance is bliss, 'tis folly to have radios. He drops his cell phone into the space vacated by the binoculars and checks his watch. It's almost disappointing to see the second hand circling so firmly. Time should have failed as well. It's early afternoon. He has more than three hours in which to explore the forests and still get home in time for doormat hugs with Francine. He puts his binoculars and his coat into a backpack, tucks his trousers into his socks, pulls his beach cap on—QUEUE HERE—and starts to climb toward the freshened sky and the silver stands of birch.

It often happens when Leonard's walking on his own. There is something about the countryside—woods, hills, the coast, the riverbanks, no matter what—that makes him feel both reckless and slightly anxious, like an escaped animal, one of those must-see wallabies, perhaps, or a family pet that has broken loose and is equally excited and unnerved by freedom. How could it not? Forests like these were where he and his boyhood friends played hidey-hunt and fought their concocted battles, carried out their ambushes, were Robin Hood and his Merry Men, were Spartacus, were fugitives. As a child, he spent countless Saturdays hiding from marauders in the branches of an oak when there were oaks, or creeping on all fours toward a suspect shed, or following the outer hedges of a field rather than cutting across on the footpath where his foes might spot him. Such unrealities, so sustained and engrossing for a child, should have been driven out of him with puberty. That's growing up. When you finally become part of the world, there should no longer be any need to act it out. Can it be possible that from all those rough-and-tumble friends of forty years ago, only he—little nervous Lennie, now almost fifty years of age—is still enthralled by these compulsions, still favors hedgerows over the open field?

He has gone well beyond the car park and is climbing up less trodden paths with no reassuring signs of humankind except the occasional nesting box and the vapor trails of jets. The forest makes its comment every time he takes a step. Leaf litter cracks and rustles at his feet, mimicking the static on the radio. Saplings, bullied by the wind, yelp and squeak like animals. A patch of restless, waving light suggests at first that someone's following—and then it stops, it hides itself. Leonard cannot help but pick up and carry the first strong branch he sees, holding it more like a cudgel than a walking stick. And then he holds it like a gun. He will defend himself. He's acting as if he's twelve years old again, a fearful and excited boy, lost in the tucks and folds of the forest, and imagining—his favored fantasy—that he's fighting Fascism in 1930s Spain. What if he falls and breaks a leg, perhaps? What if a pack of wolves sweeps out of the trees? What if Franco's men are closing in on him? How will he call for help, without a phone, without a working radio, but just the woof and tweet of distant frequencies? How can he safely reach Orwell, Perkiss, Hemingway, and his other comrades in the International Brigade? Alone in Pepper's Holt this afternoon, when he could have been on active service in a real adventure with an actual "kidnapped" girl, Leonard Lessing cannot stop himself from imagining and forging filmy memories from things that have never occurred, at least to him. He's stepping lightly through the undergrowth, in Catalonia.

He has reached the plug of weathered rock that offers views across the carbon-eating canopies into the wooded valleys of the reserve and the newly planted blocks of light-efficient, black-leaved trees, Turning Sunshine into Fuel. He is careful to be silent, watching where he steps, avoiding loose rocks and brittle timber, staying out of sight. When he's found a high nook in the rocks where he can safely wedge himself, he takes out his binoculars and trains them on the countryside, checking every angle for signs of Franco's men. *No pasarán.* His aching shoulder is a shrapnel wound. The birches are olive trees. The smudge of gray on the horizon is the fug of Barcelona, smarting from the bombs.

7

LEONARD'S BUSY IN THE TRAPEZIUM. His clothes are hardly damp from the afternoon of walking and combating Fascism in the woods, but he takes off his socks and trousers and pulls on a pair of sweatpants, still warm from the dryer. He continues to resist the news and tunes the DAB receiver to a New York jazz station and a Eurofusion band he does not recognize and does not like ("Oh, loosen up," he thinks) while hunting in the cupboard for a vase. On the drive back home, he stopped at his local shops, booked a corner table for the evening at Wilbury's, where the chef is used to naught percent diners, and bought an autumn mix, mostly garden perennials—Michaelmas daisies, chrysanthemums, rudbeckia. Already they are past their best. He has to pick up petals from the floor. He'll spruce the bunch up a bit, he thinks, with foliage from the patio, some fern sprays or sprigs of variegated bay. Francine appreciates it, praises him, when he arranges and displays the flowers he has bought or picked for her, rather than just handing them to her in a wrapped bunch with the implication "women's work." He prepares a short strong coffee in their silver macinato and rewards himself with barely half a spoon of sugar. He puts away the crockery. Wipes surfaces and handles. Pours planet-friendly disinfectant down the sink. So this is what it's like to be retired, a life of undemanding walks, role-play, light shopping, housework, nothing much to do that counts.

But this, today, is not a thought that bothers him. Today, so far, has been a chance to recuperate, to close a mortifying chapter in his life and plan the next, a better one. Fifty years of age. On Monday there will be changes. Improvements. He vows it for the hundredth time. But first he has a birthday and two days of rest, and fun. The weekend can be a breathing space.

The fusion band has finally finished its exasperating tour of Old World influences. The jazz DJ reads out the lineup. Leonard has played with only one of them. Rafaelo Vespucci, the not-so-Italian percussionist. Not that they'd ever spoken or even looked each other in the eye—the gig had been one of those show up, shake hands, and shimmy events, businesslike, unsociable. Several of the other names are familiar too. Bushy Miles (Milorad Busch) on assisted accordion, Adelina Julian on keyboards, and a reed player called Felix Marcel. It is that final syllable that sticks and hovers in the air. Leonard has to tussle with it for a moment or two before he remembers why it is shouting at him with such persistence. He mutters to himself, Marcel, Marcel, Mar Cel, and then, barefoot, walks into the living room and, sitting on the futon once again, fires up the telescreen where his Celandines have waited patiently all day. He clears the screen and starts again, clicking from Menu into Browse and on to UK Only, as he did last night. He enters the letters *c e l* with his forefinger, percussively. The memory window prompts "Celandine," but Leonard clicks Ignore, taps the Proceed arrow, and starts to scroll.

This time there's nothing horticultural on offer, nothing *lesser*, *marsh*, or *edible*, nor are there any restaurants listed or yachts for sale in Falmouth or Bath. In fact, in the opening pages at least, his target word is offered only in capital letters, most popularly an acronym for the Christian Ecology Link and then for various Centers (for Educational Leadership, or European Law, or Excellence in Learning, or Equine Leasing) and Campaigns (everything from Economic Liberalism to Ethical Lawncare). Leonard scans and skips the pages, twenty-five selections at a time, but hardly finds a single twin-cased *Cel* and certainly none quoted as a woman's name. He Narrows Search, selecting Blogs & Journals, and this time finds a less impersonal list, including, finally, a man who has signed himself as Cel and runs—he is no Celandine; a Celwyn, then—an appreciation thread for all things Welsh.

For no sound reason other than his current optimistic mood, Leonard already feels a little less distant from his stepdaughter and thereby closer to his wife. Simply hunting for her helps, even if he's only hunting on the Internet. He's enticed by the prospect that someday soon when Francine lets herself into the house, defeated by a day at school, he will be able to provide her daughter's phone number or her address or even say that he has been in touch with Celandine. And everything is well with her. And everything is well because of him. So Leonard perseveres. He tries to Narrow Search again by adding more "exact coordinates," like "Francine," "Lessing," even "Unk," but narrowing is widening. The matches that he finds expand the possibilities, even throwing up a family in Ohio who for a moment seem to be a mirror of his own except that in their case their Unk's a springer spaniel. There is a Web page and a file of photographs.

Leonard tries another list. This time, prompted by the Ohio dog, he includes "Frazzle," the pipe-smoking terrier. A loved and doting dog's a sedative. She used to hang her tail and growl with such sorrow when Francine and her daughter rowed. They hated that. The guilt of it. The dog could sometimes end the argument when even Cyrus couldn't put a stop to it.

Unusually, the engine takes its time, then clogs on failure for a while before declaring "No Results." The screen's clear, for once. The header asks, "Did you mean, frizzle dog celandine francine?"

He tries again, removing "Francine" from the list. Just six results, and none is promising. But still it feels like progress, to have his options reduced to manageable numbers. His final try is "Frazzle Terrier." Four choices now: a pet-food company in Spalding, Lincolnshire; two student blogs, one of which thinks "frazzle-dazzle" is a term denoting razzmatazz; and a link to a profile page on a networking site. He opens the last of these, a mess of graphics and shouting fonts, almost too colorful and busy to read. He left-clicks for the Go To option, types in "Frazzle Terrier" again, and ends up on the closing entries of a completed "Personal Data Questionnaire." What is your favorite meal? (Pasta with seafood.) What is your favorite drink? (Boulevard Liqueur. No rocks.) What is your favorite animal? (Frazzle, my old terrier. She died.)

Leonard is anticipating disappointment now. This questionnaire is teasing him by striking chords. Yes, Celandine was that rare teenager, one with an appetite for fish. And yes, she was always fond—even when she should have been too young to know the difference—of sweet and sticky spirits. But such preferences could easily apply to thousands of young networkers. Even Frazzle cannot be a unique name for a pet. He scrolls up, speed-reading answers, hoping for stronger evidence and more coincidences but not finding any, until his cursor hits the ceiling of the questionnaire and its opening Q&As. His eyes flood instantly. He feels hollow, weightless even. He has to gasp and cough at the same instant. He has to wait for his eyes to clear and for his coughing fit to stop before he is able to study the screen again and absorb what has been written. This fish-eating networker is female. She is twenty years old. Green eyes and chestnut hair. Her name, she says, is Swallow.

It is with an agitated hand that Leonard finds the Friendship box and, limited to thirty words, completes the sentence "Dear Swallow, I want to be your online friend because . . ." He types: "i hope youre celandine. were missing you, your mum and me. its time to be in touch again. my birthday tomorrow. 50! come to the party please please PLEASE." There's one word unused. He puts in "Unkx," erases it, both name and kiss, replaces it with "Cyrus." Before he has a chance to lose his nerve, Francine's daughter's stepfather, the peacemaker, selects Submit. He falls back on the futon, weightless still, and offers up a nonbeliever's prayer.

He would have slept. He is tired enough. This has been a day of peaks and troughs. But after only ten minutes of a shallow, dream-plagued nap, Leonard is roused by the spoken word. The music that has been playing loudly in the kitchen has ended finally and there is someone talking, not the cosmo DJ whose voice has been bluesy and unhurried but a spiky clock-watching American newsreader. There has been a fleeting mention of Maxim Lermontov, Leonard reckons. Yes, there it is again. On-screen, he selects a rolling news network and bloats the box so that he can both listen to the newscaster and read the headline straps that gust across the screen in colored bands: red for news, blue for trading reports, green for sports. He hangs the cursor on the red band and, with an agitated hand again—why's that?—waits for a prompt. It comes as "Siege Enters Day Three." He captures it, and once again he is live in Alderbeech and only meters from the hostage house.

This channel's reporter is an Australian stringer, speaking slowly and deliberately, as he is feeding stations in Europe, Asia, and America, where his viewers might not have English as their mother tongue. "Maxim Lermontov, a Canadian citizen, is not unknown in global security circles," explains the journalist, as the familiar photographic still of Maxie's face and hair replaces Alderbeech. "He has been linked in recent months to the faction called Final Warning. This group has carried out armed attacks on banks, financial institutions, and international corporate organizations. It was Final Warning which in July 2021 attacked the FU-MI Corporation headquarters in Seoul, when an employee and a female passerby were killed in an exchange of fire. Killed by *police* marksmen, I should say. It is not known if Lermontov was among that group of terrorists, but certainly his suspected connection with Final Warning and its associated American wing, Terminus, is causing considerable alarm among British security forces at this time."

The journalist turns his body sideways and the camera shifts from him and Maxie to the hostage house. "What is certain," he adds, a little out of focus, "is that some sort of detonation—a pistol shot, perhaps, though this is disputed—has been heard from inside the house today and that the British police and British authorities are quickly losing patience. So now, this latest development, this secondary, related kidnapping, makes the securing of a speedy and nonviolent resolution all the more urgent and alarming."

Leonard drops onto his knees and kneels within a meter of the telescreen. His heart is beating far too fast. His throat is dry. But the Australian has gone, and the weather chart is scrolling wind and temperature values for Saturday.

He tries another bank of channels but finds only the briefest summaries and not a mention yet of any secondary, related kidnapping. The home-based networks are still constrained by blackout filters, it would appear. He knows at once he has to phone, though what he'll say when she picks up is not clear to him. I want to be your online friend because . . .

Lucy's number is stored in his handset's memory from that morning's conversation. He calls and, still on his knees before the now muted telescreen, counts the ringtones up to eight before the answer service picks up his call and Lucy herself says, "Hi, I'm out of reach right now. Do what you have to do . . ." Leonard shuts her off. He had better not record a message and reveal himself. But he cannot leave it there. He also has the number for the Emmerson house phone. He keys the number for a second time, and it has hardly rung at all, it has hardly made a sound, before his call is answered by a breathless older man. Leonard knows the voice but cannot place it immediately.

"Is that the Emmersons'?"

"Correct."

Now Leonard has it. It's Lucy's obliging grandfather, the one who provided him with information about the "stolen" bike. Grandpa Norman, wasn't it? There are urgent voices in the background, distressed, Nadia possibly. *Who is it? Is it her?* "Shh. I'm listening. Hello, hello." Leonard presses End and closes down the call.

He is on-screen again. Heart drumming, he locates the same female reporter from the first day of the hostage-taking, togged out in a button-through work suit and with her hair clipped back but now standing outside the Home Security headquarters with "a newly released press statement." In as motherly a tone as she can muster, she explains that "a seventeen-year-old girl who cannot be named for legal reasons" has been abducted by "a vigilante group" who are threatening what they call *equivalence* and *parity*, that is to say that any harm that befalls any of the hostage family will be visited on the abductee. "What my sources can reveal," she says, stepping toward the camera to impart a confidentiality, "is that police are also keen to talk with Lucy Emmerson, the British daughter of the Canadian suspect who early Thursday identified her father to the security forces as Maxie Lemon." A sidescreen offers yesterday's material with yesterday's relentless rain, a long shot of the security barricades, a group of men in uniform, a solid adolescent girl in a red beret and dark clothes, her back turned to the hostage house, either speaking closely to her cell phone or crying. "Given existing reporting restrictions, we can only suppose . . ." the reporter begins to add, but Leonard hears what he knows to be—how many times he's longed to hear that sound—Francine's little car, parking in the mews outside.

Now he is truly flustered. He'll be discovered again. His wife has recently developed a heavily tolerant expression whenever she returns from work to catch her husband on the futon, his face lit up by the telescreen. "And so the world goes by," she's said on one occasion. "You live in two dimensions, Leonard. Nowadays." And when he's argued that "two dimensions are better than the one that most people exist in—they've no idea or interest in what's going on around the world," her reply has been accurate and devastating, despite the lightness of her voice. That's when she's named him a sofa socialist, a television activist, an Internet poodle, a vassal of the silver screen. She's said, "You've no idea what's going on *off-screen*, in fact. You've no idea what's going on *in your own house*."

"Oh, yes. What's going on? In your considered view?"

"Nothing, nothing, nothing. Not a thing. The weeks go by and everything's the same. In my considered view."

She is right to say these things, of course, to fear what they've become—since Celandine. Yes, he's addicted to the broadcast world and to the great and flat expanses of the Web, no doubt of that. Look how he spends so much of his time compulsively jumping from channel to channel, hopping from Web site to Web site, skipping from station to station, swapping from phone to phone, as if the richness of his life depends on a blizzard of media snow. Look how unnerved he was earlier today at Pepper's Holt watching the frequency scanner on his van radio shuffle through the stations but unable to locate a signal. How briefly isolated he has felt, and panicky, to find himself with *No network provision* on his cell phone. He shakes his head, shakes it at himself, in disapproving disbelief. This is a form of slavery. He's sacrificed the daylight for the screen, and see, the afternoon has disappeared without his noticing. The window glass has flattened with the dusk. If he doesn't turn the screen off now, he will be caught, red-eyed, red-faced. He will be shamed again.

He's just in time. Here is Francine's door key in the lock, and the chirrup greeting of the house alarm, the clatter of her shoes and bags, her work-worn Friday sigh that says, Thank God, I'm home, the squeaking hinges on the toilet door, another sigh. Leonard's on his feet at once. Not quite caught out. Caught out at what? He hurries to the kitchen, but there's no time to gather foliage from the patio or find that vase. Francine's standing at the kitchen door already, removing her grip and pushing her fingers through her hair. Leonard's blushing, unaccountably.

"What have you done today?" she asks.

"Played a bit of saxophone. Wrote half a song. Went round the park." He will not mention Swallow / Celandine just yet. Francine must think he's spent a screen-free day. Besides, in the hour since he discovered the Frazzle-loving girl on the networking site, his confidence that she is almost certainly his stepdaughter has waned. Coincidence is all it is. A dog, a bird, but nothing definite.

"Jog round the park, did you?" Francine indicates his sweatpants and raises an eyebrow.

"Got wet, got changed," he says.

"I tried to phone, but you were dead."

Leonard blushes more deeply now. What can he say? That the park has no network provision. She'll know that isn't likely. That he's been out to Pepper's Holt. "Again?" she'll ask. "That's twice this week."

"I left my cell here, turned off," he says. "I was only going to the shops. For these." He hands the autumn mix to her, still wrapped. She smiles. She kisses him. She says, "They're beautiful." But there is something missing in her face and in her voice. She sees his gift is incomplete; perhaps, she sees her husband has not given it his usual loving touch.

They do make love before they go out to the restaurant. Francine has decided that they will, they must. She caught him watching her reflection in the mirror this morning, watching her pull on her clothes, put back her hair, apply her lipstick, and she has seen the worry in his face and recognized his steadfast love for her. She knows they have drifted and she blames herself for that. She blames herself for being sharp with him, for parting from him in the morning and at night with dismissive quips like "That was then" and "Too late now" and "You need more exercise." He brings her breakfast in the morning, doesn't he? He brings her Florentines. He buys her flowers. She wants to be kinder to him, more giving and more generous, more physical, no matter that she feels as hollow as a shell. She phoned him this afternoon without success to say just this: Tomorrow you'll be fifty years of age. Let's make your birthday memorable.

Francine rests her face against her husband's shoulder. "Is that the poorly one?" she asks. Her voice is husky and a little strained, as it often is by Friday evening, at the end of a week of speaking loudly and firmly to a nursery class. "Let me rub your poorly shoulder. Let me rub it better." She's talking to a four-year-old.

Leonard has not recognized what she intends for him, not yet.

He thinks, She's acting tired, she looks and sounds exhausted. Perhaps she won't be pleased that he has presumed to book a table at Wilbury's and would rather take it easy at home, read, have an early night. Perhaps he ought to phone and cancel, then she can rest and he can waste another evening chasing bulletins, up till late, alone with the telescreen and his anxieties, enslaved, while Francine sleeps upstairs with hers.

Today's events have panicked him. He's trembling. But Francine thinks his trembling is caused by her. She nuzzles him. She turns her mouth to his. Soon their different troubles have been largely set aside for a short while, while she unbuckles him and he unfastens her and, fused at the chin and nose, they negotiate a stumbling way into the darkened living room and fall onto the futon, where finally—it's been too many weeks—they satisfy a less-than-childish fantasy that does not require a passion for the Spanish Civil War. They imagine making love while they are doing it. They cast themselves as lovers in a film, a hero and a heroine. And no, she's not too tired when it is over to shower quickly, blow-dry her hair, and apply—while Leonard, who has fixed their tonic aperitifs, watches from the bedroom chair—more lively makeup than that morning's and a splash of scent. She selects an outfit that she knows pleases him, a boxy emerald jacket and a straight black skirt. At once she looks less businesslike and less child-resistant than she did on her return from work. She finds a flattering silk scarf and tries out jewelry, turning to her husband and then the mirror for approval.

"Well?" she asks, giving a twirl, like a teenager.

"You always look beautiful," he says.

"Oh, yes? That's the tonic talking."

"I've only had a sip."

"It only takes a sip at our age. Come on, then, you—let's stagger down to dinner. I'm starving. I could eat a plate of wood."

"Would that be medium or *bleu*, madam?"

They walk the kilometer to Wilbury's arm in arm. A decent autumn night, with stars. They'll do their best when they are seated at their corner table in the restaurant, intimate and slightly drunk, waiting for their vegetarian options to be plated and brought out, to put a brave face on their worlds, their private, inner, hidden worlds, not to express or share how anxious they are still, or why. So this Friday finishes, and Leonard's decade finishes, at peace, an anxious, loving, troubled, transitory peace.

8

LEONARD LESSING IS FIFTY YEARS OLD AT LAST. As usual on a Saturday, he is the first to wake, but even he has slept much later than usual. It is a minute or two before nine. His stomach at once feels bloated with worry, but that is not unusual lately; this waking anxiety from dreams he cannot quite recall can last all day. He's used to it. The first heavy thought that burdens him consciously is that he has not yet discovered any details of Lucy's "kidnapping." The second, troubling in its own way, is that today is his birthday and that he will be obliged to socialize. There will be plans for him. Plans and traps. A dinner party, probably. He'll be too unsettled to entertain or be entertaining unless he tidies up his life a bit. If he's quick he can be downstairs in time to watch the news headlines and also check his mailbox for any reply from the girl he dare not think of as anyone but Swallow. He will need to be careful not to disturb Francine. If he is heavy on the mattress or tugs the duvet too carelessly, she will wake, and then she will want him to stay where he is so that she, for once, can prepare breakfast for him in bed. She can be the waitress. He can be the guest. And then she'll want to sit with him while he drinks his tea and opens the presents and cards she will have wrapped for him. Possibly they will make love again. High days and holidays, and anniversaries.

Leonard rolls over, transferring his weight as gently as he can, and slips quietly out of bed. The floor and air are wintry. Beyond the curtains, the sky is still dull, but the patio and garden show lustrous and satiny. The first frost of the year. But Leonard does not rummage for a sweater or a dressing gown. He steals out of the room, bare-chested and wearing only his snooza shorts, wraps a towel around his shoulders, and descends into the hall, where there are already several birthday cards waiting on the mat, together with circulars, and leaflets for a takeaway. Just at the moment when he stoops to gather them, a shadow falls across the door window. Someone rings the bell and, just for good measure, raps the knocker too. He expects it is a birthday delivery of some kind. But when he straightens with a handful of letters and leaflets and reaches for the lock handle, he sees at once through the brittled glass that there are several people standing on his porch. Large men. Instead of opening and answering, he goes into the little dressing room where he and Francine keep their bikes and coats, kneels on the floor, and pulls back one slat of the blind a centimeter or so.

Three men at least. Not anyone he knows by sight. There might be others farther along the path, hidden by the shrubbery. Certainly there's movement. Shapes and shadows. Probably they are salesmen of some kind, cold-callers or political canvassers, or, given the numbers, some evangelical church group, and he will be required to stand on his front mat, half clothed and shivering, and account for his energy and Internet preferences, or his party and voting affiliations, or his expectations of paradise. If he stays still and out of sight for a minute or so, then surely they will take the hint and go away.

Leonard sits with his back to the wall, his head below the

sill. He can't be seen, he's sure of it. This is a tried and tested hiding place that over the years has saved him from encounters with tiresome neighbors, charity volunteers, and unexpected friends. He's becoming homophobic, Francine says: "*Homo sapiens*, that is." He flexes his shoulders and neck. He studies his naked toes. He runs a finger down the front forks of his street bike and promises himself that he will ride it more often, just as soon as his shoulder repairs. The doorbell rings again, more heavily, and someone is rapping with keys or a metal pen on the dressing room window. Evidently Leonard's flipping of the blind was noticed. The callers know his name as well. One of the men has his forehead pressed against the pane and is repeating, "Mr. Lessing, sir, please come to the door."

Reluctantly, Leonard starts to stand. He knows that practiced tone of voice. But Francine is in the hall before him, barefoot, in her crumpled linen nightie, and is already pulling at the lock before she spots her husband rising to his feet. "What on earth—?" she says, though Leonard is not clear if that is aimed at him—his cowering, his seminakedness—or at their visitors, who, once the lock is sprung, are pushing back the door and, unlike the most determined salesmen, canvassers, or evangelists, entering the hall uninvited. And without wiping their feet. The first of them, a casually dressed man in his early thirties with a two-day growth of reddish beard, holds up his ID fob. "NADA," he says, the misleadingly feminine and cozy—unless you're Spanish—acronym for the National Defense Agency, not quite the police, not quite the SAS. The second and the third are older men, plump and neat and, it is clear at once, more polite, though both are evidently carrying handguns under their jackets. They could be brothers, except that one has a local accent and the other is a Scotsman. They show their own IDs—regular police officers—and hold up a printed document with the house address written out in heavy ink at the top. It's a search and entry warrant, they explain.

"Why's that?" asks Francine.

"Mrs. Lessing?"

"Yes, that's me."

They've come for Francine, Leonard thinks. It's all to do with her. His body blushes with relief, a little guiltily. What has she done? Or what has happened at her school? A kid's been hurt, perhaps. Didn't she mention some incident the other day? A broken arm? Then, suspecting worse, his body blushes cold again. Three officers—and now he sees another one in uniform standing at the outer gate—is quite a force. Something personal and certainly more tragic than a broken arm must have happened for so weighty a response. It's Celandine, he thinks. There's no one else. And as he thinks it, Francine thinks the same. She almost sinks onto the ground; her face is instantly as white and crumpled as her nightie. "Is it Celandine?" she says, talking to the older men. "Has something happened to our girl?"

"Who's Celandine?" the NADA agent asks.

"My daughter. Celandine Sickert."

"How old's she?"

"She's only twenty."

"Is she at home?"

"She went away . . . last year."

"Where is she now?" His tone is browbeating.

"Do *you* know where she is?"

He does not even shake his head, but turns to his two colleagues and says, "So let's get on with it."

"Get on with what?" Leonard feels he ought to speak, and firmly. These are Franco's men. "This is not acceptable," he says, with as much dignity as a shivering man in his underclothes can display. "This is a family home. My wife has not done anything, I'm sure. Make a proper appointment if you must. You could at least have wiped your feet. In fact, you ought to take your shoes off at the door like any other visitors." He wags a finger at the costly floor timbers—British cherrywood—and shakes his head, though there's not a mark on them.

"This is not a social call," the young one says.

"It certainly is not."

"Can we suggest you pop into your living room, the pair of you, and give us twenty minutes?" the Scotsman says, attempting a smile but already spreading his arms and herding them toward the door of the teleroom. "Sit there." He points toward the futon. "We'll not be long. If all is well."

"Can we at least dress ourselves?"

"No, sir. Stay exactly where you are."

"I'm cold." Leonard regrets admitting it at once. It has made him sound too timorous and frail. *Foolish fragile feeble flimsy frail,* he thinks.

The Scotsman puts a reassuring, warning hand on Leonard's upper arm. Bare skin. "We'll not be long," he promises.

"I also have a shoulder condition." Leonard winces at the policeman's touch, more from embarrassment and cold than any honest pain.

They are not long. But they are noisy. Francine and Leonard listen to the thump of feet on the floorboards above, the unlocking of cupboards and the slamming of doors, the rolling open of drawers. They hear the scrabble of a dog, and finally see it, a rangy, heavy-hipped Alsatian, with its handler, first on the patio, picking up the scent of cats, and then tugging on its lead toward the little outbuilding and the garbage trolleys. The Scotsman has not left the room. He's minding them, but he has the good manners not to stare directly at them as they sit, with four bare knees, four bare arms, and their nightclothes. He does, though, study Francine, watching her reflection in the window glass. He can smell, as Leonard can, the sleep on her, the loose ends of the perfume she used the night before. He has every reason to admire her legs and hair. He does not turn when she and her husband start whispering. "I'll ask you not to talk. Just yet. If you don't mind," he says, and then adds—requiring no reply and not inferring any approval either—"Interesting place you've got." By interesting, he means eccentric and suspicious.

Within thirty minutes they are done. The policeman with the local accent puts his head round the living room door and tells his colleague, "Not a sign. We're clean," and Francine and Leonard are thanked for their patience and asked to go upstairs—without a minder—and to dress. "What's going on?" they ask each other, as soon as they are out of earshot and pulling on the first clothes they can find in their disordered bedroom.

"It's something to do with you, I think," Leonard says. "With school?"

"You think it's Celandine?"

"It isn't Celandine. They haven't even heard of Celandine. That isn't it."

"What, then? What do you think they're looking for?"

He shrugs. "Search me. Whatever it is, we haven't got it, have we? Or they haven't found it." Some kind of error, they decide. Some farcical blunder.

"The wrong address entirely?" Francine suggests.

"They have your name. They called you Mrs. Lessing, didn't they? They do know who you are."

Their house has almost emptied. Only the NADA agent remains. When Leonard and Francine return downstairs, ready to demand explanations, he is standing in the living room, studying the row of historic framed jazz posters on the wall—old concert programs signed and personalized for Leonard by Carla Bley, Dave Douglas, and Natty "the Gnat" Nicolson, an older generation of jammers.

"Play an instrument?" he asks, addressing neither of them in particular and not waiting for an answer. He stabs his finger at the folder he is holding. "Everything is here," he says. "The tenor saxophone, yes?" and he looks up, smiling, much amused, it seems. "Happy birthday, Mr. Lessing. It's today. Correct?"

"Some birthday," Leonard says.

"Apologies if we have spoiled the festivities. Some questions, though. Then I'll hope to leave the two of you in peace." He flashes his photo fob and agent ID for a second time but holds them steady, requiring Leonard and Francine to verify the details. His name, Leonard is unnerved to read, is Rollins, though Simon rather than

Sonny. He pulls his folder open and holds up a photograph. "Do either of you know, have either of you seen, this girl?"

"No idea," says Francine, spreading her hands and fingers as if to say, Enough of this.

Leonard takes a half step forward. Puts a hand out. "Let me see," he says. He knows the face at once. It's clearly Lucy Emmerson, aged about fourteen and not yet sexy and theatrical but puppy-plump and bored. The hair, though, is unmistakable, already thick and piled. He holds her portrait with both hands, because he's shaking slightly. Not Francine, then. He's the one they've come for. It's about the "kidnapping." Why had he ever doubted it? He makes his mind up straightaway. This photo's three or four years old, an imperfect likeness. He can lie about it if he wants. It's best not to volunteer any information but to stay his hand. There's nothing on his conscience, nothing illegal anyway. Whatever they have found to link him to this girl's disappearance cannot be against the law, unless buying alcohol for a minor or driving with wine in his bloodstream is a serious enough crime to warrant the attentions of so many men. This is just routine, he suspects. Heavy-handed and routine. Someone, maybe Nadia, has mentioned his long-past connection with Maxie. The police are simply checking, as they should, given that they must believe this kidnapping is genuine. He will not betray his new young friend. He owes her that.

"It isn't Celandine, that's for sure," he says.

"You've never spoken to this girl? Lucy Katerina Emmerson. Either of you?" He lets them shake their heads before turning to another printout sheet. "Then please explain the phone log that I have for calls made and received within the past forty-eight hours by phones registered to you. Thursday night, ten-seventeen p.m.: a male using your cell, Mr. Lessing, calls Lucy Emmerson's grandfather, seeking her home number. Ten twenty-eight p.m.: a male using your cell, Mr. Lessing, speaks to Lucy's mother, claiming to have located her stolen bike—"

"What is this, Leonard? Is this you?" Francine has whitened again.

"The same male also talks with Lucy herself, according to her mother. More about the bike, she thinks. Friday, nine-oh-two a.m., that's only yesterday: Lucy Emmerson calls this same number, Mr. Lessing, from her own handset. That conversation lasts, let's see, for thirteen minutes. There's more." He smiles again. Rollins is warming to his task. "Five thirty-six p.m., last evening. Somebody, could be anyone who has access to your handset, Mr. Lessing, reaches this young woman's answer service but, in spite of being invited to 'do what you have to do,' chooses not to leave a message. Two minutes later, five thirty-eight p.m., a man using your cell again, Mr. Lessing, speaks to Miss Emmerson's grandfather at the family home. And that conversation lasts for just four seconds. Though long enough for us to make a note of it—"

"Bravo," says Leonard.

"Now, let me show another face to you." He does not even hold it up for Francine but hands it immediately to Leonard. It's Maxim Lermontov, a recent formal photograph with a police detention tag attached to it and a committal number. "Ring any bells with you?"

"It's the guy who's taken hostages."

"Know him personally?"

"Used to. Once. Long time ago."

"Seen him recently?"

"Haven't seen him since, oh, 2006."

"Been in touch in any other ways?"

"No. Not at all."

"Final warning. What do those words mean to you?"

"They mean what they mean in plain English."

"But otherwise?"

"A protest group. A violent protest group."

"How would you know that, Mr. Lessing?"

"From the television. On the news. Yesterday. I watch the news. I keep myself informed."

The NADA agent shakes his head. "This makes no sense to me," he says, and chins a smile at Francine as if to ask if *this* makes any sense to her. He shows he's happy when she shakes her head. "Your wife is mystified."

"Explain," she says. Either one of you, she means.

"What do we have?" Rollins continues, turning now to Francine as he might to a baffled colleague for help. "We have a girl your husband says he's never met or spoken to, and yet some male has used his phone to contact her or someone in her family—what?" He turns to his folder, quickly counts the log. "Five times at least. Five times that we know of. We have a hostage situation thanks to a guy armed to the teeth, a guy who's been a friend of your husband, a guy we've been informed by Lucy's mother was someone Mr. Lessing here was involved with"—he checks his paper once again—"in Austin, Texas. Snipers Without Bullets." He turns to Leonard again. "Is that you?"

"It was. For about two days. Eighteen years ago. This is very tenuous."

"Possibly."

"Then wouldn't you be better off arresting burglars?"

The young man nods and closes his folder. He's looking less amused. "Better watch the old blood pressure, Mr. Lessing. Deep breaths are called for, don't you think? Might well be sensible. Let's leave it there for the moment, shall we? Unless there is something helpful you can contribute."

Leonard takes a calculated risk. "I haven't wanted to mention it to anyone, but it's true, Lucy Emmerson and I have been in touch. Once in a while. Over the years," he says. "I'm like her kind of unofficial godfather. So obviously I tried to talk to her by phone when all this stuff blew up with Maxie. That's all there is to it."

"Mr. Lessing, let's be straight with each other before I go and before it's too late. You understand the penalties, I'm sure, for withholding information in security matters, for wasting police time."

"You're wasting our time, that's the truth of it."

"Mr. Lessing, people's lives are in danger here, not just the girl's. This is serious. This is perilous. This is what we need to know. Your final chance. Can you throw any light, any light at all, on the whereabouts of Lucy Katerina Emmerson? Or who it is that's taken her?"

It's true, it's mostly true, what Leonard says. "I haven't got the foggiest."

THE HOUSE WILL HAVE TO WAIT, Francine says, when her "fathomless" husband starts slamming drawers and fretting about the disarray—open cupboards, piles of clothes and bedding—that the officers, like teenagers, have left in their home. "Leave it, leave it, leave it," she insists, making him sit on the futon in front of a muted telescreen—pushing him, even—while she remains standing, her arms crossed, being heavily patient as if she is dealing with a bulky infant. Leave it, she means, until her anger has subsided. Leave it until she knows how big this problem is. "Now talk. No bullshit either, Birthday Boy."

He tells her almost everything: his failure on Wednesday evening to pass on information to the authorities, his surreptitious Thursday visit to the hostage house, the talk, the drink, the cigarettes with Lucy Emmerson, her genius idea, his loss of nerve, his Friday decoy visit to the woods, the log of phone calls that of course have been so simple for the police to trace. "Such amateurs," Francine says, still standing. She doesn't mean the police. "You know what maddens me the most, Leonard?" He shakes his head. He doesn't want to know. "It's not the lies. It's not your secrecy. God knows I'm used to that. You think I care anymore? It's that you never even offered me the chance."

"I was protecting you," he says, not really knowing what he means by it.

"Protecting me from what? Another one of your backdowns? Protecting me from offering an opinion, from saying, 'Yes, let's have her here, your little hush-hush goddaughter. Let's help this poor girl reach her father in some way, let's all do what we can to put an end to this monstrous nonsense with the hostages in Cedarbeech—' "

"Alderbeech."

"Protecting me from making you do something ill-advised for

once, not rational, not sensible? You weren't protecting me. You were protecting you!"

"You wouldn't have wanted me to go ahead with it. Would you?"

"I would have wanted you either to call the police and tell them what you knew or to . . . to . . . *arghh.*" Here she tightens her fists, knuckles up, and shakes them at Leonard. "I would have loved you for it, actually."

"If I'd brought Lucy here?"

"Of course, of course, of course. What do you take me for?" She brings a fist down on her open palm. It always quiets the class. "Right now I'd really like to beat you up."

The worst is over. No one's hurt. Francine and Leonard are sitting side by side on the futon—not touching, though, and for the moment preferring to listen to the television newscaster rather than face each other anymore. The news blackout has been relaxed, it seems. Whereas yesterday live coverage from Alderbeech was rationed and controlled, today the wraps are off. The UK station that they settle on provides a menu for the hostage scene: Background, Security Briefing, Mother's Plea, Latest Developments. They open the last of these. It is "the standoff's fourth tense day" already. A routine has been established. Here are St. John Ambulance Brigade officers, stripped of shoes and coats, delivering yet more pizzas for the hostages and the uncooked food and unopened tins and bottles that the hostage-takers have required. Here are helicopters "standing by" for reasons that are not specified. Here again are photographs of the three suspects, not just Maxie now. An international brigade.

The female that Leonard once suspected could be an undiminished Nadia Emmerson has been identified as a mixed-race Filipina called Dorothy Paredes, known as Donut. In one photograph, she is still a pretty student with faculty colleagues at a Chinese restaurant. Christmas 2013. She's smiling, just a little tipsy, with her arms around the shoulders of two pixelated men, one of whom is tugging at her ponytail of sleek black hair. A later photograph, released this morning by Interpol, shows a thinner woman with cuts and bruising to her lips and cheeks. Her jaw is swollen and her hair is cropped. The second man, an older, grizzled-looking Nicaraguan thought to be Donut's lover, is Tony Ramirez, also known as Rafaelo Matamoros and, less convincingly, Pancho Mancha. Both are "wanted on four continents" and both are "unpredictable."

There is also a picture of the hostages: another Christmas shot with a laden table, bottles, candles, and a turkey; four seated and delighted carnivores twisting to face the camera in the dining room of the hostage house ten months ago; and the slightly out-of-focus image of a half-crouching man who has evidently just arrived in the shot after setting up the camera on automatic delay. His mouth is hanging open breathlessly, not quite ready for the grin. The others are holding up their knives and forks in front of cheesy smiles: two boys of seven and nine years of age, their faces partly concealed; a middle-aged woman with heavy earrings—that day's gift, perhaps—and thin sandy hair, scraped back beneath a paper hat; an older, white-haired woman whose wedding ring on her thin hand catches and reflects the camera flash.

Leonard punches his way between the various reports, hardly daring to speak other than to make a muttered comment at the screen, until he finds the information that they need, the latest word on Lucy Emmerson. The girl has simply disappeared, they say. Her disappearance was not planned: she has not packed a bag, taken any clothes or toiletries, or withdrawn her savings from the bank. Her tobacco pouch, her purse, and her cell phone have been discovered in her room. The police are in possession of a ransom note "with detailed threats" that links her kidnapping to events at the hostage house and to the suspect now unequivocally identified as Maxim Lermontov. The police do not specify what threats, but they are concerned for her safety. They do not say that she is Maxie's daughter. They do say that raids are being carried out today on "suspect premises."

"That's us," says Francine, almost pleased.

Finally, under the menu selection titled Mother's Plea, Francine and Leonard find themselves observing a room crowded with journalists and film crews. Two senior policemen, a female community liaison officer, and Nadia Emmerson make their way across the screen to take their places behind a trestle table.

"It's the mother," Leonard says, though she is not the woman that he knew. How could she be? It's eighteen years. What had he seen in her? he wonders. "My God, she's changed. I'd walk right past her in the street." But Francine shushes him and edges forward on the futon.

Nadia Emmerson looks dazed. Her face is stained and shiny, stressed and tight with tears and sleeplessness. The liaison officer nods and puts her hand on Nadia's arm to a salvo of flashes from the cameras. Nadia's shoulders drop to field a sob. Another salvo catches her. But still she finds enough courage and willpower to start reading her statement and her plea, not looking at the cameras but at the tabletop. "If you are watching this," she says to Lucy's kidnappers, "then please don't think I do not understand why . . ." But then her throat clogs up with queuing sobs, and try as she might, for awkward moments she cannot summon the breath to continue. The words, written out in capitals on the paper in front of her, are beyond speech. In fact, she does not have the strength to stay a moment more. She stumbles out of the room, to a final, heartless fusillade of flash. The liaison officer has to carry on for her and read the paragraphs in her flat, measured voice, picking up exactly where Lucy's mother left off: "Mrs. Emmerson says, 'I do not understand why you have carried out this act. You hope it will stop violence in some way. But you have threatened violence yourself. Against my little girl. She's only seventeen. I beg you, let my little girl come home.' "

"Well, Birthday Boy, my undeserving Birthday Boy," Francine says, rising to switch off the screen, then standing at the window to glare at the retreating frost, "what are you going to do?"

"For my birthday?" Leonard sees too late that her eyes are glistening.

"No, you idiot. You selfish bloody idiot. What are you going to do about that?" She throws a cushion at the darkened screen. "What are you going to do for that woman, that mother? Did you hear her at all? Did you look at her? Who gives a damn about your birthday now?"

"What am I supposed to do? You tell me."

"You might at least pretend to care. That'd be a start."

"I care. Of course I care."

"Well, care enough for once to get up off your arse and act on it. What's happening?" Leonard spreads his hands and shrugs. "My God, to think I found you brave and dangerous when I first saw you in Brighton, at that concert."

"Please, Frankie, cut it out."

"What, it's too painful to hear the truth? You were playing like a madman on that night, like a demon, even. Live. I might not have wanted the recording, but I sure wanted the man. That's the truth. What I couldn't guess back then was that the jazz was the only thing about you that wasn't"—she hesitates—"decaf."

"Well, that was then," he says feebly. Her truth has wounded him.

"What's weird is that you don't seem to give a damn what people think when you're playing, at a gig. But when you're not onstage, that's all you care about, all that English blush and stutter that you do. Don't cause a fuss, don't give offense, don't make a noise, don't show it when you're angry or upset—"

"I'm getting upset now."

"Well, good."

"I have to be a demon onstage, no choice," he says finally, doing his best to miss her point. Decaf? It is a dreadful word. "That's what a jazzman has to do, to survive the gig." Jazz is a refuge from a hazardous world, he wants to say. It's not a hazard in itself. He is not courageous when he's playing, not mad and not demonic, just *less* frightened. He's Lennie Less Frightened, mapping out a landscape of his own making where it is not truly risky to take risks. "It isn't me. It's just an act. The music makes me brave."

"Let's have some music, then, Captain Braveheart."

THEY'LL TAKE THE BUZZ 900, Francine's hybrid runabout. They dare not use the roomier and faster van. They have, she says, quick to enjoy the subterfuge, to keep below the radar. It's probable that Leonard is still being monitored—his phone, his Internet use and e-mail account, his vehicle, at the very least. Perhaps that's why he's not been taken in for questioning despite the flimsy and unsatisfactory explanations he offered for his phone calls to Lucy. The police and NADA might hope he'll lead them to the girl, the place where she is being kept. It's possible their house is bugged. It's possible the van is tagged. But the Buzz is a community pool car, not registered in either of their names. "Let's go," she says, "before you duck out of it." He finishes dressing, though he hasn't showered yet, or shaved, or even found time to locate his spectacles in the clutter of their bedroom.

They leave their house by the back garden, like burglars, and walk unnoticed through their neighbor's garden and side gate. There's no one outside watching them. They walk once round the block, as dawdling as dog walkers, checking for unwanted company, before returning to the car. No stalkers at their backs, so far as they can tell. Still, they have to be discreet and take the country route again, where license-recognition pillars are thinner on the ground and there are no Routeway chargers to register their highway fees and distances. Leonard checks the wing mirrors obsessively at first, but as soon as they have cleared the suburbs and estates there is too much empty road behind them to suggest a shadow. Quite what they'll do when they reach Lucy's house—Leonard has retrieved the scrap of card from the Florentine box on which he noted the number and address on Thursday night—and how they'll get to talk with Nadia Emmerson without being noticed, they are not sure. They've not discussed it, actually. They'll extemporize—one note and one step at a time.

At first, with her husband at the wheel, Francine travels in silence. She is both burdened and elated. Undecided still. Once they have reached the country roads and there is spasmodic scenery—a nagging, undulating screen of protected hedgerows with vaults and cupolas of more distant woods and hills—she brightens up, sits straighter in her seat, breathes less reprovingly. "I'd better use *my* cell," she says, and busies herself calling the eight guests for that evening's birthday dinner party.

"Tell them you're not well," mutters Leonard, instantly regretting it. And, then, "Say that I'm not well."

Francine's not the sort to tell a lie. Nor is she the sort to break a confidence. "Something problematic has come up we've got to fix at once. We're driving out of town," she explains, managing to disguise the tension in her voice. "Don't ask. It's too embarrassing."

"That'll set their tongues wagging," Leonard says, but does not add what he's thinking, that sometimes fibs are best. More considerate, for sure.

Francine, convincingly warm and regretful on the phone, is clipped with him again. "Let them wag. So what?" But at least they're talking now.

"I'm truly sorry about the dinner party," Leonard says, a touch too stiffly, after he has spent some minutes planning how best to broker peace with his wife now that he has sulked for long enough.

"It's not important, is it, now?"

"No, but it was kind of you. As usual."

"A total waste."

"It was a thoughtful . . . thought."

"There's presents too. And cards," she says flatly. "You haven't even opened them."

"Who gives a damn about my birthday now, you selfish bloody idiot?" he says, risking the mimicry at her expense. "I've got another one next year. In fact, I've got one booked every year until I'm a hundred and one."

"You hope. Not if it's up to me, you haven't."

"Is that a threat?"

"I could've throttled you this morning." At last Francine smiles at him.

"Still want to throttle me?"

"No question, yes, but not while you're driving. Not while you're driving my car. Not while I'm in it, anyway."

"It's ages since we've driven out of town together."

"More fun than a dinner party, isn't it? Less work! Less fattening!"

"It is more fun, if me and you are getting on."

"We're talking, aren't we?" She runs her tongue along her bottom lip and looks at him. "And have you told me everything?" Leonard pulls a face. "Deep breaths are called for, don't you think, Mr. Lessing? Actually, Lessing is the perfect name for you. Lessening. Keeping it moderate and—"

"Yes, yes, I've heard 'em all before. From you."

"Well, have you?"

"What?"

"Told me absolutely everything?"

Leonard laughs. "Show me the man who will tell his wife everything. What is it that you think I ought to tell?"

"The truth might be interesting. The backstory. We've got all day."

"None of it's *interesting*, exactly. Let's put some music on."

Francine punches him softly in the arm. "I don't want music now. No, absolutely not. Do what you're asked for once."

They sit in silence for some moments more, until they turn off the lorry route and reach open, quieter stretches of road. It isn't quite the satiated, loving silence they enjoyed at Wilbury's, but at least they have agreed to a working truce. Leonard reaches out with his good arm and takes his wife's cool hand. His birthday's saved, so long as he will talk.

"Now we are sitting comfortably," Francine says, adopting her schoolteacher voice, "let's begin at the beginning."

"All that lousy David Copperfield kinda crap?" Leonard says evasively. He can see where this is heading.

"No, Austin, Texas, Maxie, all that meat."

"It'll be embarrassing." But only if he tells the truth.

"Embarrassing for whom?"

"Well, not for you."

"So what's stopping you? Go ahead, embarrass yourself. But no embellishments. This isn't jazz."

9

WHENEVER LEONARD REMEMBERS AUSTIN and all that follows, as he must now for Francine, it is not long before the evening at Gruber's Old Time BBQ intrudes itself, insists on being dwelled on once again. It seems, and is, an age ago, a time—the end of October 2006—when he is barely thirty-two years old, and as the single surviving heir unseasonably wealthy from the sale of his mother's house. For the first time in his life, he is able to please himself—free of family ties, unexpectedly sprung from debt, his music training completed, his reputation as (yes, he boasts about himself) both adventurous and reliable onstage, "all styles," growing. "That's when we all met up," he says. "When I was still political."

Leonard has campaigned with Lucy's mother, Nadia Emmerson. She is a spirited, tough-minded woman. He dates her once or twice, nothing more romantic than a campaign rally or the cinema. Nevertheless, because she is both lively and provocative, and like-minded too, he cultivates high hopes that eventually—if only he can dare to ask—they might become more than comrades. Their romance thrives in his imagination. When Nadia is there, he doubles his political exertions in order to impress her, phrase-making excitably at meetings and leafleting with such speed or picketing with such fiery commitment that Perkiss would be proud of him. He even writes a strident piece for brass with Nadia in mind and fantasizes playing it at the head of some great march. But she has already accepted a visiting lectureship in politics at the University of Texas, commencing at the end of August, so their affair is brief and unresolved. "Come out and see me," she has said more than once, a casual, noncommittal invitation that seems, in her absence, more promising the more he thinks about it. So, with his mother buried, the house finally off his hands, and half promises of session and recording work in New York, he e-mails her—rednadia@engol.com—explaining his misfortune and good luck, and presumes to say that he is missing her and plans on visiting, as she's suggested.

Her reply is not discouraging. Yes, she has a loft apartment with a spare box room where he can "throw his coat." And yes, she'll be pleased to see him too, and catch up with his news. There is work to do in America, she says, ever the activist—wealth disparities need attending to, and then the war, the health-care crisis, the pirate corporations running everything, support for project families and victim neighborhoods. She's joined Snipers Without Bullets, a local group of "Texan troublemakers." "We've got something monster in the pipeline!!!" she writes. She knows that Leon, as he has taken to calling himself, will want to play his part. She can keep him busy, if he's up for it. She'll "welcome his political vitality." It's not exactly what he hopes to hear. She doesn't mention Maxie or even that she isn't living alone in Austin. She doesn't mention that the loft is his. But he is there at the airport, on Nadia's arm, the thickest head of hair in Texas, a handsome exclamation mark among the plumpers waiting at the foot of the exit escalator, and genuinely pleased, he says, to have another British visitor. Leonard tries not to let his disappointment show, but he cannot doubt that Maxie is at best a tiresome complication to his plans and preparations, and to the hopes—and contraceptives—he has packed.

They live in East Austin, between the looping railway track and Seventh Street, in what is a mostly black neighborhood of 1920s shingled bungalows and tarpaper shacks lately designated "cool" by landlords seeking higher white rents or undefended lots on which to build slab houses, McMansions, or "space-maximizing" apartments. Where there are still bungalows with porches, rocking chairs, loud dogs, and wide neglected yards, billboards are promising NEW FUTURE HOMES in "authentic Austin," with every convenience from granite kitchen counters to poolside Wi-Fi access. "This quarter used to be *real* Austin," says Maxie, sounding on early acquaintance to a British ear both hick and hip. High twang. "Now it's just becomin' *real* estate," though what he introduces disapprovingly as his "residential livin' unit," a dull square three-room condo sparsely furnished with thrift-shop bargains, is neither authentic nor cool. "We're the problem, white folks bustlin' in," he adds, with what seems to be conviction. "They oughta kick us out and pull this buildin' down. They oughta drag us from our beds and murder one of us. That'd scare the yuppies off. I'm recommendin' it. Works every time. You kiddin' me? White flight."

Indeed, the neighborhood is already culturally bipolar. From Maxie's box room's narrow balcony are views across a new "zen garden"—hard landscaping, a single cherry tree, and litter that stays beyond the reach of winds or brooms—toward a complex of new galleries and jewelry stores. There is an expensive coffee shop, an arty bar called Scofflaws, another bar called the Four T's. Yet twenty steps across the street are the unadorned front gates of a poultry supply depot that employs only Mexicans and that, once locked at night, becomes a crack corner. Just a half mile downtown, and downmarket too, is an art-free strip of single-story tinnies: the Roadrunner Cocktails Bar, the Big Shot Grocery, a couple of thrift stores, the Reno Hotel ("Rooms by the Hour"), and, painted black and yellow in tiger stripes, behind its daily pall of smoke, Gruber's

Old Time BBQ, with—for *almost* downtown Austin—its ironic promises "Hunters Are Welcome" and "Best Motorcycle Food."

Leonard ventures to the store on his first evening in Texas, driven from the loft by Nadia and Maxie arguing and then not arguing. He has pretended to be watching CNN for almost an hour while his hosts whisper loudly at each other in their room. He hardly dares to overhear, as he fears they might be arguing about him, that he is less welcome in their home than they have pretended, even that Maxie has discerned Leonard's amorous objectives. Finally he taps on their door—four beats to the bar—with his fingertips. "Off out," he says, disturbing them as little as he can. When their door swings open in response, Maxie has her in his arms, laughing into her hair, as unrepentant as a boy. Her face is flushed and childlike. For the moment she is no longer mad at him, it seems, though clearly she's been crying.

"I'll take a stroll," Leonard says. "Just checking out the neighborhood."

"Get some juice," she says.

Maxie comes with him into the hallway and downstairs as far as the street door. "She's tense," he explains. "It ain't you."

"You sure?"

"I'm sure because . . . Guess what? She's gonna have a kid."

"Nadia's pregnant?"

"That's the only way you get a kid in Texas."

"Do I congratulate?"

"No, don't say anythin'. Just get the juice. I'll let you know what she decides when you get back." Maxie reaches out and pulls at Leonard's coat. "This is gonna be embarrassin'," he says, pushing his fingers through his beard.

Leonard nods. He understands at once. "You'll need the spare room now, I guess?"

"Whoa, take your time. That's eight months down the road, if that's a road she wants to take. You know? For me, I'm only sayin' that the time's not . . . at its very best. The kid's no bigger than a cashew nut, she says. It's no big deal. No"—he leans further in and whispers—"I'll let you know if we . . . we're gonna go ahead or if . . . well, if we'll have to put a stop to it. Hey, man, what I have to say to you, now this is strictly private stuff—"

"I understand." But Leonard still does not understand.

"I said you would. That's what I said to her. Because what with your mother's house an' all and how the dollar is right now, not worth a bean, you're better placed than us to be a little generous. I hate to even mention it, but if it comes to it, hard times and hard decisions, man, could you let me have a thousand dollars, say? Twelve hundred tops. Just to lend a hand. You know, like rent? Except not rent."

"For an abortion?"

"Volume, Leon, please! She's pregnant, dude. She isn't deaf. Okay, get juice."

Leonard's indignation, and jet lag, send him two blocks down the street in the wrong direction, away from homes, away from the stores and traffic, into an industrial block of empty warehouses, abandoned tire-and-muffler-fitting stores, and railroad sidings with patches of sagebrush on their berms and—eerily—a pair of turkey vultures killing time on a power line. Ry Cooder country, he thinks, trying to recall the *Paris, Texas* sound track, which he has attempted to play once or twice. Despite the heavy, gluey air, he takes deep breaths. He balloons his diaphragm. He licks and purses his lips, practices his embouchures, blows vowels. All preparation for the saxophone—and his way of staying calm in any circumstances, even when, as now, his instruments are not at hand. A police car cruises by and turns, fixing Leonard in its headlights. It is only when the driver rolls down the window to stare at him and shake his head that Leonard stops miming notes, checks himself—and checks the neighborhood. It's clear he's lost, and vulnerable. He's nervous, suddenly. This part of town is too shadowy and deserted for a newcomer—for this newcomer, at least.

By the time Leonard has retraced his steps, gone beyond the lofts, and caught his breath, he is less incensed by Maxie's casualness and his damned cheek for dunning money for a termination from a man he's only met this afternoon, a stranger who has just arrived. He'll not part with a dollar, though, he decides. Except for rent. He will pay rent. That's not unreasonable. And he will contribute toward the groceries. But as for funding an abortion—not a cent, not a cent unless it's Nadia who begs for it and possibly not even then. She needs to hear what might go wrong, long-term: his sister's suicide, his broken mother's subsequent deliberate decline and early death, at hardly fifty-eight years old, the nephew never born. "No, not a single cent," he says out loud, but it is only to himself and to the sidewalk. He's practicing. He'll stand his ground. He lets himself imagine it, the line of reasoning: mother, sister, nephew, all of it. He rehearses each phrase, imagines Maxie storming off, imagines Nadia's relief. Then he lets himself drift home to England, where Nadia is with him, rescued from the Lone Star State and in her final weeks, in great wide skirts. Her hands are resting on her unborn child. Whose child is it? *His* child—it's simply done. He only has to say it to himself, envision it. Then Maxie never was. Dragged out of bed, kicked out of town. His building's down. He's murdered, possibly. And it is Leonard who will help her to take deep breaths and push. Meanwhile, he takes deep breaths of air himself and parps the saxophone again for her—a skipping variation, "Mack the Knife." For half a minute he is admirable and brave, a husband and a father to be proud of, until he's summoned back to Austin first by the wolf call of a train and then by vehicles and voices that to his tuned ear sound dangerous.

Leonard has never been at ease abroad. It always seems that anything he does outside of England is a sham, even in America, where at least the language is familiar, if not the same: *Here I am, being local*, is his running commentary. *Here I am, blending in; here I am, not acting the outsider. But fooling nobody*. He is still nervous too, despite the distance he has almost run from the warehouse block—nervous of the dark and light, nervous of the street but uneasy about leaving it and pushing open doors, even the partly open doors to the brightly lit Big Shot Grocery with its wall-mounted amplifiers blasting hip-hop at the sidewalk and its come-hither kitchen smells.

Leonard is not unduly paranoid. Strangers truly pick on him. He's twice been beaten up in pub car parks, one a robbery (his instrument case, with his first beloved saxophone inside), the other without any cause or not any cause expressed except in punches. And he's been threatened countless times by men (and women too) who haven't liked his voice or his opinions or what they take to be his "attitude." His attitude, he knows, might come across—because he's tall and scholarly and has reed-player's lips—as supercilious. He admits that he can also sound intemperate, extravagantly unbending in his politics, though he prefers to characterize, mythologize himself as a plain and simple man of solid principle. He's even invented a working-class background, useful in both jazz and politics, as it validates his stridency. At antiwar and antiglobalization meetings, at the more sedate China Solidarity vigils and Carbon Conscience pickets, and on the Asylum Support and Open Borders committees (his current campaigns), Leonard is the one who does his best to strike the fiercest notes, who calls for action every time, as Mr. Perkiss would, who says they should not surrender an inch to anyone but "be a limpet, cling to principle." As far as possible, and certainly in his private life, such as it is, he matches what he says with what he does. No private health care for Leonard Lessing. He takes public transport when he can. What remains of his inheritance has been ethically invested. He carries an Amnesty credit card ("Buy One, Set One Free"). He plays for no fee at benefit concerts and charity gigs but does not accept corporate engagements. He has never crossed a picket line or stepped away from a trade boycott or defied an embargo. He does not patronize multinationals like Tesco, CaliCo, and Walmart. He will not wear clothes that have been sourced from sweatshops. He always checks the labels on his life.

Leonard cannot fool himself, however, with low-cost gestures such as these. He knows full well that he is at heart too civil and reasonable and too readily embarrassed to be truly militant on the street, no matter that the noises he makes indoors declare otherwise. He recognizes the flattening truth about himself: that he is a man of extreme principles, hesitantly held. So many activists of his acquaintance, the ones he envies, are the opposite, he thinks—comrades who seem to have weak principles but are still quick to shout and punch for them in public until they get their way or break a bone or two. Leonard might equal them in shouting, but he's never been the sort to punch. Never will be, probably. Perhaps that's why he makes a noise. Perhaps that's why he's ended up in jazz instead of in some more polite and rational form of music. Yes, the dynamo at meetings, like the all-styles hero on the saxophone, is tame and timid when there are risks and ferocious when it's safe. That's dispiriting.

So here is Leonard, shopping done, jealous, anxious, and annoyed, walking as invisibly as possible along the sidewalks of a Texan town, hurrying out of this run-down neon neighborhood where everything he notices augments his nervousness: the black men who call out to him from the poultry depot gates, the bony girls smoking cigarettes outside the bar, the two Mexicans idling, elbow to elbow, in their cars and talking unconcernedly while traffic waits in the street, the smell of chicken carcasses. He has expected to feel displaced and self-conscious for a while, the first few days. It's Texas, after all. He has not expected, though, to be assailed by such discordance, so many disconcerting odors, sights, and noises. Nothing is familiar or comforting. Here the thud-slap of someone running at his back, a siren from an ambulance, a loudmouthed television set, the clanging of a shade-trees mechanic, even the sudden starter motor of a Frito-Lay truck are played in different keys from what he's used to. They set his teeth on edge. They strike, then leave him jittery. He is convinced—how can he doubt it now?—that this journey to Austin will prove to be a costly blunder. He's traveled—what, five thousand miles?—to pursue his love, if truth be told, for Nadia. Instead, he is her English gooseberry, and the unwelcome occupant of the box room and the single bed in a town with which he feels incompatible. Nadia is tearful at the window now, he thinks. Maxie's at the street door waiting for the rent. There's bound to be an argument, a scene. "Not a single cent," he says again, but this time he has doubts.

By the time Leonard gets back to the loft, carrying a Big Shot paper bag with orange juice and some other groceries, he is feeling much less ruffled. He has decided what to do. Cut and run. It's his highway code: be cautious and be sensible, obey the danger signs. He can easily promise to lend them money but do nothing. He can say that it will take up to a week to clear the British bank. That way he'll neither have to be part of their plans nor be forced to sound a judgmental, moral note about abortion or his sister's suicide. After all, it's Nadia's right to choose, not his. He shouldn't bully her. No, he'll avoid that argument, fly east to New York, spend time there—see MoMA and the Met, visit the Hall of Jazz Greats in Harlem Plaza, sit in on a few gigs, improvise a holiday—and then go home, to the country where he best fits in.

The mood in the loft has transformed during Leonard's short excursion. Maxie is not waiting in the street. The scrounging abortionist is no longer even in evidence. He has washed and is drying three glasses, not for orange juice but for wine. There's music on the CD player, something French cum African with banks of percussion and exuberant horns. Their little table has been dressed for a meal: three sets of silverware, unmatching plates, and saucer flames. The microwave is humming brightly, and rattling. Nadia has changed into a loose white top that makes her face seem pinker and healthier than before. Aren't her breasts already plumper than they were in England, where she was overzealously flat-chested?

"I think I'd better move on somewhere else quite soon," Leonard says, standing at the window, his face hidden, almost tearful. Nadia's skin is blooming, especially in the fluctuating mix of arctic/tropic microwave and candle lights. "Tomorrow, possibly. I know I'm in the way."

But "Absolutely not!" "No way!" Nadia and Maxie will not hear of it. They both come up and put their arms round him. He has to stay, at least until the "showdown" in the coming week. "Boy, don't miss that. We need your manpower. We're gonna shake this city up a bit. Smile for the cameras." Leonard offers them his plucky smile.

Snipers Without Bullets, it transpires over dinner from two packets and a can—bean and tuna bake, a local pecan pie—has a membership of two. A third voice (Leon's) would be welcome. "Essential. Crucial. Indispensable," Maxie adds, bringing more wine to the table but topping up only his own tall glass. It's Maxie's "private enterprise," Nadia explains, "his plague on all their houses. You know, not just the fat cats, the military and the Republicans, but Democrats as well . . ."

"And fuckin' liberals." Maxie is becoming more sweeping and profane by the glass, more twangingly and less persuasively American. The alcohol—or something else, done out of sight—has made him noisy, volatile, and jittery. Nadia, though, is calm and quiet and prettier by the sip.

"We want to make a difference—and Maxie thinks that liberals will never make a difference," she says. "Voting isn't enough. Having an opinion isn't enough. *Caring* isn't enough." Repeating what Maxie thinks is clearly all that counts.

"Fuck them. Liberals are the front-row enemy. Prime target. Wipe 'em out. They've got this city by the balls. Do you hear what I'm sayin', man?" Leonard both nods and shakes his head. Maxie is only striking attitudes, though he's striking them a bit too tritely for Leonard's tastes. It's harmless boozy talk, he supposes, amusing more than bullying. "Hear this, then, heh? We're pretty certain Bush is comin' into town . . . yessir—"

"Next Saturday, to be exact," interjects Nadia, being his dutiful British secretary.

"We know he'll spend the weekend at his snake pit in Crawford bein' Audie Murphy."

"What's that?"

"That's wearing jeans, basically," says Nadia.

"It's wearin' jeans and pullin' wire . . ." Maxie's beard is truly bristling.

"The Bushes have their place out there." The secretary again. "Prairie Chapel Ranch. It's White House West—"

"It's Funk Hole Number One, is what it is. Where he goes hidin' from the people. Buried hisself out there five whole weeks, that man, when Iraq was, you know, gettin' difficult. Folks are layin' dead. And he's out on the ranch, fixin' gates and clearin' mesquite and bustin' broncs and muckin' stalls and being everythin' 'cept the fuckbrain president. Cowboy George sure does love to dirty up when it gets tough." Maxie is performing only for Leonard now, facing him excitedly across the table, talking fast and showing off. "How do we know what he's gonna do next weekend? We know it 'cos we have a comrade workin' there. The sister says they've set aside a patch of brush and cocklebur for the president to clear and there's been Secret Service personnel crawlin' all over it in case somebody's left a thorn out there and he could scratch his thumb. We know it 'cos a comrade workin' in the canteen at Fort Hood army base has seen the signs. Air Force One is scheduled for a drop, and there's a chopper on standby all week. You gettin' me, Leon?"

"I'm getting you."

"There's more. We know that the Bush bitch is coming down from Crawford into Austin on Saturday. That ain't no secret, point of fact. It's there in black-and-white, on the first page of the program for the Texas Book Festival. She's come to patronize y'all. She's gonna give a little talk, no shit . . . except it's all bullshit . . . in the Texas State Capitol. She's gonna give a little talk on 'Libraries and Children's Literature' because, guess what? She used to be a little girl herself."

"And she was trained as a librarian," adds Nadia. "Books for kids."

"Except Iraqi kids, natchoo."

"You know, the Reading First initiative. The No Child Left Behind bullshit. It's Laura's special thing."

"Don't call her by her fuckin' name. Jeez, Nadia. You countin' her among your friends? That's what the problem is, right there. Too much respect."

"Maxie's got no time for her," says Nadia, rubbing Maxie's arm by way of recompense for her slip of the tongue.

"Too right, I don't. She deserves what's comin' at her Saturday." Both Snipers Without Bullets look at Leonard, inviting questions. He doesn't ask, "What's coming at her Saturday?" as they expect. He wants to ask, "You'll keep the baby, then?" He says, "You ought to pick on Bush, not her. The president."

"It's him we're aimin' at, you kiddin' me? I said up front, he's comin' into town. The man himself. How do we know? We know 'cos George Senior has tickets. He says he and Barbara will be hoppin' across from Houston to listen to the speech, and little George is bound to wanna see his mom and pa for the day. George'll show, I'm sure of it—"

"You're using Christian names yourself," Leonard says, emboldened by his single glass of wine. He only means to defend Nadia.

"I'm usin' 'em without respect, and that's the difference. I'm usin' 'em to differentiate. We're talkin' 'bout four Bushes here. You hearin' me?"

"How could I not?" Leonard can't decide whether he is exhilarated or annoyed by Maxie's unembarrassed stridency or simply doesn't trust it, the mix of street talk, Texas drawl and twang, and campus condescension.

How Nadia's been taken in by such a showman is an irritation and a mystery.

"So don't get the British smarties, Leon, por fayvore. Either you are with us or you ain't."

"With you where?"

"Not in the silent fuckin' vigil on the Capitol lawns that those blowhards of the American Civil Liberties Union and Mrs. Pussyfoot of the Texas antiwar coalition have organized. No way. No, sir. We're gonna take our shit into the House chamber and we are gonna dump it in his lap. AmBush, we're callin' it."

"Sounds good."

"Too right, it does sound good. And it is gonna be a breeze, my man, 'cos we mean it and we've got it organized. Tell him, Nadia. Tell our comrade what we've gotten ourselves."

"Well, number one, Maxie knows a schoolteacher, and number two, she's been invited to"—she hesitates—"the Bush wife's speech, and number three, she's handed us her tickets!"

"Three tickets, Leon. One, two, three."

10

LEONARD STAYS ANOTHER WEEK, and is relieved to do so. He is not well enough for travel yet. What at first he has presumed to be jet lag and then mistaken as a cold has left him coughing, sneezing, and itching. His eyes are red and weepy. His lips are dry and sore. The lotion Nadia offers him gives no relief. "Welcome to Austin, the City of Sniffs and Tears," Maxie says, by way of explanation. "What you have gotten is either the last of this summer's dander fever or the first of this winter's cedar fever. Allergy planet. We live with it." Don't make a fuss, in other words.

Maxim and Leon, or Comrades Gorky and Trotsky, as Nadia refers to them, spend their days—while she is at the college teaching class—training for AmBush, largely at Leonard's expense, in the Four T's. As its name implies (*Newsweek* has judged that Austin ticks all the *T*'s for "a creative city"—tolerance, technology, talent, taste), it is a bar intended and designed as a watering hole for the neighborhood's new yuppies, the aspirant professionals, the opinionators and tenure slaves who, since the advance guard of students, gays, and artists softened up and bleached that quarter of the neighborhood, have already started moving in their businesses, their offices, their yard art, and their families. It is here, on the afternoon of his fourth day in Austin, that Leonard unpacks his saxophone. The first time in America.

It's always a comfort to lift his instrument free from its nesting case, to check and finger its glinting, complex engineering, the key stacks mounted on their axle rods, the pillars, needle springs, hinges, and leverages, the tooling and the soldering, which against all seeming logic unite and conspire to make this "singing tube" the most harmonic of the reeds, and the one most like a human voice, capable of everything from murmuring to oratory. As a child with a "good ear," Leonard was captivated by the saxophone rather than his parents' preferred clarinet or oboe, not despite but because of its fussy, varicose technology, the way its fittings and its moving parts dripped and melted from the tube like hardened candle wax. "It's easy, man, it's like puffing a cigar. You breathe through it, not into it. Just don't put the wrong end in your mouth," he was told when, as a teenager and on an impulse, he bought his first cheap saxophone, the only affordable left-hander in the shop. The salesman was not being entirely frank about how easy playing it would be, but there was some truth in what he said. Despite its size and visual complexity, Leonard found his instrument less complicated to cope with than he feared. As a single-note instrument, its fingering system was relatively simple, and its generous bore and extended octave range flattered even the beginner. Leonard took to it speedily, keen to prove his parents wrong—the clarinet and oboe seemed docile by comparison—but not so keen to let them know how effortless and satisfying his progress was, or how music felt as personal and clandestine as sex. When they were out, he practiced in front of the long mirror in their bedroom, sometimes naked even, serenading his own reflection and never quite forgetting that salesman's sensuous advice that he should play it like a cigar: the long dense tube that's held between the fingers, fits between the lips, and puffs out melodies as pungent and weightless as smoke.

Leonard's current Capitaine—acquired only weeks ago, with money from his inheritance—is a much grander instrument than that first workhorse. He calls it Mr. Sinister, his southpaw friend. It's customized: everything from the hand engravings on the cone to the details of the mouthpiece at the business end was designed especially for him by a Belgian atelier. Even his reeds have been modified: they're longer than the usual heartwoods, favoring clarity and nuance over the brittle brightness of that first cheap instrument—and of too much postwar jazz, in Leonard's view. Just holding it is comforting. Today he's keen to show it off.

"I'm all set to puff on my cigar," he says to Maxie, though Maxie seems determined not to pay him any heed, even as his English houseguest clips Mr. Sinister to his neck strap and blows almost inaudibly across the mouthpiece to excite the air column for the first time in America. Maxie's jealous, Leonard thinks, wishes he could be this cool. He'll wish it even more when I start playing.

It has been exhausting, living Maxie's lazy, energetic life—the late mornings and late nights, the noise, the tricky, ranting, high-revved conversations and the intimidating charm that leave Leonard shaken and unnerved, the couple's almost unrestricted lovemaking, their arguments, the day-for-night in low-lit bars. Leonard is not bored exactly. In fact, he's more flattered than perturbed to be paraded in the neighborhood and introduced as Maxie's British friend, for Maxie is to all appearances a local celebrity, a man that everyone—the Mexican construction workers, the prostitutes, the users and suppliers, the painters and jewelers, the storekeepers, the surviving black families—knows by name and seems to like. To be perceived as Maxie's friend is "the key to the city," Nadia has said, quick to exaggerate on her lover's behalf while her lover sits listening, interrupting only to correct and embellish the details. The sight of him and his great stack of hair seems enough to make even the meanest-looking passersby smile, or wave, or stop to talk. He has the happy knack of flattering the listener while referring mostly to himself, and somehow even when he isn't talking still remaining the focus of attention.

"Maxie's everybody's Everyman. The original twenty-four-carat, emblematic, whacked-out, freethinking American." (Nadia again, quoting herself.) "He's been to college and dropped out. He's been in prison—"

"Yeah, way more than once. Property is theft. Violence is the poor man's repartee and stuff. Carnage, mayhem, mutiny. I like to shake it up a bit, is all. Tumultuous! I do my thing and then I do my time."

"And now he's going straight—"

"I'm on parole."

"He's been a junkie. Made it clean. He is an immigrant. His parents brought him here from Vancouver when he was three months old."

"I'm Russian, man."

"You're Russian out of Canada."

"Canucksmontov. It's all the same. Both realms of ice and snow."

"He ran away from home when he was seventeen—"

"Sixteen!"

"Correction, sixteen."

"Fifteen! Fourteen! What's the difference?"

"He got radicalized the hard way. On the street and in the county jail. And now he's fighting landlords in the neighborhood."

"I'm Robin of the Hood. That's British, right? Hey, do we have to go through this?"

"He's kind of a . . ." She hesitates to use a campus word her lover might feel bound to ridicule, but decides to risk it. "You know, an exemplar? A paradigm?"

"She says she's gonna write a dissertation on my life, when AmBush is over and we're done with that. Or shoot a documentary. Hey, you can write the sound track, Leon, and play it on your saxophone. How about that? You *can* blow that thing, can't you? Or is it just for bling?"

So now this afternoon, against his better judgment—his lips are swollen still, and his breathing is impaired—Leonard has Mr. Sinister out of the case and ready to play at the Four T's. He finds Dutch courage in some bottled Pearl, drunk from the long-neck at the bar, asks for the cowboy metal on the CD player to be turned off, and, despite Maxie's careful lack of interest, steps up to the dais in the corner of the room where that evening the Javelina Sisters are scheduled to appear with their accordions. At first he has an audience of six, all men, including Maxie and the bartender. The other four, sitting in a window booth—white site engineers, with their hard hats on the table—eye his horn suspiciously; wrong bar, wrong time, wrong instrument, is what they're thinking, he suspects. And so—to acknowledge but also to deal with the point, and to test his inflamed lips and lungs as well—he begins with "Midnight at the Lavender," the Simmy Sullivan number that he played at his graduation concert and that surely is familiar even to Texans. It has the most hospitable of ten-to-ten swing beats. Nothing frightening. No bragging multiphonics—yet. He plays well, despite the handicaps, though he does not attempt any of his usual circular breathing or his signature ram and flutter with the tongue. His lips feel tender on the reed, but this bestows his tenor with an unusually smoky, quavering tone. Even so, the four go back to work, without so much as a nod to Leonard, halfway through the tune, leaving him an audience of two, one of whom, the barman, is watching a television courtroom show with the sound turned down. A few strident phrases might cause the man to turn around and come back to the counter, summoned by the jazz. But no, the louder notes only send him closer to the television set.

Leonard doesn't allow himself to mind. This isn't the first unresponsive venue he has played in. There have been worse—everything from highbrow, disapproving conservatoires, where free-form jazz is considered feral because no one can allow that any civilized music is beyond scoring, to function rooms where the bridegroom's mum demands "something dancey" and "Auld Lang Syne" is unavoidable. It has been a blessing on such occasions that the saxophone is to some extent an anonymizing instrument, a sort of mask. The drummers, pianists, and bass players confront the audience with open faces. Their agonies and ecstasies are on display. But the saxman's face—when he's playing, anyway; and when he isn't he can turn away—is mostly shielded by the instrument: his cheeks are puffed, his mouth is crammed, his eyes are often shut. Whatever he is thinking does not show.

What Leonard's thinking now is that this lunchtime gig could prove to be yet another blunder. Welcome to Austin, the City of Gaffes and Blunders. Embarrassment Planet. Learn to live with it, he tells himself. Don't make a fuss. Luckily, he has been taught by experience to hold his nerve, even when no one at all is listening. That's when a jazzman can at least pay true attention to the music and to himself. He can soliloquize. As Marty Johannsen tells it, "Play it for the mirror, even when the house is packed." But Leonard cannot quite convince himself of that, on this occasion. It's only Maxie he's been targeting. He's planned to wipe the Sniper out with jazz. But Maxie, after watching Leonard for a few minutes, is now leaning on the bar, his back turned to the room, and looking through the adverts in the *Daily Texan*. He reads out sections to the barman. He evidently does not feel obliged to exaggerate any interest in the music. If only Nadia could be here, at Maxie's side, shushing him to pay attention, Leonard thinks. She's heard him play before and she has been admiring. She's claimed she's envious of Leonard's level of artistry. He's overheard her say the saxophone is a sexy instrument and that "Leonard is more complex than he seems. He has the most beautiful hands." Such endorsements have raised his hopes with her back home. Yet he has not been able to get even remotely close to her since his arrival in Austin. He hasn't even dared to congratulate her on her pregnancy. ("Volume, Leon, please!") Life here is arranged and conducted on Maxie's terms, and Maxie isn't even pretending to pay attention to what he himself has asked for and arranged, this impromptu concert in the afternoon, this effort to impress. It is infuriating.

Leonard labors on. He does his best to invigorate the room with notes, begging to be noticed. He follows "Midnight at the Lavender" with the nagging push and pull of "In the Wee Small Hours of the Morning," and, now that he has established a crepuscular theme, "Night Hawks," and the bluesy, pensive "set 'em up, Joe" phrases of "One More for the Road," from which he plans to segue into the blithely happy chorus of "First Light" and back again. He's keeping it serene, adagio, and laying back on the beat, even though his heart is pounding presto with irritation. That's something he must conceal. The music can be hot or cool or hip or blue, the four great humors of the form, revealing and iconic words that Leonard loves despite their overuse. Even if the player cannot claim these attributes himself, if he's never truly hot or cool in private, if he's never hip or blue in life, he must seem so onstage. Jazz must not display itself as peevish or impatient.

The music is an appeaser, finally. Each note moderates the fury that Leonard feels toward Maxie and the barman, and soon enough he has become almost as pensive and serene as the tunes he is playing. Now they can ignore him all they want, the two men at the bar. He doesn't care. He's the barroom king, no matter what they think. He presses on and plays an almost perfect second half to the set, resisting any outbursts of invention, just flattering the room with melody and melancholia. Oh, how he loves the saxophone, the old brass *J*, his Mr. Sinister, its shiny, rounded generosity. Maxie, Maxim Lermontov? What instrument can Maxie play, other than beating his own drum? What's Maxie got to boast about? He extemporizes the answers to this final question on Mr. Sinister, with notes: *a fan_cy name, a Russ_ian dad / a head of craz_y hair / a time in jail, five years on drugs / no sense of birth con_ trol.* Leonard feels himself distend. His solar plexus supersedes his brain, so that soon (he knows it's true) he's strong and sexy on the dais in the bar, no longer playing bearlike from the shoulders as a chippy trumpet player would, shoving at his notes, but playing cool and catlike from the hips, and cool and catlike from the knees. It's exhilarating to be at the center of such harmony, even though he's not the center of attention. When he has finished playing he will be a man renewed. Music reinforces him. The days ahead are clear and welcoming. While the music lasts, he's man enough to face up to the president.

Leonard's concentration is splintered by, first, the faces of a few black kids pressed up against the window, their pink palms spread like suckers on the glass, and then by new arrivals in the bar, a woman and two older men in business casual. They have been drinking elsewhere, it would seem. They're noisy, scraping chairs and talking loudly. The woman stares across the bar at Leonard, pulls a face, and says, "Jesus, what is that?" Maxie answers them. Whatever he has said causes hilarity and high-fives. "Jazz?" she says, as if the word is new. "Can't dance to that." Maxie mutters something else. The new arrivals shake their heads and grin. Maxie's talking and they're listening. He's satisfied now, the charming main attraction once again. They're buying him a drink and clacking bottles in a toast, oblivious to everything except themselves. One of them throws a dime. It catches Mr. Sinister on the bell, playing its own, uninvited note, followed by laughter and finally some applause from the bar.

Leonard stops midphrase, kicks the coin across the room, turns his back, then lifts his instrument to fart a final pair of notes. *Eee-nuff!* He plays them shoddily, out of key, a raucous road-rage protest, a pay-attention-to-me-now discharge, a squall of petulance. There's more laughter from the bar, though it's directionless. No one wants to catch his eye. He packs Mr. Sinister away as crossly as he can. He blows his nose and clears his throat. He has bitten his lower lip so fiercely that he can taste blood. But the cowboy metal album is being played again and Leonard is either forgotten or ignored, even when he bangs his way across the room and leaves the bar without a word. He goes back to the loft alone in what Maxie later describes to Nadia as an "artistic tantrum." "Has to be the focus of attention," he says. "Plays that thing like no one s'posed to talk. What's the deal? Everyone in Austin plays an instrument. That dude is half a bubble outta plumb. Jeez, Nadia. On top of everythin'."

The *everything* is not Nadia's unintended pregnancy, as Leonard first presumes, but an event that Maxie claims is "unnervy." "Got government spies on my tail," he says. Boasting almost. That afternoon, abandoned by "my British pal, supposedly," he was walking back to their apartment alone and more than a little drunk when an older man he recognizes but cannot place rolled down the window of his Jeep and called out "Maximum!" from the far lane of the street.

"Maximum's his prison name, you know, his tag," Nadia explains.

"What am I gonna do?" Maxie continues. "I go across. I think I'm gonna know the guy. Some yardbird from the block. But when I duck and look at him, he's not the species. Perhaps an officer, I think. But then he says, 'Word to the wise, Mr. Lermontov. Best not turn up for Mrs. Bush. I'm just sayin,' for your long-term benefit.' He's achingly polite, you know, trained up. That tells me FBI or Secret Service. A goon. 'Tend to your own knittin', pal,' is what I say. 'This is a democracy. Did no one tell you that at G-man academy, or were you too busy jerkin' off to James Bond DVDs?' But he's not stoppin' for the conversation. He's away. Jeepin' outta there."

"What does that *imply*?" asks Leonard, meaning, What does that imply for AmBush and for me?

"It don't mean shit, as far as I'm concerned. It's just a fishin' trip. They're trawlin' through their database, is all, and I've popped up. I'm known to them. I'm on the list. No sweat."

"We going to call it off? They are expecting you. You'll not get past the police checkpoints."

"The heck I won't. This is where the fun begins. They're lookin' out for Maximum, but Maximum is goin' in disguise. That's what that *implies*, comrade. That *implies* we've got the edge on them. They only know so much. Now we are advised: what we have here"—he spreads his arms, trying to embrace the pair of them at once—"is two mysterious British Snipers, not on anybody's list, not yet, one emblematic American in camouflage, and a ticket to the circus each. The president is fucked. He's gonna get his ears torn off."

ON THE EVENING BEFORE Laura Bush's Saturday appearance at the Book Festival, Leonard—hoping to mend fences after what Maxie describes as his tantrum at the Four T's—offers by way of thanks for their hospitality and for "the fun" that he is having through the day in Maxie's company to treat them both to a last supper. He wants their reassurances that all is well and will be well. AmBush frightens him.

"Take him to the barbecue," Nadia suggests. "Leon, have you ever had a Texan barbecue?" He shakes his head. "Then let's go there. We don't have to drive out to Coopers or anything. There's that funny little down-home place right along the street. We can't let you go back to England a smoked-meat virgin."

Gruber's is not busy at this time in the evening. The street outside is still hectic with commuter traffic and with pedestrians. On the sidewalk, exhaust fumes blend with wood smoke. The smell of motor fuel overwhelms the subtler, deeper smells of oak, mesquite, and pecan from the smoldering hardwood coals of the pitmaster's open fires out back. "These are not exactly boney-fidey," Maxie explains. "This is just pretend. If you want a full-on Texas barbecue, you'll have to drive an hour south. Coopers, same as Nadia says. But that"—he points at the racks of kitchen-cooked meat, the sides and carcasses, the slabs of brisket, the bubbling sausages, which have been laid out on the coals for show, Hill Country style—"now that's authentic meat. There's no pretendin' otherwise."

One of the Gruber boys, working the coals under woodcut signs that promise LOCAL SPOKEN HERE and SERVING AUSTIN'S ORIGINAL HOT SAUSAGE, wipes himself on his apron and shakes hands with all three of them, using only his fingertips. He recognizes Maxie, of course. "So what'll it be, sir?" he asks, too shy to use Maxie's name. He points at the ready meat with his serrated slicing knife.

"A bit of everything, man—beef, *cabrito*, pork."

"Some Elgin sausage?" Nadia suggests with a passable Texan accent.

"Clearly a vegetable brochette is out of the question," says Leonard, more primly than intended. He has not expected this display of unforgiving flesh.

"You do eat meat?" asks Maxie. "Get the man a pail of collard greens."

The Gruber boy stares first at Leonard and then at Maxie, and then at both of them again, his mouth half open, though it's not clear whether he is in awe of Maxie or is simply taken by a British accent.

"Just joshing you. I'm not a vegetarian as such," Leonard says. He doesn't say, I am a hearty carnivore, slaughter me a hog, bring on the raw and bloody steaks. These days, back home, the only meat he eats with any appetite is chicken, and not so much of that. He does not truly believe that Meat Is Murder, as some vegan diehards claim—though certainly it's slaughter—but he can't be certain, so he has trained himself to go for fish and vegetables instead, at least when he is eating in company.

It does smell good at Gruber's, though, he must admit. He is reminded of his mother and her customary Sunday lunches, with the skewered joint of beef or the cracklinged side of pork and the heirloom carving knife at the center of their table. Those meals were wonderful. This might be too. Anyway, he reasons, Maxie and Nadia are his guests, it is his treat, and he will have to go along with it, wonderful or not. Eating beef in Texas is something unavoidable, he supposes. He won't cause much of a fuss. "Let's make no bones about it—bring me the head of Alfredo Garcia," he says, attempting two jokes that no one even smiles at except himself and, finally, the Gruber's boy, who says, "I seen that movie. It's way cool." But Leonard is feeling slightly nauseous already. This is far too *real*, and surely not hygienic. "Feelin' peckish, herbivore?" asks Maxie.

Inside, they collect bottled beers and sides of pinto beans and coleslaw with poppy seeds in polystyrene cups, find a trestle table to themselves in a corner, under a pair of mounted buck deer heads, and wait for the staff behind the counter to call their order number or shout Maxie's name. Leonard does his best to seem at ease, though he is not at ease. Tomorrow worries him. This evening worries him. And Maxie's herbivore remark has been infuriating. He must stay calm and *cool*. No tantrums here. No British petulance. To steady himself, he reads the labels on the easy-squeeze bottles of relishes and mustards. He studies the cloudy murk of a one-gallon jar of Ben E. Keith pickles. He peers inside the plastic bags of bread, hoping for wholemeal but finding only extra-thin white. Bread from the fifties, he thinks. Pickles from the devil's larder. Hell's kitchen. Constipation, here we come. But says, not quite waggishly enough and causing Nadia to blare her eyes at him, "Man, I could eat a dead bear's bum."

Once the barbecue arrives, wrapped in butcher's paper, Leonard tugs at the unfeasibly large steaks with his fingers for ten or so minutes as everybody else is doing, but all too quickly has had his fill of meat. Rather than sit back puritanically, too soon, while Maxie and Nadia finish off the cuts, he busies himself with the free-with-every-order jalapeños and dill pickles until his eyes begin to smart.

"This is the *real* real deal," says Maxie, relishing that perfect Texan trinity of beer and beef and company. "Cowboy style!"—by which he must mean *no finesse*. Leonard cannot imagine anything less European. Or customers less European. Everyone is either wearing jeans and gimme caps from cattle-feed companies or they're done up for two-step dancing with cowboy boots and button shirts, doing their best to seem like red-blooded Texans rather than employees of Motorola or UT. It is now that Nadia pulls her camera from her shoulder bag and asks the charmless Gruber girl to take some pictures of the three of them. "Get in the bottles and the meat," she says. They are the indoor shots, flash bright, that Leonard takes home to Britain. The only evidence that they have met, that he has eaten barbecue. There they are, posing side by side in Gruber's hot-meat abattoir, in a bygone, unhygienic age. The room is blue with smoke. The archive date is 10-27-06.

"JUST CHEWING POLITICS," he says whenever, in the years ahead, he recounts how this Austin evening finished so badly. "Just talk, that's all."

Leonard is relieved when finally Nadia and Maxie retire from the fray, defeated by the size of their order. He's ready to go home and sleep the evening off. But he will have to wait. The eating may be finished, but the drinking has only just begun. An hour later they are still sitting round the detritus of their meal, with a third and fourth order of beer. Leonard is more than a little drunk—but, in his view, not so drunk as to be talking incautiously. He is not being too specific. He has not mentioned the president by name. He has not referred to the Laura Bush event. He has merely said exactly what he feels about the current wars in Iraq and Afghanistan, about the torture camps at Guantánamo. Surely that is reasonable.

But Leonard is chewing politics too loudly now and in an accent that clearly is not Texan. He is showing off, of course, wanting to seem lively and stalwart for both Maxie and Nadia, making up for not enjoying meat and for being fearful of the next day's plans, for being called the herbivore, for being guilty of a tantrum. The Brit is being *antsy*, as the saying goes. He is looking round the room as if he is a tourist checking out the artifacts (the rattlesnake skins and diner photographs) in a heritage building staffed by costumed volunteers. He is smiling far too readily. He is making eye contact with strangers, who turn away, or lift their chins at him, or fix him with hard expressions. He leans forward to try to read, out loud, the full text on the T-shirt of an overweight man sitting with his younger wife at the table opposite. It says, "Get Out of Your Rut and Spend Some Time with Us and You Won't Be Disappointed." Above is "Bullseye Sportsmans Bar and Grill." Leonard smiles for the missing apostrophe and catches the wearer's eye. He grins again, the British protocol. "Nice shirt," he says. "Get out of your rut, indeed!"

But realizing that the closing word is not quite right, too pipingly BBC, he adds, "Indeedy-doo-doowa! That's jazz."

"Time to take you home." Nadia is more uncomfortable than amused.

"Take it easy," Maxie says, grinning suddenly. "There's still bottles on the table."

Three bottles later Leonard stands unsteadily, at Nadia's prompting, to settle the check, but he diverts off to the restroom first, not only to urinate but also to find some privacy to belch and to wash his hands, rinse away the meat before he handles dollar bills. The men's room—called Gouchos, although some pedant, some clever frat boy, has already scored out the first *o* and corrected it with an *a*—is at the end of a long unlit hall with cinder-block walls. Halfway along, Leonard passes the man with the T-shirt swaying from drink and too wide for the hall. Leonard squeezes to the side as best he can, into the recess of a fire door, but still their shoulders meet. Not a painful clash but an awkward one. Leonard offers his apology.

He is standing and still straining to empty his bladder when the restroom door is opened. Whoever comes in does not step up to the remaining stall at the narrow urinal but waits at Leonard's back, breathing badly. Leonard does his best to hurry up. But Texan beer is cold and gassy and slow to pass. He turns his head a little and offers a placatory smile, just at the moment when the newcomer reaches forward and shoves him, once, in the middle of his back. He is off-balance anyway. His left hand is holding his open trousers, his shirt front, and his belt away from the urinal; the right hand is directing what remains of his stream. He manages to stay upright but bangs his forehead against the wall in front. The blow is softened only marginally by the decades of chewing gum pressed into the grain of the cinder blocks. Ridiculously, he apologizes again, though how he can have counted it his fault he cannot say. His assailant mutters something. Not an apology, clearly. But more like "Shit" or "Git" or "Shirt." He shoves Leonard again, this time higher up, in the shoulder, spinning Leonard round. The man steps back, just in time to avoid the final splash, which catches the lower parts of Leonard's trousers and a shoe. Still, he nods with recognition. It is the T-shirt man again, smiling almost, evidently pleased with what he's done.

Leonard is not fearful yet; he only feels the victim of a boyish, childish prank. He can almost hear a childhood adversary shouting in his ear, "Leonard's wet his pants again," then everybody rushing in to stare and point at him: "Leonard Pissing Lessing! Leonard Pissing Lessing! Get the mop, someone." This man, though, is saying nothing, just smiling to himself and clenching his fists. Leonard starts to tuck himself away and do up his zipper, his eyes cast down. He knows he ought to speak, make light of it, perhaps. But T-shirt Man is turning now and heading for the hallway.

So it's like that, thinks Leonard, swiftly sobered. That's what happens when you bang into a fat man in a hallway, in Texas anyway. You take a shoving. And you take another. And you have to go back to your table and your friends wet around the ankles.

The restroom's hot-air dryer is not functioning, so Leonard tries to fix himself with toilet paper, but it is the manly, nonabsorbent sort and merely spreads the damp. Fortunately, he now has the Gouchos to himself, and so he has a chance to catch his breath and settle his pounding heart. He's close to tears and, now that the danger has passed, indulgently angry too. He almost draws blood, biting his lower lip again as he did in the Four T's. He has to calm himself and get back to the embarrassing safety of the dining room. DAB, Leonard reminds himself. That's what he's been taught at music school. When you are waiting in your dressing room with fifteen minutes yet to go before the concert starts and you are shaking like a palsied leaf, then DAB—divert and burn; do something brisk and physical to burn the fear away. Leonard waves his arms around, though that is difficult in such a narrow space. He'd like to kick the restroom door or punch the walls. But he is sensible. Divert, don't hurt yourself. Indeed, he does feel better almost at once. He pumps his arms to a count of thirty-two and then waits for a moment, more than a moment, washing and drying his hands several times.

His hands are shaking anyway, so rubbing them with the thin toilet paper stops the trembling. He counts to sixteen and back again to naught. He'll give his inexplicably resentful fellow meat-eater time to leave the hallway.

Leonard need not return to the dining room at all. He can easily push through the fire door in the hall and escape directly onto the sidewalk. Wouldn't that be wisest? Wouldn't it make sense simply to go back to the apartment alone and at once and let Nadia and Maxie figure it out for themselves? He can say that he was drunk, confused, got lost, misunderstood their plans. Whatever he does, inventing excuses will be easier than facing T-shirt Man again or walking back to the table looking damp and smelling urinous. He's lost enough face already: the disappointment that Nadia and he will not be partners, the news of her pregnancy, its continuing uncertainty, his timid Englishness, which Texas has made unignorable, the demanding prospects of tomorrow's AmBush.

The problem is, he has already walked out sulkily on Maxie, at the end of that humiliating performance in the Four T's. It was a mistake and not one that he should repeat. It wasn't worth the dime. Besides, he's said this barbecue will be his treat. If he runs off without picking up the check, they will think he simply doesn't want to pay his whack. He can guess what Maxie might say. "That British dude is tighter than tree bark. Won't help us out with, you know, doctor's fees. Won't even pay for supper. What do we get for our fine hospitality? A carton of orange juice, is all."

No, Leonard must face the music, so to speak, and go back to the dining room. He splashes his face with cold water, washing away the taste of meat and lip blood and the sting of pickle. He listens carefully. No sounds close by, just water, distant traffic, and music from the bar next door, a thrashing bass. A deep breath, then, and he will push the restroom door back. He gives it a solid shove, but the door will not open entirely. It sticks halfway. He puts his shoulder up against it and tries again, too soon to realize that what he thought was the toilet cistern refilling is in fact his old assailant's wheezing lungs. The man's been waiting—and evidently smoking—in the hallway behind the restroom door. Now he's even less amused, and has as his excuse the pair of knocks he's taken from the door handle and the sudden loss of his half-burned cigarette. "Sorry," Leonard says for the third time, closing the Gouchos door behind him. He says nothing else. His chin is punched, a heavy rising blow, his head banged back against the cinder-block wall with a porous thud. He bites his tongue. Another blow. His nose this time. Another blow.

The punches do not hurt exactly, but they are shocking, shockingly efficient, as if a chiropractor rather than a boxer has carried out some restorative procedure on his face. He's been straightened out. His skeleton is realigned. Even the impact of his skull on the wall seems soft at first. But, so soon after washing away the taste of meat, Leonard's mouth is full of blood again, not cooked, not smoked, but fresh and privately familiar. Now T-shirt's fingers are wrapped round Leonard's throat and he is hurting, finally. His feet are barely touching the ground. All his weight seems to be hanging from the man's thick arms. His face is turned against the cold cinder blocks. He feels as weak and helpless as an overcoat being hung up on a hook.

T-shirt is muttering under his breath. Leonard makes out the word *Brit*, repeated as a curse. "Look," he says, as best he can, given that his windpipe is so constricted. He means to offer more apologies, an explanation, some recompense perhaps. That seems urgently wise. "I'm sorry if—" His assailant unexpectedly backs away, goes limp in fact, releases his throat hold so that Leonard drops onto his knees and is staring into the man's rodeo belt and gut. T-shirt hovers for a moment, halves in height, his eye whites, now level with Leonard's own eyes again, suddenly visible in the low light of the corridor, and then he falls forward onto Leonard's shoulder, a sudden penitent, exhaling like a punctured cushion.

"Jesus," Leonard says, flattened almost, fearing/hoping that the man has had a heart attack, a stroke. He's fat enough. Evidently from the stink of his breath and his fingers he is a heavy smoker too. Leonard is already beset with awkward possibilities. What should he do? What should he tell the monster's wife? Who'll take the blame? "Jesus Christ," he says again, and starts to push against the leaden body pressing down on him.

"Jesus won't help you," someone says. T-shirt Man is rolled aside. Leonard is being pulled by his wrist. He does not recognize his savior straightaway. Then he sees the hair. It's Maxie. Maxim Lermontov. He has blood on the knuckles of his right hand and a short gray-and-black handgun in his left. "So get up off your knees," he says.

HE WAS GONNA KICK YOUR ASS." Maxie is sitting at the window with a tablecloth round his shoulders while Nadia combs out his hair, pushing back the long, loose strands from his forehead, reluctant to begin the conscript cut for his disguise.

"You don't know that." Leonard is still angry and embarrassed, but Maxie does not seem to understand his discomfort. "You had a gun. I saw it in your hand."

"That's the best place for a gun."

"Where the hell did that come from?"

"It came from right under my shirt. Like this." Maxie produces his pistol again and swings it on his forefinger.

"I mean, where did you get it from?"

"Down the street. Go get one yourself. You hand the man the money and he hands you a pistol. This sweetie's a Taurus 1911. Rock-solid."

"Why would I ever want a gun? Why would you? Don't point the thing."

"They've got guns, that's why. If it's in their toolbox, then it's gotta be in yours. That's how the revolution's won. That's how the shitty world is changed. We're talkin' Russia 1917, Cuba, Vietnam, um, you know, armed rebellion, the just and mighty barrel of a gun. You shoot first and you don't get pronounced first. That's pronounced *dead*, Leon. Game over. If it wasn't for the people's firepower, there'd still be czars . . . back home."

"Well, that's debatable." There never have been czars in Canada.

"And you know what? If you'd had a sidearm under your belt tonight, in the restroom, you could've shot the fat guy's pecker off. Job done."

"Why would I do that?"

"That's what he would've done to you. That's what he's gonna do next time he catches sight of you."

"You absolutely don't know that." Leonard turns to Nadia for support, but she only raises her eyebrows.

"Oh yes, I do. Abso-fucking-lutely, man. I know his brand—he owns three, four guns, one for each of his bellies. He's drunk most nights on Shiner Bocks. He don't forget. He don't forgive. And the sticker on the fender of his pickup doesn't say KEEP AUSTIN WEIRD. It says DON'T MESS WITH TEXAS. Yessir, he was always fixin' to kick your ass as soon as you started speakin' through it."

"Why would he want to kick my anything? That's crap."

"That's what he's kickin' outta you, my friend. Because you're British and you're talkin' about his president in not so many words and this is Texas U.S.A. and that man's havin' dinner with his wife and they're both patriots, they're red-state, redneck, red-blooded Americans. And then you're lookin' at his tits, like he should lose some weight or what. And then you're tellin' him you absolutely love his shirt, indeedy-dee-doowah. Nice work. That's gonna make you friends round here. Plus that guy was in a meat stupor. That means he's like a stag in rut. Don't mess with him. If he wasn't gonna beat up on you, he was gonna beat up on someone else. He was in the zone for poleaxin', all three hundred pounds of him. Then you show up, some British guy who's dumber than a box of hammers, and as good as put your chin up to be clobbered. Go right ahead. Take aim."

"So you say."

Maxie laughs, genuinely amused, happy to be arguing. "Believe me, comrade. Even I was tempted to beat you up and I agreed with everythin' you said, except about the shirt. So."

"You were tempted to beat me up? That's nice."

"Nice I came and hauled you out of there. Nice I know the basic rules of engagement, like kick butt or get butt kicked. One day you'll look at your big smile in the mirror and know who to thank for havin' any teeth left. You'd never play that cheesy saxophone again. How'd that be?"

"I don't think he meant to do me any real harm." *Cheesy?*

"You don't? Now who's to say? You don't negotiate with guys like that, is all I know. This is what the world is all about. You always have to stand up to those punks. Or always be a loser. That's my philosophy."

"Well, my philosophy is that discussion is always better than concussion. I might've calmed him down myself if you hadn't interfered."

"You think?"

"I was just explaining to the guy—"

"You're in the restroom with your zipper down and someone sticks his shoulder in your back. And you explain? And you apologize? That's not the way we deal with dickheads in America. You should have pissed all over him. Instead, what do you do? Listen to me, Leon. What do you do?" Maxie knows the answer. Leonard pissed down his own leg. Leonard pissed on his own shoe.

"What could I do? You saw the size of him. How many times do I have to repeat myself?" Leonard adopts an American accent, more East Coast than East Austin. "I was gonna *speak* to him."

"Jeez, Leon, who are you, Neville Chamberlain?"

"Oh, please."

"That's a conversation I'd have liked to hear. You've got two fat lips and some guy's fist halfway down your throat and you want to open a peace conference. Where's the brains in that?"

"Where's the brains in sending someone back home or to his wife, well . . . *bleeding*? Bleeding and unconscious."

"He won't be goin' home. Not yet. He'll be needin' stitches.

He'll be needin' crutches. He was lucky, point of fact. I could've shot him in the knees and he'd be limpin' till he dies. Fuck him, anyway. And fuck his wife."

"And you're supposed to be against the war."

"Leon, now I'm warnin' you. Don't cheapen it. Don't get confusin' this or that, because the way I feel, all dandered up, I might be tempted to take a poke at you myself, just in the name of fair play. And parity."

"What kind of father are you going to make?"

"He'll be the perfect dad," Nadia says, interrupting finally, her hands still resting on his full and springy head of hair. "No need to make it personal."

Maxie stands, stretches out, and takes hold of Leonard's shoulder, a fifty-fifty grip, loose enough to be mistaken as friendly contact, firm enough—after it is held for far too long—to hurt a little. "Best keep it calm, Leon. Don't say another word."

"Maxie, this is all I want to say. You went too far. You frighten me. You're hurting me. You really hurt that guy."

"Yes, I did. Oh, boy, I hurt him bad."

"Congratulations."

"It's deserved. We walked all over him."

"You walked all over him. I didn't touch the man."

"Well, yes indeedy-deed. Comrade Leon walks away unscathed."

Leonard pushes Maxie's hands away and turns toward his room. "I'm not unscathed. I'm hurt." He points at the cuts and bruises on his face and flexes his shoulders. "I'm hurt real bad," he adds. "By *both* of you."

"Real bad? You've no idea what real bad means. The fat guy knows."

"Enough." *Eee-nuff!*

"See, that's it, you're still runnin' off . . . Some two-trick circus pony you turned out to be, either runnin' off or down on your knees—"

"Leave him. Let him go. You guys are ugly drunk. Let's fix your hair before the evening's completely spoiled and wasted." Nadia pushes Maxie back onto his seat and holds up her scissors, clicking the blades. "Sit still and stop talking, unless you want to bleed," she warns. She lifts the first tress and pulls it clear of his scalp, starting at his widow's peak. "You're sure of this?"

"Just cut."

"Farewell, the lunatic fringe."

"Amen."

When Leonard comes back an hour later—he has to show he isn't in a sulk—his face and nostrils wiped clean of blood, his bruises dressed, his trousers changed, Maxie has become a different man. His black mustache and sparse and adolescent beard have gone. Nadia's cut has almost reached the top of his head. All the hair around is harvested and cleared. It's only stubble that remains, black bristles on white, unweathered skin, and two inches of Mohican, standing straight and vulnerable as wheat. He's nothing but an exclamation mark. A crest. A military plume. But already Maxie is virtually unrecognizable. The familiar piled hair made him unmistakable. Perhaps that's why so many people greet him on the street. They recognize the hair and think they know the man. The loss of hair has aged and brutalized him—criminalized him, in fact. His lips and nose seem huge. His eyebrows—till she trims them too—hang heavy on his face, like bats. And once the Mohican is gone and Nadia is rubbing Maxie's scalp with the same tea tree oil that Leonard has rubbed into his bruises, the original Sniper Without Bullets has disappeared entirely. Nadia holds up the mirror. "You clean up good," she says, though she does not sound impressed; regretful, rather.

"He looks like a skinhead," suggests Leonard. "Or like a serviceman."

"What kind of serviceman, Leon? Am I fixin' TV sets or swimmin' pools? Or am I fixin' for Uncle Sam?"

"We're speaking different languages. In England, servicemen are . . . army personnel. They don't fix anything. That's for sure. You look like a marine."

"No bull. Just look at me. Back to the bone. Ain't that a head of hair?"

"Looks more like rawhide than a head of hair." Leonard disapproves of what he sees, of what the haircut has confirmed.

"Yessir, I'm all spit-shined and polished up. So hats on, ladies. Let's go greet the president."

11

IT IS A SAPPHIRE, late October day, warm enough for shorts or hiking pants, but Leonard does his best to dress conservatively, a Bush supporter, though to dress like a Republican in Texas does not necessarily mean the light jacket, trousers, and button-down shirt that he has chosen from his few British clothes. It could mean the cowhide boots and the pair of Wranglers cinched by a buckle bigger than your brain that the president favors for himself at weekends. Or even the full black and unlikely business suit that Maxie has, without a word of explanation for its provenance, taken from his closet. His court suit, possibly. He looks less like a skinhead now, and less like a serviceman. His scalp stubble is only thirteen hours old but has already darkened. Today he seems most like an excitable Baptist pastor heading for a prayer breakfast or gospel brunch, with, at worst, a nerdish streak. No one can see how muscular he is, or wildly menacing, or know for sure what he has tucked under his shirt.

"My, don't you look the part?" Nadia says, picking off bits of fluff and thread from the back and shoulders of his suit.

Maxie is surprised and elated by the sight of himself, it seems. He turns and twists in front of the mirror, changing his expression. "Well, look at me. I'm Tony Perkins for the day. So welcome to the Bates Motel. Your shower's ready, Mr. President." He glimpses Leonard's tense, unsmiling, damaged face in the mirror. The men have not yet exchanged a civil word this morning. The fug of last night's fights and squabbles has not cleared. Besides, Leonard is too nervous to be civil—and he is hoping to engineer a final row, something upsetting enough for him to take offense and run from Austin in a righteous huff, flying out while Bush is flying in.

"Buck up, Leon," Maxie says eventually. "That's yesterday. Today is gonna be your fifteen minutes of fame. We're on active service now. Be big about it, man. Step up to the plate." He pulls Leonard toward the mirror, gently, playfully. "Be sweet." For a moment the pair pose, an arm round each other at the waist. Leonard knows that he has been defeated. There's no escape. Then Nadia, still in her pajamas, comes up behind and rests her chin where their two shoulders form a cleft. "See what I see, right there?" asks Maxie, not entirely without irony. He jabs his finger at the mirror. "I see the Three Musketeers. Ain't we the Bushbashers today? Ain't we the warriors?"

"You don't look good," Nadia says, on tiptoe at their backs. Leonard can feel a soft breast pushed against his shoulder blade. She smells of warm cotton, a more provocative odor than any bottled scent.

"You don't like the cut, lady?" Maxie rubs a hand across his scalp. "Feels like baby seal to me."

"You'll do just fine. No, I mean Leon Trotsky here." Nadia pulls Leonard away from the mirror and sits him on a high-backed kitchen chair in the bright light by the window. "You look too weird like that. They'll never let you through. I'm going to have to fix that face."

"Boy, yes," says Maxie. "A little field surgery. Hide those gaping wounds."

Nadia stands between her one-time British boyfriend's legs and dabs off the remnants of dried blood on his lips and jaw with a Q-tip. She cleans him up with arnica gel. "Bit shiny now," she says, holding Leonard's chin and turning his face into the light. "What we need"—she rummages inside her cosmetics bag—"is this. This is going to minimize the shine. This is going to make you matte. Grab hold." She drops the moisturizer into Leonard's hand and leans into him.

"Jesus, have you seen what's in this stuff?" he asks, squinting at the small print on the tube and reading out the listed ingredients. "Palm oil, propylene glycol, cyclomethicone, stearic acid, hydroxylated milk glycerides, talc . . ." But Leonard is only trying to distract himself. The closeness of Nadia's breasts to his eyes and face, that half-buttoned pajama top, that bedclothes smell (is it the smell of pregnancy?), the pressure of her knees on his when she opens her legs to crouch and peer at his cuts and bruises, have made him start to sweat, and worse. He wants to reach out, lay his hand across her abdomen, and bless the child. He wants to touch her everywhere. That's why he's come to Austin, isn't it? Not to be caught up in some madcap plot. "Cetyl alcohol," he reads, while Maxie stares across the room at him, shaking his head. "Sodium magnesium silicate, tocopheryl acetate . . ." He's trapped. There'll be no flying out. He no longer wants to find excuses, actually. What he most wants, for Nadia's sake, is to be her bold comrade. "Titanium dioxide, paraffin—"

"Enough already," Maxie says. "Paraffin schmaraffin. Who gives a shit? Let's go. Come on, Snipers, hit the street."

AmBush does not work out quite as Maxie hoped. The three participants set off at different times and follow separate routes downtown. Leonard is the first to leave. Following instructions, he walks along Seventh as far as the interstate and then cuts across the Red River district toward the southeast corner of the Capitol and its encircling lawns. He couldn't get lost even if he tried. The sunset-red granite building with its commanding dome and its zinc-skinned goddess of liberty presiding over Austin is almost never out of view.

Leonard is carrying his passport, six ten-dollar bills, his ticket to the Laura Bush address, a Book Festival program, and spare keys to their apartment. "Penny plain is the order of the day," was Nadia's advice. She wrote her dissertation on Mondavi's resistance handbook *Infiltration and Identity* and so knows the tested protocols of blending in, including the recommended contents of their pockets. Avoid too little and too much, is the rule; carry nothing to raise alarm, nothing to reveal your plans should you be stopped and frisked. She dropped an apple in Leonard's pocket as he left the loft, "for authenticity, while you're in line. Apples are the most innocent of fruit, Mondavi says."

"Go tell it on the mountain. Let my apple go! Lermontov says." Maxie is in a strangely expansive and skittish mood, now that AmBush draws close.

Leonard is eating his apple as he crosses San Jacinto Street. He does his best to keep to an unsuspicious pace as he nears the southern entrance to the Capitol and the already bustling festival tents in the streets beyond. He can hear some poet reading too close to the microphone, and there is laughter from a second tent and then applause. The adjacent streets have been closed to traffic by the Austin city police. Their cruisers are parked across the roadway. Only official vehicles can pass. Leonard is expecting to be challenged and half hoping to be turned away. He will have failed, but he will have done his best, or seemed to, anyway. To Nadia. Yet no one pays attention to him or any other pedestrians, even the ones who have not dressed like Republicans. The city police are entirely relaxed, just taking it easy with their thumbs in their belts and their backs against their cars. Why not? The day is mild. The president might wave at them.

It is not until Leonard has walked through the southern entrance gate that he sees anything of note: a family of five, three girls and their parents, dressed up Sunday smart and waving the

Stars and Stripes together with a photo portrait of a uniformed young man. His name and dates are written underneath: *Pvt. Alexander M. Sharp,* 1987–2006. Leonard calculates the young man's age and makes the appropriate face. It is a dreadful war, he reminds himself. It's in this family's interests that he's here, on active service, though they might not appreciate it now. One of the girls has a T-shirt inscribed "Lubbock Loves Laura." The father has a Bible in his hand, which he waves at Leonard and anyone that passes. "Support *our* troops," he says. "God bless America." And Leonard offers him and his family "Good afternoon" in return.

Although there is more than an hour yet before the scheduled arrival of the president and his wife, there is already another protest group gathering among the rose beds, lawns, and monuments on the west side of the Capitol and loosely circled by state troopers in their Boy Scout uniforms. This is the "silent fucking vigil" that Maxie has talked about, organized by the Texas antiwar coalition. Their message is laid out on a banner on the grass in front of them in letters three feet high and made from photographs of all the soldiers who have died in Iraq so far—Alexander M. Sharp included, presumably—and some Iraqi civilians: TROOPS. OUT. NOW. BRING OUR BOYS HOME. There are about thirty demonstrators, but the numbers are growing by the minute. They are working hard to show restraint and dignity, facing forward in two rows like veteran soldiers, doing their best not to fidget, talk, or seem amused or even angry when a younger, tattooed man, not one of them, calls out repeatedly and manically, from behind their backs, "Bring our girls home. Save one for me."

Leonard could step up and join the vigil here and now. This is more his type of protest than the one he's caught up in. He could happily stand in the second row, his bruised face well hidden, staying quiet and grave, until the president goes home again. These are people he can be at ease among. He understands their etiquette. Not one looks less than peaceable. He's tempted to stroll across and offer them his smiles, more sincere smiles than the ones he gave to the family from Lubbock, until he is invited to take part. But he has to toe the AmBush line—and that means staying distant and discreet, not drawing any attention to himself or seeming to be anything other than a man who's keen to hear the first lady talk about children, libraries, and reading. He turns away and kills time by walking round the building, looking at the monuments, "all the fucking brass and marble," as Maxie has described it. "Monuments to whom?" Leonard asked. And Maxie replied, much to his own amusement, "Well, it sure ain't Willie Nelson. And it sure ain't Reckless Kelly." What Leonard finds instead are tributes to a Texas that is both historical and cinematic: the heroes of the Alamo, Texas pioneer women, the Spanish War veterans (though not the Spanish War that Leonard cares about), the Boy Scouts of America, the Pearl Harbor survivors, the fighting men of the 36th Infantry Division, the heroes of WWI. Its lyric is vainglorious, "God and Texas, Victory or Death" rather than "Come lie with me, my Texas rose."

By the time Leonard has examined most of the many monuments and numbed himself by reading the legends and dedications, as he had tried to numb himself that morning with the moisturizer ingredients, the atmosphere in the Capitol grounds has modified. The vigil has been separated from its banner and pushed back fifty yards toward Lavaca Street and the festival tents, where the protesters are required to be dignified, disapproving, and silent out of sight of the Capitol's main entrance. The save-a-girl-for-me campaigner, after being frisked for drugs, is "taking a walk," as advised. A platoon of state troopers has created a security corridor through which the ticket holders for the Bush event are required to walk. Secret Service men, in suits not dissimilar from Maxie's but wearing sunglasses, ear sets, and chest holsters, stand on the Capitol steps watching everything and everyone. Security at last. Leonard's throat goes tight and dry in seconds. He wishes he had kept the apple now. Eating it would give him something innocent to do while he takes stock, while he identifies his options. He needs a coping strategy.

It is only when he sees a now familiar shorn-headed man walking confidently toward the Capitol steps that he is prompted—is obliged, perhaps—to show himself and get in line, a few yards back from Sniper No. 1, and begin the shuffle forward into the shadow of the dome. He's frightened every step of it. Self-conscious too. The bruises and the cuts are bad enough, but there is also women's makeup on his face. He spreads and smudges it when he wipes away his sweat. There are flesh-pink marks on his jacket sleeve. He takes deep, cooling breaths. This is Leonard's single chance to prove and validate himself in Texas. Maxie has made that much clear. "Be big about it, man," he said, meaning that any other option would be *small.* So Leonard stays in line, fixes his eyes on the scalp ahead of him, and concentrates on Private Alexander Sharp, his cruelly wasted life. What's the problem, anyway? What's he frightened of? He reminds himself of Nadia's reassuring gloss, delivered over breakfast that morning when Leonard admitted to feeling nauseous: This is just a demonstration. At a seat of government. In a democratic state. Against an elected leader. What could be more natural or more American than that? All he has to do, as agreed in every detail, is wait until Laura is at the podium, and when, as she must, she says *child* for the first time, simply get up on his two hind legs and shout toward the president.

"Shout what?"

"Jeez, Leon, speak your mind. Just make it loud. And keep it short and simple, yeah? All I'm sayin' is, in circumstances such as this, 'Out' is way more eloquent than"—Maxie holds up his clenched fist, Mr. Perkiss style—"than 'Let's battle for the death of the fascist insect that preys on the lives of the people.' You won't get deeper in than 'Let's.' You hearin' me, my good advice?"

Leonard hears him. He'll plagiarize the giant-sized words from the silent vigil on the lawns. He'll call out clearly and with a space between each word, "Troops . . . Out . . . Now." That's his opinion, after all. U.S. troops and UK troops. And, as Nadia reminds him, as a Briton in America, he has the right, a duty even, to speak his mind; that's what alliance means. "Respect with honesty—like, show them that you care by telling them the truth." Anyway, it hardly matters what he shouts. As Maxie says, he cannot expect to get beyond the first two words before he's bustled away, maybe pushed and shoved a bit, maybe questioned fiercely by one of those men in sunglasses, and then probably turned out onto the street as soon as the Bushes have returned to Crawford. The worst that can happen is that they all get slammed into Travis County jail for a night of "sobering up" with all the other weekend criminals, the drunks and speeding drivers, the wife abusers and the crackheads: "That's why you're carryin' those six ten-dollar bills. Protection money, man. You gotta watch your ass."

For a moment Leonard imagines being put into a cell with Nadia. Then something worse: he's sharing a cell with T-shirt Man, whose eyes are black and whose wounds have not begun to close. "So, Brit, do you love my shirt today?" he says; his great hand takes the wad of ten-dollar bills and reaches out for bones and saxophones to crush. Leonard shakes away the thought and next imagines—hopes, almost—that rather than a jailhouse beating, he gets heroically deported. The police and FBI see he's British, not a U.S. national, and feel obliged to treat him gently. They're allies, after all. They run him out to the airport and they put him on a plane, untouched, unscathed. They add his name to those not welcome in the U.S.A., along with other progressive icons: Fidel Castro, Graham Greene, Paul Robeson, and the Marxist drummer Eber Hardt, one of Leonard's idols, a complex and percussive man. They stamp his passport DEPORTEE, and—his heart jumps a beat at this—they say he won't, "as in never," be allowed back in again. "Don't even try it, bud. You're not welcome here. You disrespect our president."

But what kind of jazzman can't work in America? That's unthinkable. Eber Hardt's exclusion all but ruined his career. What Leonard does today might scupper his career as well. There is a dollar cost to everything. He shuffles forward in the line, trying not to panic but to persuade himself there isn't any danger of exclusion. He must believe in order and civility, that in America men in uniform and men who work for agencies will show restraint and moderation as a matter of training, as a matter of course, as a preference. They won't throw random punches or flout the rules or trample on his rights or send him home to Britain on a whim. Leonard will not be the victim of a beating or a rubber stamp for deportees, just the appropriate victim of procedures, and such procedures will not be capricious or violent. In America, it must be safe to exercise a right of protest, even a noisy one. Safer, probably, than exercising a right to barbecue.

Leonard lifts his head. He's calmed himself at last. Ahead of him, Maxie has engaged some strangers in the line in conversation. He's talking, as ever, but he is talking quietly, matching his demeanor to his suit and haircut. The elderly couple he has singled out seem fascinated with him. The man even takes hold of his arm briefly to mark a joke that Maxie's made. So Maxie will reach the ticket and security check in respectable company. He looks just like a decent Texan now, on home leave from his army unit or his aircraft carrier, with his proud mama and pa, attending on his president. Leonard has to nod his head in admiration. Maxie is a true professional, a skilled and practiced blender-in. Leonard ought to do the same, associate himself with someone in the line. But he does not trust himself. His mouth is far too dry to be convincing. He'll give himself away at once. Two words from the tongue-tied British weirdo with the makeup and the scars and they will call the police, he's sure of it. So as the line progresses into the south foyer of the Capitol and begins to ascend the stairs toward the second floor and the legislative chambers, he stays quiet and studies every detail of the festival program, hiding his face, hoping to look busy. There is a color photograph of the first lady on the opening page, among the "highlights" and a long list of other participants. Who are these writers and celebrities? He'll have to ask Nadia to recommend some new American novels. Frank McCourt, Kinky Friedman, and Gore Vidal he knows, with varying degrees of vagueness. But other names—Gutkind, Salinas, Obama, Minutaglio, Hinojosa-Smith—are unfamiliar, except that they seem to tell the same story about America as any U.S. movie credit sequence or war memorial or heroes' monument: that the country is a melting pot.

Leonard pivots on his heels to look down the stairs, wondering if there are any black or Hispanic faces and to see if Nadia has joined the line yet. His back is turned when the commotion starts on the second-floor landing. The line of ticket holders breaks loose abruptly, creating space for the fracas like playground kids. Guests step aside or press against the banisters and walls. There is shouting. Maxie's voice. Three men in black suits are struggling with each other at the top of the stairs, just before the ticket check and access to the representatives' chamber, where Mrs. Bush is slated to speak.

"Ticket or no ticket, you're not coming in, no way," the smallest one is saying. "Now just step out of line, sir." He reaches out and takes hold of Maxie's wrist. "Make it gentle. Move away."

"Don't even touch me, asshole." Maxie throws a punch, but it falls short. The third man speaks into his lapel radio—"Backup, backup"—while his colleague repeats, "You're not going in. Just walk aw—" He catches Maxie's second punch full on the cheekbone and the push-and-shove begins again, dangerously close to the stair top. The older man who shared Maxie's joke a minute or so ago is backing away from the scrum, pulled clear by his wife. He's holding his ribs and looking both shocked and bruised. The backup beef arrives in the shape of three DPS officers in their light brown uniforms. They hardly make a noise but just reach out and take hold of a limb apiece, as quickly and as undramatically as three shepherds taking up a ram. It lasts a minute at the most. This is democracy at work. Order is restored with firm civility. Maxim Lermontov is hoisted off the ground. Neatly, though not noiselessly, he is carried, cursing like a teenager, in his deceiving suit along the hallway, out of sight, and very nearly out of Leonard's life for good.

Leonard, still in shock but oddly satisfied as well—he's smiling, can't stop himself—has taken his seat in the chamber before he catches sight of Nadia. When he left the loft this morning with her apple, she was wrapped in towels and standing, barefoot and pink-faced, at the mirror drying her hair. Now she is dressed, of course, and prettier than he has ever seen her. During their brief flirtation over politics in Britain, she always wore walking boots and trousers and kept her hair fiercely brushed back from her brow. She'd not worn makeup, or certainly no makeup that was anything but functional. Sunblock. Lip salve. Moisturizer. Dermatitis cream. Nothing colorful. Here, though, when he sees her walking down the left aisle of the chamber looking for her place, her lips are painted red and her hair is teased into a wavy bob so that she looks less like a Sniper and more like a neat schoolteacher or librarian. She's wearing a granola-patterned linen pantsuit with a butterfly brooch on the lapel. She seems a little taller too. Heeled shoes, perhaps. She looks composed. She cannot know that Maxie has been—what, arrested or just marched out of harm's way? Leonard's tempted to hurry after her, whisper the latest developments, and hint that they'd best call off AmBush entirely.

Regrettably for Leonard, this eventuality has already been allowed for in their planning. There was always the possibility that one or more of the Snipers might fail to get inside or within shouting range of Dubya. Whoever's left, whoever does get into the chamber, must see the whole thing through, and alone if need be: as soon as Laura Bush says *child*, "Stand up, point toward the president, and shout what you have come to shout, and then resist removal by clinging to furniture or to your neighbor. Grab your neighbor's belt or necklace. Don't let go." So, as instructed, edgily obedient, Leonard stays where he is, near the right aisle, two rows back from Nadia on one of the chamber's heavy leather chairs, at a representative's desk with its own telephone and voting keypad. He watches her and hopes she will turn and see him watching. Then he can make the cancel sign. But once she has found her seat, she is immobile, like a worshipper at church, frozen in thought, focusing on the pulpit.

Even Leonard is more composed now. Maxie's removal or arrest has unburdened him to some extent. He does not have to prove himself in front of the American. He does not have to fear excess—a hidden gun, perhaps; more violence. He only has to be a plucky comrade for Nadia, and he is practiced at that. Many's the time that he and she have stood shoulder to shoulder in demonstrations or on pickets in Britain, chanting slogans harmlessly. He can do the same today. With any luck, Maxie will be locked up. He deserves it, Leonard thinks. Punching a Secret Service agent must be worth a night in jail. Then he and Nadia can spend the evening together at the apartment without Maxie's brutish presence. Finally. Today's three contrasting views of her, in pajamas first, and then the wet-haired woman in her towels, the pretty woman in her suit, have made Leonard think once more that possibly he could make his move on Nadia. Or that he ought to at least try. With Maxie absent for the night, with AmBush successfully or unsuccessfully behind them, and with Nadia's pregnancy acting on her mood, it could just happen that she tumbles into Leonard's arms. He'll ask if she will fix his face again. She stands between his open knees . . . It's just a feeble fantasy—he stops himself—but still he returns within seconds to contemplate them making love: this time she lets her wet towels drop, she reaches up on her high heels and lets him kiss her lipsticked mouth while Maxie watches through his prison bars. This will be his sweet revenge for last night's incident at Gruber's, for the Texan's painful, spiteful, fifty-fifty grip on his shoulder, for his turning his back on the saxophone, for—here Leonard's anger shakes him hard—the clatter of that thrown dime. All Leonard has to do is hold his nerve. The worst he'll have to do is shout three words.

By now the oakwood chamber is almost full. All the seats are taken and ticket holders have occupied the galleries, but there is still no sign of any officials or dignitaries on the dais at the governing end of the room, under the canopied square arch with its IN GOD WE TRUST inscription, the national and state flags, and the Lone Star chandeliers. Leonard studies the festival program again, trying to steady his hands and keep his eyes off Nadia, until with hardly a prompt the audience goes quiet, all of its own accord, and attendants come from the back of the room and take up positions in the aisles and in front of the dais. Laura Bush enters through side doors, from the Speaker's office. There's no mistaking her, her ordinary smile. She is escorted by some tough old Texan reptile that Leonard recognizes from the local television news, by an awkwardly neat festival chairwoman, and by a younger woman in a black shift dress whom someone in the row behind identifies as Jenna Bush, the daughter. The audience applauds, and Leonard mutters to himself, "Child, child." He wants the word to be set as a spring that snaps him into noise and action the very instant it is aired, right on the first beat of the bar, or at least before he has the chance to think. He needs to feel as triggered as an athlete waiting for the starting gun.

Of course, there's someone missing, isn't there? Leonard straightens at the thought. Where is the president? He did not accompany his wife when she entered with her daughter, that's for sure. He isn't on the dais. Leonard raises himself a little in his chair and inspects the front row of the chamber, where the dignitaries are seated in reserved places. None of them resembles George W. Bush. None of them has the president's distinctive wiry crop of hair or his stiff shoulders, always halfway through a shrug. And none of them resembles George Senior or the president's mother, come to that. He swivels round and swiftly checks the rest of the room, the galleries even, but not a sign. Laura and Jenna are the only ones. If the president and his parents have come to Austin, as Maxie has said they would, then clearly they will not be attending the first lady's keynote speech, unless they're doing it in disguise or are crouching behind the woodwork of the upper balcony. So, thank heavens, Maxie's "private enterprise," his plague on all their houses, has proved to be a thorough waste of time. A totally inefficient squandering of time. There is no Maxie and there is no president. AmBush has turned into a farce.

For the first time that day, the rigid knot in Leonard's stomach loosens and unties. He is a happy man. Their plans can be abandoned. He will play jazz in New York. The Four T's will not be his only gig in America. Bravo. Bravo. But his relief is still uncertain. Nadia will see, of course, that the president has not arrived and that AmBush should be called off. But almost certainly she cannot yet know that Maxie isn't there. There is no predicting what she might do if she still thinks he's with her in the chamber.

Laura Bush is talking at the podium. She looks, he thinks, a lot like Nadia might look in twenty years' time, if she dyes her hair and smiles. Both women are dressed similarly, in fact, with churchgoing small-town white-bread values in every stitch of their clothes, although Laura's pantsuit is more pearl than granola, and she has a textile bloom on the sprigging of her lapel rather than a metal butterfly. But the lipstick is almost a match. So, oddly, is the hair. They could be mother and daughter, Leonard thinks—Laura, Jenna, Nadia—and the mother comes across as personable rather than viciously Republican, even though she's reading from the page a little stiffly. It's something dull about the administration's billion-dollar-a-year "national reading initiative" that is targeting "low-income children." Children! Leonard almost jumps. But no, that's not it. The word he fears is singular. He looks across at Nadia. She seems unstirred. All is safe and well, perhaps.

It is four minutes, actually, before, at last, Laura Bush says the word. But Leonard's missed it. He is in a reverie. This time it's Maxie sharing cells with T-shirt Man—and T-shirt Man has two big friends with him. Maxie is apologizing. Maxie's pissing down his leg. Maxie's head is making porous thuds against the wall. Leonard's never hated anyone this much, hate and envy, all in one. For a moment it's almost as if the commotion from the front of the chamber belongs to Leonard's reverie and Maxie in his prison cell. But all too soon Leonard is half out of his seat, like everybody there, and trying to find a clear view of the dais. Nadia is on her feet, shouting, "Shame! Shame! Shame!" and has already pushed her way into the aisle before anyone has a chance to seize her arm.

Leonard sits and lowers his head into his hands. He squeezes his eyes shut. He doesn't want to hear or watch. Nadia sounds so screechy and so British—and so inefficient. Uncool, in fact. Unhip. Unblue. "Shame!"—constantly repeated as she dashes toward the podium in her high shoes—is an aimless slogan. Shame on what? Shame on the war? Shame on the planned withdrawal of troops? Shame on libraries? Does this woman have no sense of what's appropriate? He's overestimated her. America has poisoned her.

Maxie's knocked her out of shape. Does she not understand or care that the president's not here and that this is only the president's unelected wife, supporting libraries? All Laura Bush is calling for is that kids should read a book in bed at night. Everyone heard her saying as much a minute ago. Now where's the shame in that? She's just the meek, accommodating spouse. She could be married to a Democrat or to a pacifist and she would still want dads and moms to read their children nursery tales. This is silly, Nadia Emmerson. This is impolite. Sit down.

In fact, Leonard almost stands and shouts "Sit down," as others are doing, rather than the "Troops . . . Out . . . Now" that he has planned. But he stays where he is, his face pressed into his hands, while pregnant Nadia succeeds in getting to the podium before any of the Secret Service men stir in their suits to block her access to the president's wife. Indeed, Nadia has jumped up on the great oak Speaker's table and has kicked off her spiky shoes before the first protector, a beefy, uniformed state trooper, has succeeded in grabbing her ankle and succeeded too in toppling Nadia off the table and onto Laura Bush. There is an audible clash of heads. Inexplicably, Nadia has not attempted to roll off her victim but is both gripping her by the lapel of her pearl pantsuit and pushing her back over her chair. Laura Bush takes hold of Nadia's hair but does not tug at it. They're wrestling. It's an erotic fantasy made flesh, the blogs will say.

Now guns are drawn. Almost everybody in the audience is on their feet, shouting for this embarrassment to end. The Secret Service men have come alive at last, as have some men from the audience. Texan Volunteers. Heroes of the Book Festival. Nadia is pulled back across the table by twenty hands and forced onto the floor. Again there is a crash of heads. She screams and tries to shout, "Troops—" but is silenced with a hand across her mouth before she's lifted up by ankles and by wrists and bundled away, through the governor's door. Another friend is out of sight, though not immediately out of hearing, and very nearly out of Leonard's life. Another eighteen years.

Leonard does not need to stand, or to speak. He no longer has to make a fuss. Any fuss he makes would be too late anyway and buried by the mayhem all around. Everybody else in the chamber is already making an excited fuss. What a historic tale they'll have to tell their grandchildren. The nation's first lady is being ushered from the room. She presses a tissue against her face. She holds her head with the other hand. Her nose is bleeding and blood is dripping on her suit.

Leonard lets his neighbors pass and waits for the chamber to clear round him before he even gets out of his chair. He's calm but he is shaking. He'll go back to the loft, remove his makeup, collect his bags and Mr. Sinister, and leave at once, before the police arrive. What other choice is there? He's being sensible. His only hope is that the child has not been hurt, the child who will be Lucy Emmerson.

12

THE EMMERSONS LIVE IN THE SORT of digital Smarthouse designed to satisfy both fashion and environment—slot-in, prefabricated components but cottage-styled and then overbrightened and individualized with pastel StucoLux. They have the corner unit in a block of eight, with gazebo doors, dormered upper floors, an integrated glazed atrium at the back shared with neighbors, a wall-mounted carbon scrubber, and light-seeking energy scanners whirring on the roofs. Their StucoLux is beryl green. The building could be in any new development in almost any temperate city in Europe or New England, apart from the show of tended British evergreens breaking up the architectural lines of the suburban mews in which it stands.

Leonard is surprised: he has envisaged an ill-kept, narrow terrace house with peeling timber and cats, something batty or subversive, behind the times. Francine is disappointed; these increasingly ubiquitous Compact Intelligent Households are not cheap to buy or rent or run, so why choose one? Both expected the house to be more spirited than this bland and voguish eco-pod, and more in keeping with the hot-headed Sniper and the willful, sparky daughter described during the drive south in Leonard's scrupulously selective account of his few days in Austin. "I like the sound of Nadia," was all Francine offered, when he was finished and inviting her lenient response. She kept any thoughts on Comrades Gorky and Trotsky to herself, only nodding at her husband's familiar frailties. She laughed out loud three times: when someone threw the dime at Mr. Sinister, when Laura Bush was floored, and when Leonard pissed on his own shoe.

They have left the Buzz in the local shopping precinct, recharging at a fuel unit in the rooftop car park, and walked the last five hundred meters not quite arm in arm but shoulder to shoulder. When they reach the Emmersons' block, they do take hold of each other, though, posing as a blandly contented couple, unhurried and companionable, simply walking down the street and going about their errands. At first there is no evidence of any police or security services outside the house, but the residential parking spaces are all occupied, and in a side road opposite two photographers are sitting on the bonnets of their cars, waiting for some "show."

"Let's ring her bell," says Francine at once. "Why ever not?" Leonard hasn't seen her look so energized or so amused for months.

"I can't do that. What if she isn't on her own?"

"You can't. I can. She won't know me. I can always say I've got the wrong address. Walk on. I'll catch you up." She pushes him in the ribs, halfway between an impatient shove and a playful prod. "Buck up, Leon. Ain't we the warriors?"

Leonard's heart is racing as he continues up the mews. "I can't do that" is one of those phrases that Francine has often teased him about. He knows he should at least have gone up to the door with his wife, or, better, volunteered to ring the bell himself, alone. He could pull his scarf and collar up. He'd not be recognized. It's too late now, however. What's the point of beating himself up about it on his birthday? He's already been beaten up enough today and, on present evidence, can expect to be teased and prodded for many hours more. Even so, he cannot help pretending, as he walks along the street while Francine takes the risks, that he has volunteered and that he is alone on Nadia's step, where he is recognized by her at once, though his face is masked. For a moment Leonard has her standing at her door in the same pajamas she wore in Texas on the day the Bushes came to town.

This Nadia, this one who knows him straightaway, is not the Red Nadia of old, plucky, stocky, and attractive, and, like her daughter, just a little mad; nor is she the hardly recognizable plump, sobbing mother from this morning's news; nor the sofa socialist of Lucy's description. She is Leonard's own creation, but idealized and updated over time. She has matured into handsome middle age but, like Francine, is still strident and exciting. He has visualized making love to her countless times, because he never did make love to her at all. She is unfinished business. She is his road not taken, as it were. Mostly, when they are having sex in his imagination, they are fugitives, holed up in the woods or sharing floorboards in some radical squat, passionate and breathless, waiting for the timbers of the door to splinter or the wail of sirens to bring their loving to a halt. He has also *sometimes*—too often to admit—thought of her dressed up for the Capitol. She's at her sexiest, as he remembers it. She's put on lipstick for a change. She has a brooch. She has heeled shoes. Her linen pantsuit hugs her bottom well. A fiery, pregnant woman deliciously disguised. They're waiting for the first lady to say *child.* And when she does say *child*, both Nadia and Leonard will be on their feet and heading for the podium. Yes, both of them. Now it isn't Laura Bush who's bumping heads with her, it isn't Laura Bush who takes hold of though does not tug her hair, but Comrade Leon Lessing. They will have a future in each other's arms. Ten pairs of hands take hold of him. Ten pairs of hands are pulling him. But all those Secret Service men and Texan Volunteers will not have the strength to drag him free, until Francine catches up with him and he must shake away the thought.

As it turns out, Nadia is at home but not alone. The door is answered by an officer in uniform. "Ah!" Francine lets her mouth fall loose and arches her eyebrows, faking her surprise. "Is this the right address?"

"Depends. Who are you looking for?"

"Ms. Sickert. Celandine," she says instinctively. "My daughter's place."

He shakes his head. "Wrong house, I think. I'll ask." He turns away from the front door to reveal a woman—Nadia—standing at the dark end of the hallway, her face scumbled by shadow, her shoulders down. What had she hoped for when the doorbell sounded? "Anyone you know called Sickert Celandine—"

"Celandine Sickert," Francine corrects him, automatically, and looks directly at Nadia, offering a smile to the woman. A smile of solidarity, of course. She knows exactly what it means to be fearful for a daughter, how the throat and heart are gripped by some keen torturer every time there is a caller at the door, or the trill of incoming e-mail, or someone on the phone, how the shoulders mass and sag, how the shadows gather round, how even talking is at times such a punishing and heavy task that it is easier just to shake your head than say, "Nobody of that name is here." Just naming Celandine out loud, as Francine has just done, is painful still, even after eighteen months of getting used to it. Three syllables of pain. At once the memories stack up: that final, shocking, violent clash, that unsigned farewell note ("Dear Family, I'm moving out & moving on. No need to be in touch. X"), the early days of constant hope and bursting into tears and being practical, topping up her daughter's phone until the number was discontinued, the weekly text messages she sends, the no-replies, the e-mails that are blocked or failed, and then the months of nagging dreams in which Celandine herself is blocked or failed or discontinued. She is floating facedown in a canal, or padlocked in a room, or working on the streets, strung out and pale, or—hard to swallow, this—she's safe and well and happy in her life. No need for Mummy now. Or Unk.

"What names again?" asks Nadia, stepping forward and peering over the policeman's epaulettes at the stranger on her step.

"Celandine Sickert?"

"No."

Later there is better luck, although it does not seem so immediately. After killing an hour over coffee and more questions about Nadia and Maxie at the local Starters, Leonard and Francine are walking toward the Emmersons' front door for the third and, they have determined, final time. They have a plan. If all is clear, Leonard will distract the photographers with some bogus query while Francine delivers an envelope marked "Nadia/Personal," containing the unsigned note that she has written spikily with her left hand on the back of a Starters coaster: "Lucy safe. With friends. *Not kidnapped.* Teenage escapade. Tell nobody. DO NOT WORRY." But in the event there is no need for any note. Much to the relief of the now four waiting photographers, Nadia Emmerson, dressed in a gratifyingly adventurous multicolored overcoat, steps out of her front door and gets into a silver citicar driven by a heavily built police minder, out of uniform. The uniformed officer that Francine spoke to earlier takes up sentry duty outside the house. He pops a sweet into his mouth. He looks as if he means to make it last.

"That's it, then, I suppose," Leonard says, both disappointed and relieved that the note is now undeliverable and that, for the time being, Nadia Emmerson is out of reach. He's done his best; it's not his fault—the usual chorus line. "It is my birthday, after all," he reminds Francine. "What do you say we find ourselves a country pub, with a restaurant?"

"We could."

Back at the rooftop car park, though, while Leonard is disconnecting the charger leads and settling the bill with his fob, Francine spots the silver citicar again, parked two spaces forward. The officer is sitting with the window down and with his in-screen switched on, tuned too loudly to a football channel, and muttering fan rant to himself. It's midafternoon on a Saturday. The football season's hotting up, and here's an opportunity. He's on duty, but he doesn't have to miss the match.

"She's only gone shopping, wants to take her mind off things,"

Francine says, clapping her hands with satisfaction. "And she's on her own. How lucky's that? Her ape would rather sit up here and watch the game than do his job. Thank heavens for slackers."

"What now?"

"Come on. We'll sleuth her down," she says, clearly enjoying herself.

There is no immediate sign of Nadia's loudly colored overcoat in the avenues of the ground-floor concourse, so Leonard and Francine separate. She takes all the shops and cafés in the southern wing, at a dash, in what must seem a familiar panic to passing women. She's just another scatty shopper who has left a bag behind or misplaced a child. He strides north with measured steps, peering into or briefly entering shops but trying not to draw attention to himself. There'll be security cameras and precinct guards. Despite his care, he's breathless soon, and sweating. He searches amongst the shelves of a B&N bookshop, not quite expecting he'll discover his old comrade indulging her passions in "Politics and History," but being logical and thorough. Now he's squeezing between the aisles of a pharmacy, his shoulders brushing customers and, embarrassingly, toppling rows of shampoos and conditioners. He's in the Java Café lounge, turning on his heels and scanning every circle of sofas for a glimpse of Nadia. He's checking an energy advice agency—no luck—and then crossing the concourse toward a food store. He does not even reach the automatic doors. Francine is here. She grabs his coat. "Got her," she says triumphantly.

"Show me."

"Not me. You're going on your own. This is something you must do."

"Where is she, then?"

"In Maven's, treating herself to a pair of pants."

"Not underpants?" Leonard puts his hand to his brow. He can't be expected to approach her on his own while she's buying underclothes. He wants to say, "I can't do that."

"No, *trouser* pants. You idiot." Francine shakes her head dramatically. She adds, "Are you afraid of everything, including clothes? Just go." She pushes him. She's pushed her husband quite a lot today.

This Maven's department store is just like every other Maven's in the country: cluttered, cheerful, cheap, and understaffed, with an overriding smell of cardboard and cloth and an unbroken sound track of music, offers, and announcements. As usual, Male Box is to the right of the doors, close enough to the entrance for men to find easily and be tempted to buy before they are tempted to bolt. Women shoppers are expected to be more focused and even to prefer to go beyond the menswear, kitchenware, bedding, and electronics sections to the more private carousels and racks of women's clothes at the back end of the store. The deeper Leonard ventures, trying to look purposeful, the less purposeful he feels. He's not rehearsed. He's not decided what to say. But when he reaches the far end and quickly prowls all corners of the section, there is no sign of Nadia. He's looking for her coat. She might be carrying it by now or might have hung it up somewhere. So now he prowls again, looking for a face to recognize.

She comes out of the changing rooms just ahead of him, wearing her coat and carrying two pairs of trousers over her forearm and another pair on a hanger. It's easy, then. He's walked straight into her. Now that he sees her in the flesh, even from behind, he can recognize Lucy in her: that boxy build and pale, scrubbed skin. Her height. Her walk, even. It seems just hours ago, rather than days, that he has been clipping this woman's daughter's heels with just the same uncertainty, plucking up courage in his yellow beach cap to blurt out, "I knew your father" at her back. This time he just says, "Nadia." She is either too deep in thought to hear him or she has simply buried Leonard's greeting in the noisy mayhem of the store. He tries again, closer but more lightly: "Hi, Nadia." It's as if he is a familiar neighbor. No big deal. Certainly that is what she takes him for. "Oh, hi," she says. "How's it going?"

"You don't recognize me, do you?"

"I know the voice."

"We spoke the other night. On Thursday night."

"Where did we speak?" She looks about her, uneasy now, but reassured by the nearness of a pair of women in the next aisle and a shop assistant at the till.

"On the phone."

She shakes her head and tucks her chin. She's doesn't know what he means.

"I phoned about the bike. Your daughter's bike."

She's thinking now and making fast connections. She looks at him again, steps back a pace, looks round to check that she can get away if need be, glances at his hair, then looks down at his hands. "Leon . . . Lessing?"

"That's me."

"I've told the police."

"I know you've told the police. I've spoken to the police."

"I have a policeman with me now."

"He's on the roof, watching the match. He won't trouble us."

She backs away a further step. One more step and she'll be out of reach. He stretches out to hold her arm or sleeve. But she's too quick, and getting angry now.

"Jesus, Lennie. Is that what you call yourself these days? What is going on? What do you want?" She edges round behind a display of skirts.

"I want you to know that Lucy is all right. She's safe. She's not been kidnapped. Not at all."

Nadia has dropped the trousers and has her cell out before he notices. He has no choice but to dart forward and take hold of her wrist, making her let go of the phone. It clatters to the floor. She calls, angry and alarmed, but nobody comes to help. The two women shoppers look up and exchange grimaces. A man and wife are arguing, that's all. Husbands are a pain, especially in shops. Men are bullies, all of them.

"You have to trust me, Nadia." His mouth is a centimeter from her ear. He can smell her hair and perfume. He's tugged his damaged shoulder far too hard in seizing her, and it is hurting considerably. "Don't phone the police, not now. Stay quiet, stay still, and I'll explain it all." For reasons he can't understand, except to normalize this encounter and to flatter her, he adds, "You haven't changed a bit. It's eighteen years. I'd recognize you anywhere." He waits for her to say the same to him, to say that he appears much less than fifty years of age, to say that she's followed his jazz career for years and it's "brave stuff." But her look is hostile still, and fearful. She seems in pain. He lets go of her wrist, realizing far too late that he is gripping it too tightly. What must she think of him? He's shocked and trembling. He's never frightened anyone before. He steps away, well out of reach. "Sorry, Nadia." She rubs her wrist, shakes her head at him contemptuously, then rescues her cell, picks up the trousers, and drapes them over the end of a rack.

"Let me say one thing. It's going to make you feel okay," he says.

"So talk. So make me feel okay. You better had. Where's my Lucy? Tell me that." She retreats a little further into the racks of clothes. Leonard can see she is ready to make a dash for it.

"Let's find a safer place," he says.

Leonard explains almost everything in the cafeteria on the first floor above Maven's. He tells Nadia Emmerson that he does not know where her Lucy is, but he's certain what she's done and why. She listens as he lists it all: the yellow cap, the red beret, the beer, the wine, the cigarettes, the promises he made, the rendezvous, the phone calls and the stolen bike, that morning's raid on his house.

"How old are you?"

"I'm fifty. Today."

"And Lucy? Remind me. How old is she?"

"She's seventeen," he says, almost inaudibly.

"Exactly so. Just seventeen. So which of you, do you suppose, should have put an end to this before it happened? You should have called the police at once. You should have found me. Shouldn't you? She's just a girl who wants to be a heroine. What were you thinking of?"

"I thought I'd be a heroine as well."

She looks at him and shakes her head. Her mood has softened now. Lennie Less, the heroine. "Well, she's headstrong, that's for sure."

"You were once."

"We all were once. But we grow up."

"Maxie hasn't grown up. Evidently."

"Maxie is just a pot of bile. That's all there is to him. He never really meant to make the world a better place. He only ever wanted to throw punches. Well, you saw that yourself."

"He never hit me, actually."

"Aren't you the lucky one? Indeedy-doo-wa, Comrade Leon walks away unscathed. Remember that?"

Leonard cannot pretend he is not startled. That exact and shaming phrase has not been heard for eighteen years; nor, evidently, has it been forgotten or forgiven. "You weren't the lucky one, I take it?" he asks, attempting to disguise the cause of his surprise.

"You never knew? You could have guessed. He hit me plenty of times. Oh, well—"

"That's Politics and History."

"That's love, I guess. The only trouble was, he and I both loved the same person. And now he's back in town."

"And armed."

"This is a nightmare, isn't it? I knew it would be the moment I saw him and his hair standing on my step in August. Maxie doesn't make social calls. There's always, you know, some upheaval planned. Lucy wouldn't listen to me, of course. Big mess she's made of it."

"Disastrous, I know."

"Great help you've been. Some ally. So what's new?" She's prompting him to say something about that final day in Austin, Leonard realizes. She said then, before he set off for the Capitol, "You have the right, a duty even, to speak your mind. That's what alliance means." He let her down in Texas. He's let her down again.

"I've never had a head for heights," he says, spreading his hands to surrender an apology. "Or fights."

"Well, that's the truth. Ever the invertebrate."

"What are you thinking now?" Leonard wants to move their conversation away from bruising territory. Decaf? Invertebrate? This is a consensus he would prefer not to explore.

"I think I'm feeling mightily relieved. No thanks to you. Well, hardly any thanks to you. Quite honestly, I couldn't trust you less right now. Lennie Less." She laughs at him.

"I mean, what do you think you'll do?"

"It's not your business, is it? Except you'll have to talk to someone and own up to your lack of brains."

"Not yet."

"Yes, at once. Upstairs. I want you talking to my cop. And I want my daughter back with me by teatime. Otherwise. Well, otherwise, the shame is yours." Nadia pauses for a moment, an eye flicker, no more. "Shame, shame, shame. Remember that, Comrade Leon? Ring any bells? I've not forgotten it. Nor the fourteen months I served for it. Malicious damage, public disorder, and assault. Lucy is a prison kid. Did you know that?" She offers him a nod, and then—seeing how appalled he looks—the stiffest of smiles. She's still attractive, sparky too, he thinks, surprised that he can rescue any comfort from the jaws of this defeat. She stands and turns to collect her scarf and bag from the back of her chair. "A nightmare, yes. Don't make it worse," she says. "Do yourself a favor. Go to the police at once. Before I start to yell."

Now that Nadia is no longer looking at him directly, Leonard dares to touch her lightly on her upper arm. "What if—"

"I've heard enough. Don't try to wheedle me." She shakes him off.

"I wasn't wheedling. It's just . . ." He pauses, choosing his words carefully. He has got to get this right. "I was telling Lucy how you . . ." He was going to say, used to be a militant. But *used to be* is a loaded phrase. "What a firebrand you are. Really headstrong, like we said. I have to tell you that Lucy said she's never seen that part of you. I think she'd like to see that part of you. What daughter wouldn't?"

"What are you now, a family counselor?"

"Sorry," Leonard says, not meaning it. He can see by the flutter of her eyes that what he says is reaching her. "What if . . ." he asks again. What if her daughter has had a truly genius idea? What if Lucy is correct, that believing his rediscovered child is in tit-for-tat danger might stop Maxie hurting anyone, including himself, might bring the Alderbeech siege to a bloodless end? "Could you live with not giving it a chance?"

"Nobody wants bloodshed," she says distractedly. Nobody except Maxie, that is. *Bluedsched.*

"So here's my thought, Nadia: keep Lucy's secret for a while. No one need ever know. Give her till Monday, say. Let her be the little heroine while she's young enough to care. Be her comrade here. The firebrand mum. That's what she wants."

She shakes her head. She's wavering but not enough. "Who are you to say what Lucy wants?"

He almost answers that he is her unofficial godfather. If it weren't for him and the thousand dollars, "twelve hundred, tops," that he wouldn't loan Maxie, none of this might have happened. Instead, he says, "It's my birthday, Nadia. Today."

"You said."

"So just for old times' sake—"

"Ha! What old times?"

"Allow me this. Allow your daughter this. One final thing. One final favor, please."

"Allow you what?"

"I want you to meet my wife. Francine."

"Why would I ever want to meet your wife?"

"Because if you two meet, you're bound to trust me more."

13

LEONARD PARKS AGAIN ON THE EDGES of the waste ground. There are a couple of half-erected marquees adding a dash of color—Oxford blue—but otherwise the makeshift village of trucks and buses has not changed much since Thursday, except that the earth is more churned up by vehicles and there is a collage of litter blown against the outer fence or kicked there by time-killing policemen. There is no longer any sense of urgency or excitement. Everyone is bored and regimented. Day four, it's almost 5 p.m., and nothing much is happening.

This time Leonard has company. In fact, it has been Francine's suggestion that they drive down to the hostage street. She's curious to see it for herself, and she has promised Nadia that she will phone tomorrow evening with her report. As Leonard has suspected, the two women are prepared to like each other instantly. Within minutes, after Nadia says, "You're the woman at my door," they are holding hands across the cafeteria table while Leonard acts the waiter, bringing teas and pastries. Women are so skilled at reaching out, he thinks, at finding sisters, listening. He sits with them for a while, his chair drawn slightly back, indicating that he does not wish to intrude, as they take turns showing interest in each other's daughters and their current whereabouts. He's happy to stay silent and just look at them, a jealous spectator.

Here, unpredictably together and touching hands, are—so very few—the only two women in his life that he has ever cared for. Cared for sexually, that is. Observing them so openly, and comparing them, is curiously rewarding. His wife is thoroughly familiar, of course. After nine years of marriage, they have hardly any secret drawers. He's intimate with everything she does. He knows the clothes she's wearing, what she's now wearing underneath, the dots and pigments of her skin, her range of smells; he recognizes what she says and how she says it, the characteristic language and expressions that she uses, the expressions on her face; that hanging thread; that single less-than-perfect fingernail; her slender upper body with its small breasts, the fuller hips and upper legs she regrets so much, the waist she's learned to emphasize. Francine is the breathing, vivid detail of his life, a woman in hi-def, a wife till death do part, while Nadia is just a smudge. He'll never know about her breasts and waist or recognize her underwear and fingernails, except in fantasy, this current fantasy, which causes him to close his eyes and exhale noisily: he's loving both of them. He has to sit straight on his chair and breathe less heavily.

"Are you okay?" Nadia and Francine stare back at him.

"Yes, why?"

"You're talking to yourself. You're muttering."

"No, I was only thinking . . . saying that I'm going to stretch my legs, leave you two pals in peace."

For a moment, as he picks his way between the cafeteria tables and loaded shopping bags, Leonard feels a little like a man doubly rejected. He would have preferred it if they'd said, "No, stay. We want you sitting here with us." But instinctively he sees that what he wants—what Lucy wants—will come about only behind his back and only if Francine mediates. He finds his way back through Maven's into the concourse and wanders with his shoulders down and his hands in his pockets toward the exit doors and the open air, where he will—what? Sit among the flower beds with the smokers and feel his age advancing by the minute? It would be a surrender to beg a cigarette for himself; nevertheless, it is tempting. Lucy's roll-ups have infiltrated him. Her nicotine has not cleared yet. The weather saves him, though. Yet again it's damp outside, misty and autumnal rather than showery. So he comes back into the precinct and cuts across to the bookshop. If he can't smoke, he'll treat himself—why not? He'll buy himself a birthday treat, something, anything. So far today, it occurs to him without self-pity, he hasn't opened a single card or unwrapped a gift. He hasn't even had a kiss.

He's waylaid again before he reaches the bookshop, this time by a two-meter-wide concourse telescreen showing music videos, film trailers, advertisements, sports highlights, and every hour a home news and showbiz bulletin. What catches Leonard's eye is Lucy's face, that same schoolgirl photograph that the police showed him this morning: "Do either of you know, have either of you seen, this girl?" He stands and stares, tipping his head toward the screen, doing his best to pick up what is being said above the din of passersby. A "new communiqué" has been delivered, together with a long and heavy lock of Lucy's hair. Nice touch, you clever girl, he thinks. A deadline has been set, it seems. Release the Alderbeech hostages by midnight (which midnight, when?). He steps closer to the screen, but almost at once he's required to move aside by two women with prams. So he misses the final sentences of the commentary. By the time he has repositioned himself, the bulletin has finished and the first match results are on display. He has to stand among the jostling football fans and wait for the news strapline to track across the bottom of the screen. "Unknown Terror Group SOFA Holding Kidnap Girl." Leonard smiles at that. No doubt the pundits will already be speculating what such an acronym might signify. Save Our Fat Arses, Leonard thinks. Pass the velvet cushions, please.

Leonard does not hold his smile for long, however. A moment later and he's panicking again. The half-heard bulletin, with its totemic lock of hair and the always chilling word *deadline*, snaps him free from his earlier illusions. His all-too-recent and romantic entreaties for Nadia to allow her daughter this one chance to be the little heroine suddenly seem disastrously poor advice, given for the benefit of no one but himself. He has naively hoped that when this is over and everything is told, he will be reported as a genuine comrade by her mother to Lucy, a man who backed her up, not let her down, a man who's still prepared to throw his pebble at the wall. But the revelation that Nadia served fourteen months and Lucy is a prison kid and he's a bit—a lot—to blame has darkened everything. He knows he ought to go back into the cafeteria at once and tell the two women he has changed his mind, that caution—he'll call it circumspection—is always sensible in situations such as this. He ought to do it straightaway, because at this very moment—if he has understood his wife's intentions clearly—Francine will be charming Nadia, persuading her to go along with what Leonard has proposed, that she keep Lucy's secret for a while. And Francine will agree with him. She always loves an escapade.

But if there is an escapade, costs and consequences are bound to follow it. Especially for Lucy. She's piling up problems for herself—and for her mother now. Monday is two days away, and two extra days is a deep hole into which the police might pour a thousand men, as well as dogs, helicopters, news teams, public appeals, not to mention money. One million euros? Two million? He has heard of such cases before and has been shocked by how much such operations cost—and by how unamused and vengeful the police, the public, and the courts can be when it turns out that the missing person wasn't kidnapped after all but playing games, "playing costly games with people's lives."

Leonard steadies himself. He thinks it through again from the bottom up, rehearsing the debates he has already had with himself and with Nadia and Francine for and against Lucy's "genius." It's possible, of course, that the police will merely bof and shrug when they learn the truth, as they are bound to. Lucy cannot disappear for good. She's isn't Celandine. When she does show up, they might only tell her off, issue her a caution, then let her go. That's possible. She is just a child, after all, a minor. But the more Leonard considers that outcome, the less likely it seems. The authorities will have to punish Lucy in some way. They'll have to punish everyone involved. Public opinion will insist on it. The public do not like to be *mischled*.

Leonard can imagine the headlines already: "Tearful Mother Knew Lucy Was Not Kidnapped" and "Kidnap Mother Charged." Francine will be implicated too. He has a sudden image of his wife, defiant in the courts. "I accept that you were a minor player in this deception, misled by your husband," the judge is telling her, "but nevertheless this has been a thoughtless and costly hoax and one for which an exemplary custodial sentence is inevitable." Now Leonard is almost running into Maven's and up the single flight of stairs to the cafeteria. Just before he catches sight of Francine and Nadia, still sitting over their cups with their foreheads almost touching, he has another thought. His own genius idea. He doesn't have to look a fool in front of them, by changing his mind so soon after arguing in favor of Lucy's plan. He doesn't have to tell them anything, in fact. It's just the authorities who need to know. But not the cop on the roof. He'll phone NADA, then keep that phone call to himself. What happens next is up to them. If they choose and if it serves their purposes, they can even decide to keep the matter quiet, sit back and see what comes about in Alderbeech. After all, it might be the best of strategies, even for the police, to encourage Maxie to believe that Lucy's still in danger.

Leonard uses his own cell phone, standing on the landing of the store. It doesn't matter if his calls are being bugged or logged. He isn't hiding anymore. He texts in "National Defense Agency" and connects to the number that the directory provides. It's Saturday, the switchboard is unattended, but Leonard leaves his information anyway. "This message cache is checked regularly at weekends and during public holidays," a voice informs him. "Start recording now." "This is urgent and it's for . . ." What was that agent's name? Yes, Rollins, not the saxophone colossus but Simon Rollins. "For NADA agent Simon Rollins. You visited me at home today, remember? This is Leonard Lessing. You asked if I could throw any light, any light at all, on the whereabouts of Lucy Katerina Emmerson. Or who it is that's taken her. To tell the truth, since we spoke, the girl has been in touch . . ."

NOW HE AND FRANCINE WALK arm in arm from the waste ground to the hostage street. There are fewer gawpers at the barrier than on Thursday, fewer know-alls with opinions that they want to share and spread. And there are fewer men in uniform in the approaches to the house. Nobody at all is keeping armed watch behind steel shields in what has been designated an arc of fire. Keep It Tight has been replaced by Keep It Calm. The nation is a little bored with Maxim Lermontov, it would appear. He's let them down. He hasn't starved or handcuffed anyone. He hasn't fired his gun enough. He hasn't tossed a body out of an upper window, providing drama and pictures for the evening news. He hasn't tried to master an escape or released a second video detailing future *misch-apps*. Instead, he and his two accomplices have simply run a tidy house for four days, ordering in food and toiletries like any family. It is even easy to imagine Maxie fascinating those nonvolunteers inside, the hostages for whom he will seem to presume a duty of care, the two sons especially. They will be glued to his great smile, no doubt, his sense of fun, his devastating and unstable charm, his artificial tenderness.

Tonally, today the house is like the sky, grayed out and smudged. The weather is contagious, showering the suburb in gloom. The street seems washed of energy, and muted. The afternoon is deepening as what little light there is sinks behind the rooftops. No bulbs are burning in the hostage house; all lights are doused, nor are there any in the evacuated neighboring and opposite houses. There are no moving window silhouettes or twitching curtains. Behind the barriers the television crews have been downgraded, and the remaining journalists are mostly juniors detailed just to keep an eye on things and then call for more experienced backup should anything kick off. Restricted by the police to one small area, they pass their time sitting under their fishermen's umbrellas, texting, smoking, drinking coffee from their flasks, watching palm sets. Except for one wall-perched cat, wondering why nobody is passing to stop and rub its back, and pigeons on the roof, the hostage house is not worth looking at. The only sounds are the drones of distant traffic and, occasionally, a dog barking.

Leonard and Francine walk twice across the street, hoping perhaps to catch some sign of life inside the house, but see nothing to detain them any longer.

"It looks more interesting on the television," Leonard says. He feels he needs to apologize, as if somehow the scene's lack of energy is his responsibility. "What do you suppose is going on in there?"

"They're watching television," Francine says. "That's how it works. That's the deal. We watch them, and they watch themselves. It doesn't happen on the street. It only happens on the screen." Leonard nods but does not meet her eye. She's said as much before to him, and meant it as a criticism. She thinks he watches television far too much, that the remote console is well named. He is consoled by it; he is unreachable.

"I'll mend my ways," he says, though that is what he always says. He rarely acts on it. He cannot pretend to share his wife's gadget nausea or sympathize with her refusal to engage with any of the bloatware he has downloaded to their systems.

"But now let's *wend* our ways." She's evidently in a punning, merry frame of mind. Her time with Nadia has cheered her up, illogically. Their hearts have been emptied and their troubles have been shared. They've promised that they'll stay in touch. They have agreed, as Leonard thought they would—his wife's persuasive when she wants to be; she will have swept Nadia's qualms aside—that Lucy should be allowed, until Monday anyway, to enjoy her adventure, unbetrayed, and that Celandine is bound to show up safe and well in her own good time. Both women leave the cafeteria less burdened. Excited, even.

"Back home?" says Leonard.

"No, let's break the mold for once. It's your birthday, isn't it? I haven't even kissed you yet." She pecks his chin. "Let's find a pub or restaurant. Let's have champagne."

It is the second time that Leonard walks the streets between the hostage house and the suburb's row of shops with its one restaurant (not open yet) and the same pub—the Woodsman—that he and Lucy visited two days ago. They do not go into the yard. No need for that. They are no longer smokers. Instead, they find a table in what is called the Parlor Bar & Bistro, where there is waitress service and a sundown menu of appetizers. They order poppy bread and olive dip, vegetable wedges, fried garlic and haloumi, and a whole bottle of champagne. They are the only customers. It's intimate: table lamps and easy chairs, a corner, dusk. They drink and talk and reminisce self-consciously.

"You realize I didn't mean half that stuff this morning," Francine says.

"What stuff?"

"You know . . ." She beams at him. " 'You selfish bloody idiot.' That stuff."

"So what half did you mean?"

"None of it—well, *hardly* none of it. I only mean it at the time. It doesn't last."

It lasts for me, thinks Leonard, not quite managing a beam in return. "Decaf!" he says eventually. "That got to me. It sounds like *impotent.* In all its ways. And *cowardly*."

"I didn't mean you're always cowardly . . . no, take that back." She pegs her mouth playfully. "I'll be careful. *Timid* is the better word."

"Depends who's saying it and who's accused of it. *Timid*'s not a word I like that much, to tell the truth."

"*Squeamish*, then."

"Oh, this is so much fun when you're being more careful!

Squeamish, am I now? Hell, Frankie. Get out the thesaurus, why don't you? How about *inhibited... repressed*—"

"You have a point. I'm teasing you."

"You're bullying me?"

"It's good for you. You know it is. No, what I'm saying is... sometimes I think it's just as well I'm here to bully you, because if I wasn't breathing down your neck some of the time—"

"And prodding me."

"And prodding you, then you'd just sit back and Google your life away. Admit it, you're a screen slave, Leonard. I prefer it when..." She hesitates, wanting to strike a loving, hopeful note before it's too late. She loves him, after all. And she is in a brighter mood than she has been in for months. For eighteen months. (Nadia has cheered her up. That daughter talk. That *safe and well*.) It's time to end hostilities.

"You prefer it when what?" he asks.

"When we have fun." *Fun*, as Leonard knows, is one of Francine's favorite words, but one she hasn't used much recently. It is her greatest compliment, to say that someone has been fun. "I'm going to hold my tongue from now on and be all sweetness and light, the perfect loving wife on hubby's fiftieth. Because everything has started to turn out well today, hasn't it?" she says, almost in her classroom voice. "I shouldn't admit to this, I'm being bad, but it's the truth. Dodging those awful goons back home. The drive down. Hunting Nadia in the shopping mall. Meeting one of your old flames—"

"Let's not exaggerate."

"Going to the hostage house. Drinking bubbly here. It's been enormous fun. And you've been bouncy, haven't you? We're always better together, don't you think, when you show a bit of swing?"

"Like on gigs, you mean?" Her glass is empty. He looks down at the bottle. Almost empty too.

"No, not only with the saxophone. That was mean of me. Let's see..." Now, here's an opportunity. "Remember that ECM Jazz Gala in Budapest about six years ago?"

"I do." They had sex every night. "We made love every night."

"Do you remember flying out?"

He does. He's never been that scared since. The gales were so turbulent across the runway that the pilot was forced to abort his landing a meter from the ground and toil into the storm again. They had to circle, jettisoning fuel in cyclone winds, for forty more minutes before being cleared to try again. Leonard's terror was so excessive that it rendered him powerless, motionless, expressionless, and mute, hardly able to breathe, let alone scream. He still remembers with unnerving clarity how the luggage lockers in the cabin all dropped open in one deafening *clunk* and how the coats and cases stowed above their heads dislodged and fell into the aisles. Outside, beyond the streaming window glass, the skyline of Budapest tossed and seesawed like a ship.

"I was absolutely sick with fear," Francine says. "But you were totally calm. And comforting. Boy, you hardly raised a sweat. The only one on board. I thought you were so cool that day. And *hot*! That's why we tumbled into bed so much."

"Not quite the Mile High Club."

"Now there's a thought." Francine wraps her hands around her champagne glass and stares into it, smiling self-consciously. "Truth or dare," she says finally. "Did you make love to Nadia? With Nadia?"

"When?"

"Not in Maven's, obviously."

"In Texas?"

"Yes."

"The answer's no."

"Before that, then?"

"Not exactly."

"You go blotchy when you're lying, Leonard."

"I'm blushing because I'm telling the truth. Because the answer's no again. Another failure. We exchanged slogans but no fluids."

"I wouldn't blame you if you had. She must have been dramatic then. She still looks good. Don't you think? Leonard, look at me. I'm asking you."

It is the alcohol. They're giggling, like people half their age, and Francine is reaching out to hold his hand across the table, not in the way she reached out for Nadia's, stroking it to comfort her, but flirtingly, meshing her fingers between Leonard's and lacing her legs round his below the tabletop.

"I always admired your hands," she says, rubbing his palms and the backs of his fingers. "Long and strong. Sexy hands."

"That's from playing scales for more than thirty years."

"I always liked your throat and cheeks and lips as well. From the first time I set eyes on you. You still look good. No sign of sag."

"That's blowing for a living. It gives you muscles in your face."

"I'm sagging everywhere."

"You're not. In point of fact, you're lovelier than you have ever been. I was watching you only today. In Maven's cafeteria. With Nadia."

"I saw you watching us. Bad boy."

Leonard does not look at her. "Well, you were looking . . . fabulous."

"Let's not go home tonight. Let's find a hotel," she says.

"I'm okay to drive, I think. I haven't downed as much as you."

"No, Leonard. Let's find a hotel *now*. I want to go to bed with you right now. A little birthday treat." She twists around toward the bar hatch. "Let's ask if they do rooms." She laughs. That pealing, mezzo, Brighton laugh. "We don't have to stay the night. An hour ought to do it, don't you think?"

"Jesus, Francine, what are they going to think? We haven't got any luggage, even."

"Couldn't give a damn what they think." She's standing up already and leaning over the bar, calling for attention—"Hello? Hello? Customers!"—while Leonard watches from the table, fearful and aroused.

The room is on the upper floor, an attic space with sloping ceilings and a tiny shoe-box sink. It isn't clean and it isn't comfortable.

The mattress has been compacted by five years of heavy salesmen. The pillows smell of beer and other people's scalps. Francine and Leonard do not notice any of this until they have tumbled onto the bed, pushed off their shoes, torn at each other's lower clothes, and, in the words of a song from Leonard's repertoire, *Gotten so familiar* with each other, *So fervent and familiar / That what they feel is similar / To floating on cloud nine.* They've not made love like this, so thoroughly and so spontaneously, for years. The champagne was a genius idea. It helped them find the reckless courage to make love in this unlovely place, and now it helps them try to rest, half naked in each other's gluey arms.

Francine—once she has found a cleanish towel to put between the pillow and her face—is soon dozing, though fitfully and shallowly. She's breathing heavily. Her day has been exhausting and exhilarating, packed with more drama than any term at school. It's started with a police raid, and now it's ending in a low-rent bed with sex. It has taken years off her. It is not long, though, before she begins, both in her episodes of consciousness and in her dreams, to regret the bottle of champagne and this grubby room. Now that she is sobering and submitting to sleep, all its imperfections shout at her. The furnishings are soiled and dirty. She has not been able to brush her teeth. She does not have deodorant or a change of underwear. If her car was a little longer, well, twice as long, or they had traveled in Leonard's gig van, she might have suggested making love in some dark field, closer to home. Then she would've woken up tomorrow morning in her own clean bed, with Leonard bringing Sunday breakfast on a tray. Naked if he has to. That's okay. Anything is more okay than this. Nevertheless, she stretches out. Any restlessness will not survive for long. She's used to sleeping well on Saturdays. She stores her tiredness for the weekend and then she gluts on it.

All nights are the same for Leonard at the moment, now that he is nursing his bad shoulder and has no gigs to tire him out. His sleep is patchy at best. On this thin mattress, he's wide awake at first, in fact uncomfortable, but not even trying to fall asleep.

Hoping not to, actually. He wants to think about their lovemaking, and then he wants to run through his encounter with Nadia Emmerson and his clandestine phone call before considering what could occur to Lucy between today and Monday if Agent Rollins does not pick up his messages over the weekend. He sinks into a shallow doze, dreaming madly, bruising dreams, but waking often, stirring to the night sounds of the street or to adjust his body to the shoulder pain.

He's almost glad to be rescued from the dreams by disturbances below the room, late or maybe early departures from the bars downstairs and taxis sounding their horns. He's sleeping in his underpants and shirt and feels the cold. His cock is caked and sore. He turns his back against the room and hugs himself, looking at Francine's sleeping profile just a few centimeters from his own face. She looks warm and peaceful in the strip of street light wedged across the bed. Still a handsome woman, even now that his sexual appetites are pacified. Leonard will not wrap himself round her, however. She should not be woken before she's fully rested. She might push him away. So he slips out of bed to find the jumper he abandoned so hurriedly only a few hours earlier. As he pulls it on, he turns toward the old sash window of the room and its bottled nighttime silvering of glass and stares beyond the gables on the far side of the street to what are either the first signs of a fragile, dawning sky or the ambient light of the city center. In the other directions, the sky is still huge and salted with stars. He can't decide the time of night. He'll wait until he sees some evidence—an early bird, an early van, an early dog walker, some winking aircraft lights, perhaps—before he crawls back into bed. At least he's warmer now, and while he is standing here he can let his shoulders drop to ease the ache.

Two vehicles drive idly past the pub, almost in convoy. The first is a dark gray personnel vehicle with blackened windows. So is the second. Leonard does not wait to see the third, or more, although they're on their way. He guesses at once what's going on. The siege is coming to an end. The troops are moving in.

"What are you doing?" Francine asks, an edge of weary irritation in her voice. "Come back to bed. You're waking me."

"I'm trying not to wake you. That's why I'm up."

"Well, you are waking me. I need to sleep. I don't want to be awake in this dreadful room. Not for one minute. We should have driven home last night."

"Don't say that."

"Don't say that, because it's true? I haven't even got a toothbrush here."

"I'll go and get you one."

"Don't be ridiculous. What time is it?"

"I've no idea." Leonard holds his wristwatch up to the window but can make out only the circling phosphor of the second hand—and then the headlights of another dark gray vehicle. It's clear he has to go back to the hostage house. "Anyway, it doesn't matter what the time is," he says impulsively. "We have to get away from here. I agree. It's horrible. You get some rest. I'll get the car. I'll make it quick. Drive home, okay?"

14

ACCORDING TO THE ONE-ARMED CLOCK in the pub's lobby, it is 4 a.m. or thereabouts, early hours, still the trenches of the night when even sleepers are too deep to dream. The city road where Leonard abandoned his car on his first encounter with Lucy is unusually busy, and not only with the tail ends of Saturday's club traffic and the first Sunday tram, but also with slow, determined vehicles that exit from the townway into Alderbeech.

Leonard hurries, runs almost, toward the waste ground and the Buzz, tracing the steps that he and Francine took late yesterday afternoon, hand in hand. Now he is striding down the street like some jilting adulterer or skirt owl who's abandoned his prey half feathered and half awake in creased and grubby sheets. He hopes he doesn't look as furtive and transparent as he feels. Can everybody tell from his own creased and grubby appearance—he hasn't washed or shaved for almost two days; he's still wearing yesterday's clothes, he's slept in them; he hasn't cleaned his teeth; his mouth is bruised and furry from the kissing; he smells of many things—that he has all too recently bolted from a woman's bed? In chilly retrospect, the ardors of last night could seem a little sleazy. Not that that will bother Francine in the least—well, not the Francine of old. "Sleazy does it," she once said in her Brighton days, on the one occasion she persuaded him to help her to a climax in a cinema. She is not the sort to care if the lustier parts of her nature are disclosed and acted on, the parts that need sensations and encounters. He was surprised by last night's lack of inhibition, though, and this late revival, this flaring up of Francine's younger, raw-boned self. No wonder he feels sore and bruised. And no wonder he is already planning ways of being sleazy with his wife again. As soon as possible. Next weekend, if he can engineer it. Hire another shoddy room for sex. Extemporize. Experiment. He must remember to stow emergency toothbrushes in the glove boxes of their cars.

Leonard is so engrossed by these prospects, and so beset by the cold, that he does not notice until his way is blocked that the street ahead is clogged with vehicles parked across its width. Personnel carriers are drawn up, sideways, their tires against the curb, their bodies rocking from movements within, beyond the blackened glass. A police car passes, moving slowly, with its headlights off. An ambulance does the same. The night is getting busier with maneuvers and arrivals, and the pavements are already thick with men in protective uniforms moving heavily and deliberately, not speaking but doing what they can to keep the noise down, though not out of consideration for the suburb's sleeping residents. There's something curious that Leonard can't identify at first but, when he stops to take it in, is not difficult to spot for anyone who's been in Alderbeech before, during the siege. The regulars, the men who've worked duties out here for the past few days, the foot soldiers, the local units on secondment from traffic duties and street patrols, are, as usual, wearing either their salmon-pink high-visibility jackets or silver-yellow strips. But the small groups of armed units from the National Security Forces, standing solemnly and tensely by their carriers with automatic weapons and battery shields, are wearing blacks, dark blues, and grays, and not a silver button between them. Not only are they staying quiet, they're dressed not to be seen.

It is as he suspected. "They're going in. They're absolutely going in," Leonard mutters to himself, as if Francine or Lucy were at his side, although the phrase *going in* is too low-key. Clearly something less civil is intended. What's certain is that it's rare and it's unsettling to see such firepower on active duty in a British street. *Assault*'s a truer word. *Offensive* is the perfect word, in both its senses. Here's a chance to watch it live. Francine will be sleeping now. She doesn't even have to know if, instead of picking up her car at once, he spends half an hour at the barrier again, just to be a witness. In the flesh.

The plainclothes officer controlling access to the inner streets of Alderbeech with an Uzi resting on his forearm is curtly adamant. He shakes his head at Leonard's ID fob. "That's not legit. Police personnel and residents only. You don't score," he says, indicating the way back with his chin and clearly not prepared to waste a word or moment more on this civilian. Leonard does not argue or complain, despite the young man's lack of courtesy. He isn't dressed for it. He doesn't look the part. Anyway, the decision is out of his hands now. *No pasarán.* No witnessing. He'll just have to collect the car and drive back to the Woodsman for Francine. But again, at the entrance to the waste ground and just twenty paces from their Buzz, another man, this time in uniform, spreads a hand a centimeter from Leonard's chest and orders him to stop. That open area is off-limits, he explains, "for the foreseeable." Leonard shows his ID fob once more, points to where they have left their car, promises that he will be only three minutes at the most, and then off home. The policeman whispers into his shoulder radio and nods his head.

"Go ahead, mate. Three minutes max."

"What's hitting off?"

"I've no idea."

Their tiny car ("It's built for elves," a neighbor once remarked) is dwarfed and hidden by the caravan of blank-sided vehicles and panel trucks that are now occupying almost every meter of open ground. Driving away through what narrow gaps remain will be tricky.

Impossible, perhaps. It's just as well they didn't bring the wider, longer gigmobile. There'd be no escape, except on foot. Leonard collects his thicker coat from the rear seat, and finding his yellow beach cap in its pocket, pulls that on as well. He's feeling warm and jaunty, suddenly. He whistles as he hunts between the vehicles for an easy route onto the street.

A man is in the shadows, urinating on a lorry wheel, by the sound of it. When he emerges finally, buttoning his uniform, he shines his billy torch at Leonard and the Buzz and nods a greeting. "Nippy," he says.

"It's glacial," Leonard agrees, presuming that the policeman means the weather and not their elfin car. He routinely feels for his ID and holds it up, but this officer does not bother to check. He's not suspicious in the least. If Leonard has reached this far and has a car parked among the police and NSF vehicles, clearly his presence is legitimate, despite his shabby appearance.

"What's hitting off?" Leonard asks again.

This officer is less reticent and less officious than his colleagues. He is, though, tired and cold and bored. "I couldn't say what's going on exactly, but it's about time," he says. "I've been on nights since Thursday. So have you, by the looks of it. What are you? Press?" Leonard nods, not meaning to deceive or at least not lying for any purpose. He's written pieces now and then for *Jazz UK* and *Impro Quarterly*. "I'm not supposed to speak to press." The policeman points toward the exit on the far side of the open ground and the two dark blue marquees that were being raised yesterday afternoon. "You're down that end, then. On the right. That's press."

Leonard does not step into the marquee, although he can see the journalists inside, in their showy winter hats and overcoats. A few are helping themselves to coffee; some are doing their best to catch a little sleep; others are readying their microphones and cameras. They are uncharacteristically muted. All look tense, chilled to the bone, and not in the least thrilled to be selected for this night patrol and required to prepare dawn choruses for their Web sites and their breakfast shows. He waits for a minute at the marquee's entrance flap, delayed by the coffee smells, and pretends to puff on a cigarette—it's chilly enough for breath to look like smoke—until he's certain that the officer he's spoken to is looking elsewhere. Then it takes only seconds to walk the extra meters along the far side of the marquee and into the lee of a shoulder-high, grit-dashed garden wall, where he is out of sight. Again he stops to mime a cigarette and take his bearings, though no one's watching him. He's baffled, actually. Just a few minutes ago he was standing by the car, ready to drive away. Now he's hiding in the shadows, and closer to the hostage house than he's allowed to be, closer than is wise. But he hasn't broken any laws, so far. A fib, perhaps. Otherwise, he's just slipped through their nets, unintentionally. Too easily, in fact. Three officers have questioned him and let him go. Security is lax. It's not his fault. He's come to collect his car. That's what he'll say if anybody else challenges him. He is a man without a plan—except to be nosy for a minute or two.

But as the moments pass, Leonard feels himself edging forward rather than retreating. It's not that he is being shoved by someone other than himself: "Go on, Leonard, one more step." That's familiar; he's always being urged ahead, by Francine in particular. On this occasion, he's not being shoved so much as drawn. Drawn toward a rendezvous. Another dozen steps or so and he'll be there, wherever *there* might prove to be. He sucks in air and fills his lungs, for confidence.

The public barrier where Leonard has already stood on two occasions to view the hostage house is still in place, he sees, but, unsurprisingly, there is no one waiting there, no hardcore and determined group of insomniacs to join and mingle with. In fact, apart from a pausing, puzzled cat, making humpback bridges with its spine as it patrols, the visible neighborhood is lifeless. The streetlights burn with only Leonard to witness them. Security monitors in a hundred stationary cars flash red, unfailingly and independently, deterring nobody. The nation sleeps. This could be anywhere, anywhere where nothing's going on—except there is a shiver in the air, the kind of geared-up atmosphere that perhaps it takes a musician's ear, or a cat's, to pick up on, a charged hush, the sort of breath-sucked quiet that often means the sky is jittery and heralding a thunderclap, or shooting stars, or rain.

Leonard fills his lungs again and blows out his deceptive smoke, smelling not of nicotine but of last night's garlic. This darkness, with its pulsing ornaments of light, would make a moody concert poster or an ambient video track, he thinks, pushing his hands into his coat, posing cool and blue. He's humming "Nighthawks" to himself, working his fingers inside his pockets, tapping the keys of his cell phone until it cheeps at him. He takes it out to switch it off. He doesn't want a call from Francine right now. The ringtone will only draw attention to his hiding place. He checks the street once more, but there is still nothing new or odd to catch his eye, so far as he can tell. It is what he would expect to find if the siege had ended days ago, with normality returned and the guns, the cameras, and the uniforms working somewhere else. But clearly he can't have come too late. If the assault, the offensive, were already over, finalized in the last hour or so, when he and Francine were in bed, there certainly would be bustle and noise, and the news crews would not be sitting under canvas, twiddling their switches and their thumbs, but gabbing into microphones and posturing at lenses. It does seem likely, though, the more he thinks about it and the more he shivers in the morning chill, that he has come far too early to witness the end of the siege, and for any final chance of seeing Maxie Lermon in the flesh and failing publicly. The police will surely wait for dawn to break before they risk a raid with firearms. They will bide their time until daylight is on their side. Leonard checks his watch, daring to extend his wrist out of the shadow of the wall and tell the time. It's earlier than he thought, just short of 3 a.m. The pub's lobby clock must be running ninety minutes fast. That means an even longer, colder wait for light and action, if he's to persevere. No, Francine's waiting, keen to get away. He might as well be sensible. He might as well admit defeat, set free his wife, drive home with her, stay warm, and wait for it to happen on the news. At least he will get closer on the news.

A dozen steps and Leonard will reach the press marquee, its hectic hush, its delaying coffee smells. Another forty meters will take him across the waste ground and its host of silent vehicles to the Buzz. A kilometer reaches Francine in her grimy room. Ninety or so minutes on the road delivers them to their front door. It will chirrup when they open it. But before he's even reached the corner of the wall, a restless, impish ruby light, just briefly glimpsed, detains him for a moment. Is it a cigarette? He thinks of Lucy suddenly, her skinny roll-ups, and imagines that she, like him, is hiding in the dark and waiting for her father. He stays until he catches sight of it again. This time the glow is wrong for cigarettes. Too uniform. Now it looks more like one of the car security monitors, no bigger and no brighter, except it is not pulsing. This smoldering glow is constant and moves like an unusually determined firefly, directly and unswervingly, leaving a fleeting wake of red across the weighty shadows of the street as, first, it darts along the gutter of the curb, then cuts across the pavement. It stops to fidget for an instant in the angle of a garden wall, outside the hostage house. Leonard moves along his garden wall to keep the light in sight. It's briefly lost and then shows up again, on the wooden acorn decoration of the gatepost. The firefly hovers, its beam stretching to an oval on the swell of the carving, before crossing to the house itself and, contemptuous of gravity, rising geometrically, at speed, avoiding only windowpanes. It comes to rest on the ledge below the front bedroom.

Now there is a second firefly, roosting on the lintel above the front door, and a third, tracing its way across the brickwork of the house, looking for a perch. Leonard guesses what they are—they are familiar from films: laser beams from the telescopic night sights of power rifles. He has to rub his eyes and catch the movement of another beam before he's able to infer an angle of origin and spot one of the marksmen. He is as dark and clothy as a country night, virtually invisible in his black gloves and balaclava. He has tucked himself into the shadow of a car and looks more like a heavy bin bag than a man. Indeed, Leonard dismissed him as a bin bag when he first inspected the street ten minutes ago. Now it is easier to spot the other men and their weapons. From where he stands, Leonard can see six in all, at the ready, fingers wrapped round triggers, hidden in the most absorbent shadows. Not Snipers Without Bullets. This hostage-taking, then, will end with bursts of gunfire first, and blood, then sirens possibly, and screaming vehicles, and Lucy weeping long into her life. Leonard shivers, not from cold. In truth, he partly wants the siege to end this way, with Maxie dead—the squads of armed, trained men, the splintered doors on both sides of the house, the clatter of their combat boots on floors and stairs, the six or so precise, intended shots that put an end to it and him the moment that a firefly settles on his head. That would be the way they'd end the siege in Hollywood.

There are other possibilities, of course, less neat, less speedy narratives, more muddled. Leonard can imagine Maxie Lermon hearing the shattered wood and glass, leaping from his guard duty, and reaching for his gun—he's seen him all too glad to handle a gun before—determined not to be the first to be *pronounced* and maybe firing off a shot or two at the marksmen in the street or the shock-and-awe squads on the stairs, but in too great a panic to take aim and complete this final act, the act that justifies his rapid execution. There are other scenes in Leonard's head, more troubling ones, more Wild West cinematic ones. There's Maxie Lermon executing all his innocents, that unnamed family of five. There're booby traps, there're trigger bombs, there's gas. There's Maxie Lermon, with blood on his shoulder, coming out the front door of the house with a filed-down rifle at the grandma's head, or perhaps a kitchen knife held against the youngest boy's throat. "You fire, he dies," he's saying to the police. "Bring me a car. I'm out of here. A car, a car, my kingdom for a car." And for a moment (but only in these dreams) Leonard himself is answering the call. He's driving forward. His hands are on the steering wheel of Francine's Buzz, her plucky runabout. It's crashing through the barriers. Bullets wing the car. The rear screen shatters. Leonard does not stop. The front screen fills with Maxie's face and hair.

When it happens it is quieter than in films and less heroic than in dreams. There is a soft but weighty thud first, as if a mattress has been dropped onto the ground from thirty meters up. The night is stunned. Then all at once the sleepy street springs to life. The doors of parked cars open abruptly and men in camouflage spill out onto the pavement. The hidden marksmen stand to aim their rifles more accurately at the windows and the doors. More marksmen throw back windows in the upper stories of the buildings opposite the hostage house. A pair of floodlights, concealed on the back of roofs, fill and penetrate the street, blackening the sky beyond their arcs. A now thundering helicopter, which has somehow positioned itself above Alderbeech without making a sound, trains its spy beams on the rear gardens and on the house, where a pair of men with heavy-duty weapons and clips of stun grenades can be seen sitting on the gable roof, keen to get it over with. Three armored police saloons speed in and hold off just out of rifle range, their engines racing. There is a second thud, a louder one, and then the pop of gas grenades and shouting. Inside the hostage house, the ceiling lamps, warmer than the floodlights in the street, click on in every room, almost in unison. Not a single shot is fired.

Leonard never sees the hostages. They are the last to leave their home. But from the shelter of his garden wall he has clear views of their captors. The Filipina woman, Donut Paredes, is the first to be pushed through the door and led by two armed female officers out of the front garden into the sharply lit street. She looks in better health than in the television photographs, where her face was cut, bruised, and swollen. Her hair has grown out a bit, not quite the student ponytail of her youth but black and styled. The four-day break has done her good. Her hands are cuffed behind her back, but she walks briskly, despite the restraining grip of her minders. She takes deep breaths, as if she is finding the air crisp and flavorsome. She calls out once. Not a slogan. Nothing political. Not *No pasarán* but *"Rafaelo. Te quiero."* It's when she's being ducked into one of the waiting armored saloons and sees her lover, the hardened Nicaraguan, being brought out of the house, feet first, between four hefty, clumsy officers, like a struggling boy, resisting playground bullies.

Maxim Lermontov is last. The hair is unmistakable. Otherwise he is hardly recognizable. Either he has been stripped from the waist up and forced to remove his footwear or he was in the shower when the raid began. He's slender still, but hollowed out and ribby, no longer young and toned. He's middle-aged like Leonard now. His walk attempts to be just as insolent as it ever was, but he's barefoot—it's not easy to shuffle insolently without shoes. His near-nakedness and the biting cold of the morning, together with the runny eyes and hacking cough caused by whatever canisters and sprays the police have used on him, have robbed the Final Warning warrior of any majesty. He's shivering. His head is down. His mouth is dripping phlegm. He's looking like a cornered animal.

Leonard steps into the street, just as the day's rain starts with a bilious thunderclap. He should announce himself, at least. He remembers the advice from Austin: "In circumstances such as this, just make it loud. And keep it short and simple, yeah?" Leonard pumps his lungs and spreads his legs. Habit almost makes him mime a saxophone. But what—apart from "Shame, shame, shame"—can he call out, except their captive's name? Maxie. Maxim. Max. No, anyone could use those names—the police, a press photographer: "This way, Maxie, for the cameras." Almost instinctively, then, and on his third or fourth step toward the cars lined up to take away the Final Warning trio, Leonard yells out, "Maximum." It does the trick, amazingly. Maxie lifts his head and stares across at the familiar man who is now striding toward him. Unexpectedly, he recognizes who it is at once, though he evidently can't recall the name—that very stiff and very English name. "It's the fuckin' herbivore," he says, and tries to take a step into the street, pulling away from his escorts for a second. Leonard hurries forward now, at jogging speed. "It would have been ill-mannered and unfriendly," he explains later in his many interviews, "to not say hi at least." He doesn't know what he should do when he and Maxie meet. Shaking hands is out of the question. The man is handcuffed, like his comrades. A hug would be presumptuous. They never were that close. Besides, Leonard's damp already from the rain. He doesn't even know what he should say, except "I'm taking care of Lucy."

The shout of "Maximum" has not just alerted Maxie. In less time than it takes to say *Kapow, you're dead*, Maxie has been thrown to the ground. His cheek and naked chest are on the wet tarmac, a knee is pressed against his shoulder, his hair is bunched and gripped tightly at the back. Automatic guns and tasers are swiveling, fingers on their triggers. Three red laser lights dance on Leonard's jacket. Fireflies again. They're shouting at him now, a hubbub of instructions: "Stay where you are," "Get down, arms out," and "On your knees." Three men in combat uniforms are running at him, their nightsticks drawn, their hot breath smoking in the morning chill.

Leonard does not doubt what he should do. Don't hesitate. Retreat. He turns his back on them and starts toward the waste ground and the safety of the Buzz. It's Budapest again: his terror is too deep to spot, but he is mute and powerless with fear, hardly able to breathe, let alone walk. He does walk, though, and tries his best to move as nonchalantly as a man who does not understand what hurry means. He aims to be so slow and insubstantial that the red laser lights he knows are trained on him will pass straight through his back and head and pale into the night. Half a second and he's dead.

Their lasered target succeeds in taking another dozen steps. Before he has reached the corner by the press marquee and the posses of journalists and camera crews just released to inspect and film the hostage house, the three night runners catch the herbivore. The first blow that he takes—a kick, in fact, clinically delivered—is to the back of his calf. It topples him. He's down before he feels the pain. The second is a knee, rammed into his frozen shoulder. He feels that pain at once, and yells. The third blow is a silencing and stunning punch to the jaw. It clicks his head back sharply, knocks off his beach cap. All he hears is someone shouting, "Make him safe, make him safe." The men are frisking him, simply pulling out his pockets and pushing their hard fingers into his niches and his angles. "He's clean and he's made safe," one shouts eventually. Another advises, "Keep it easy, lads." A third, his mouth a centimeter from Leonard's ear, is whispering, "You hear me, pal? You so much as twitch and you are getting tasered. That's fifty thousand volts, understand, you fuck? You'll never want to twitch again. Be a hero or be sensible. Your call." Leonard cannot know, but it will seem that he is being both.

Francine is awake by now. Awake and tired. It's not nearly dawn, but she slips out of bed and looks into the street to see if Leonard has come back with her car. She's not sure how much time has passed since he went out. It can't be long. He will have walked to where they parked in less than fifteen minutes. He'll be back quite soon. She checks her phone: no messages. She speed-dials Leonard's cell. It's off. She'd better dress. It will be good to have an early start, get home and make the most of Sunday. She waits at the window, like a trawler man's wife. The street outside the Woodsman is quiet. The parked cars have it to themselves. Again it's raining, and the wind has lifted from the east, bringing in a Russian chill that rattles the windows of the room in hostile gusts. It is a Sunday morning wind, the sort that says that it will be okay to stay all day in bed. But this is not a bed for staying in, and so the weather must be faced. She pulls the sash window up and leans out into the cold as far as she can, so that she has views across the rooftops toward Alderbeech. She sees a helicopter and what looks like the hard white glow of floodlights. At once she knows what they must signify—the siege is finally over. Lights, camera, action—that's how it always goes. So that's where Leonard is, standing at the barrier and watching. She knows better than to wait for him. When her husband is spectating—at anything from a tennis match in the park to a fight outside a pub—he seems to lose all sense of time. He has to stay and watch from his safe distance until there is no drama left. So Francine settles the hotel bill by posting cash in the early-bird payment safe and sets off toward the car by the route that Leonard is bound to use himself on his return. She expects to spot her Buzz and husband at any moment. She will wave, and he will pull across to let her in and take her home. A pleasing prospect. Everything is pleasing, even the rain. The walk itself is deeply satisfying, and not only because she has escaped that room. She feels unexpectedly young and sensuous. She has not washed or changed her clothes. She has not cleaned her teeth. What makeup she had on last night has smudged across the pillows on the bed. Her lips are bruised from kissing. Her cheeks are wet and flushed. She's warm and satisfied. In ways she does not even try to understand, the helicopter and the distant blush of lights suggest a rescue she has feared would never come. Everyone is rescued, actually, not only the hostages and not just Lucy Emmerson, rescued from herself, but Leonard and Francine too, and—dare she think it?—Celandine.

It is almost two hours since Leonard left her sleeping. The approach streets to Alderbeech are calm and unpopulated. A typical predawn Sunday. The waste ground has already almost cleared. There are a few detachments of uniformed men there, clearing up, and the mobile lavatories and canteen are still in place, though locked and shuttered. Francine goes directly to the Buzz. There is no sign of Leonard, but that is no surprise. She cuts across the waste ground, past two marquees not noticed on her first visit, and enters the hostage street under the bluish flooding of police lights. She sees at once there is no barrier for Leonard to be spectating behind. It has been dismantled and its parts are piled up on the pavement awaiting collection. For the first time in more than four days the street is open to traffic and pedestrians, but there are none yet. If she were Leonard she would want to see inside the hostage house and investigate the full length of the street. That is where she expects to meet her husband now, on the pavement. She thinks she sees him standing a hundred meters farther down, beyond the lights. She waves and starts in his direction, walking along the far-side path, not even pausing to stare into the house, past the single policeman who is at the gate, keeping guard and getting very wet. He watches her, glad to inspect this attractive older woman, walking with a swing, and relieve the monotony of guard duty by wondering what has made her seem so spirited so early in the day. Apart from this one officer, there's no activity at the hostage scene. No doubt the policeman's many colleagues are tired and catching up on sleep. Forensic teams will come in when it's light, she thinks. Film crews will return to finalize reports. She hurries on, but the figure she has taken for Leonard turns out to be a dog walker, a dog that barks and warns her off. She'll wait for Leonard in the car. She's sure she has a spare key in her bag.

On her return—on the nearer pavement—she does stop to stare into the house. It seems untouched, determinedly undramatic, dull. Most of the curtains have been drawn. The only light is in the porch. The only movement is a cloud of moths. It's hard to even dream up a figure standing in the shadows, holding a gun at shoulder height and pointing it at Leonard in the street, as he's imagined it: *Kapow. You're scathed. Kapow. You're dead!*

"All over?" she asks the policeman.

"Done and dusted," he replies.

"Anybody hurt?"

"One of our guys took a tumble. Family wasn't touched. Three individuals in custody, and hardly a scratch on them. All foreigners. That's about the size of it. Nice work all round. Top job."

Francine offers him her widest smile and keeps on smiling as she crosses the street, heading for the entrance to the waste ground by the two marquees. It is there that she spots, with immediate alarm, what looks like Leonard's yellow beach cap swept up among the litter, the recent pile of paper coffee cups, pop cans, and takeaway wrappers. She doesn't pick it up at once but turns it with her foot, expecting to discover some other logo on its peak—but no, its slogan is QUEUE HERE, just like Leonard's. Now she bends for it. The cap is damp and heavy in her hands, caked with mud. She shakes and stretches it, then turns it inside out, hoping not to find her husband's stage name, Lennie Less, inked along the rim.

15

THE WONKY, UNEDITED VIDEO of Leonard's detention in Alderbeech during the early hours of the morning is greeted by clapping and whoops when it is first aired on the wall screens of NSF's debooting and debriefing rooms. There's little else of dramatic interest for the news networks to broadcast and nothing else for the armed incident squads, now going off-duty, to applaud; the hostage rescue itself was disappointingly routine, with at best a bit of shouting but not a shot fired or a punch thrown. So Leonard's late, unheralded appearance on the street was a godsend in a way. The weirdo in the yellow cap provided their only opportunity, after more than four days of dreary vigilance, to let off a bit of steam. "That's copybook, that is," one of the officers calls out, as the intruder is brought to the ground in three easy movements. "Step up, those men. Rosettes all round."

Elsewhere in the building, in the rooms above the custody suite where the four detainees are being held in separate cells, the responses among members of the NSF command team are not so celebratory. It's not only that the first broadcasters of the video, already syndicated round the world, have failed to pixilate the faces of the arresting officers. That is an easy fix. A phone call, or a text reminder of the National Security Standards in Broadcasting, and it's dealt with. There are greater problems, less easy to massage or to solve. What is now clear is that what they flagged up as "a delicate and risky" security operation has proved to be an embarrassing anticlimax. According to the brisk report just delivered to them by the duty CO, the siege could have been ended much earlier "by a couple of coppers on a tandem." When the armed squads stormed in, according to the first reports, everyone inside the hostage house—the family, the gang—was asleep. It was Operation Wakey-Wakey, not so much Shock and Awe as Rouse and Arrest. All but one of the hostage-takers' guns were soon discovered to be replicas, and the single working revolver was unloaded, with no trace so far of any spare ammunition. There were no barricades, no booby traps, no ropes, just evidence of takeaway food, the stink of cigarettes, and unusual tidiness. A jigsaw puzzle of London's Tower Bridge lay almost completed on the living room table. Add to that yesterday's tip-off from NADA that the Emmerson kidnapping and SOFA's grim threats of "an eye for an eye" were nothing but a stunt, and the whole standoff begins to look absurd. "No need to make any of that public. Yet," one of the team says. "Embargo it." Unfavorable details such as these can be buried in the minutiae of the official incident report, he suggests. And the report itself can be delayed for a week or so, at least until the public and the press have lost interest, as they will.

It is less easy, though, to know how to handle the embarrassment of the wonky video, especially with the summit leaders scheduled to discuss freedom and security in two days' time and all the world's press already in town and hungry for a British story to tide them over. What is needed, just to offer balance, is a strip of film showing a heroic and risky intervention by the NSF. A few injured officers paraded for the cameras would help. But there is nothing. They can't even hope anymore for some drama associated with a rescue or release of Lucy Emmerson. Some shots of a pretty teenager, hurt possibly but certainly tearful, would have played well on the newscasts. Instead, the nation is getting up to watch three of the security force's celebrated "burly bastards" knocking to the ground, with what commentators are already describing as excessive force, a shabby, middle-aged member of the British public who is guilty of little more than straying.

The command team plays and replays the video footage, looking for a PR spin but finding none. The liberty lobbies are going to have a field day. No question about it, the first kick is rule-breaking; this civilian is clearly offering no threat. He's walking off, in fact. The man's back is turned. His arms are down. He is not attempting to run. That kick cannot be justified. Nor can any of the subsequent blows: a knee in the back and a fist to the chin are not appropriate, especially given that the target is offering no resistance and is, to use the parlance of the force, already tarmacadamized. The video's sound track—enhanced by NSF techs—is little help. It worsens matters, actually. It can't be long before the news networks enhance the audio for themselves and hear exactly what was whispered full to camera into the arrested and incapacitated man's ear as he lay stunned on the ground: "You so much as twitch and you are getting tasered. That's fifty thousand volts, understand, you fuck?"

"Yes, understood—and all too bloody well." The officer turns off the telescreen. "That's bloody tasered us, that's what that's done." The other commanders shake their heads in glum agreement. This is a mess. A classic case of excessive and unwarranted, which at best will earn the NSF another roasting in the liberal press—especially when it transpires, as it must, that their captive was not a danger at all but just a nosy parker—and at worst will have its payoff on the streets. Riots, possibly. The mood is jittery already. And it could escalate. The "demo mob" has a hero and a martyr now.

"What was he doing there, anyway?"

The duty CO checks his report sheet. "Picking up his car, it says."

Leonard has not yet seen the news reports or video. He has been sleeping for an hour or so, despite his bruises and the narrowness of the banquette in the custody cell. The night's events are tumbling. He makes no sense of them. He mostly dreams of Maxie crashing through the windscreen of the Buzz. But when the command team sends for him, he's dreaming that he and Maxie have escaped from Alderbeech. Together. Bullets wing the car at first. Then they find themselves in empty neighborhoods with no one in pursuit. "I came for you," he says to Maxie, the streetlights turning into stars, a sudden blast of light. "Comrade Leon saves your sorry arse."

The sudden blast of light comes from a set of interrogation lamps, pointing toward the ceiling. The duty CO stands at the end of the banquette, grinning stiffly and holding Leonard's coat, belt, and shoes and an envelope containing his cell, ID fob, and keys. His instructions are to bring Mr. Lessing up to the visitors' lounge without his seeing a television screen and to sit him in the soft-backed chair facing the window, out of harm's way. It is here that he is served a canteen breakfast on a tray while the service paramedic dresses and photographs his wounds and makes light of "the rugby damage" he's received. A middle-ranking female officer has been instructed to placate and scold the prisoner before releasing him. He should leave the building persuaded that it's best to make no fuss. Certainly any complaint for wrongful arrest or a claim for damages would be "mischievous and unwarranted." She shakes Leonard's hand and offers her regrets for the "necessarily firm" treatment he received. The three men responsible have already been suspended from all duties, she explains, glad to see that he looks surprised and guilty when he hears the news. But the truth is that Mr. Lessing has been foolhardy, in her view and in the view of anyone who saw him on the street this morning. Straying into the middle of a security operation is never wise. But—she's checked—he has not broken any laws. "We can congratulate ourselves," she adds, pleased with her bantering tone and the phrasing she practiced before walking into the lounge, "that this is still a nation where straying is not a crime but merely inadvisable. And inconsiderate. And best not repeated." There will be more questions to be answered, possibly, but not in custody. He can expect a home visit, perhaps. But in the meantime, it might be better, judicious even, if "discretion is allowed to rule the day, on both our sides. We will not be releasing your details to the press, out of consideration for your privacy."

She does not say that her next task is to preempt any problem he might cause by ghost-briefing some of the NSF's pet dependents in the press, telling them what she's learned from a NADA leak just a few minutes ago: that this Leonard Lessing might not be as squeaky as he seems. Somehow he's linked to Maxim Lermontov and to the not-so-missing girl. He has history as a militant, some Texan connection. He is known to be someone who has provided information to the police. He's been spotted in a cafeteria with Mrs. Emmerson. Foolhardy, indeed. She shakes his hand again. "Now, let us reunite you with your vehicle, Mr. Lessing. You look as if you'd benefit from . . ." She pauses, judges that she'd better not be personal. "From forty winks."

Francine is sleeping in the car, her mouth hanging open like a child's, when Leonard is finally returned to the now almost vacated waste ground a little before 10 a.m. She must have checked out of the room as soon as it was light and waited at the Buzz for his return, not panicking, even though his cell was off, but finding comfort in logical and reassuring explanations for his absence, as he'd expect of her. She's always level-headed when she has to be. His yellow cap is clutched in her hand, he sees. That's puzzling, although he can't say why. He has to reel back through the events of the morning before he recalls losing it and where. It's all a haze at first. He can clearly remember the early walk through Alderbeech, the conversations that he had—"What are you? Press?"—the two marquees, the engulfing shadows of the garden wall. Each step of it is still crisp in his memory. It's crisp until the fireflies start to glow. But when the mayhem begins, the snatch squads and the stun grenades, the heavy boots, the heavy fists, the hoisting of his body in the air, the impact of the metal wagon into which he's thrown, the shouting and the threats, he cannot concentrate or be certain of the details. Is that concussion or champagne? Is it himself or Maxie Lermon whom he can half remember crashing to the ground? The scene itself has lost its definition. Victim and witness are the same. All he remembers now is haste and pain. Everything is physical.

Leonard rubs his chin. It's dislocated, possibly. It's tender, for sure, from the tip into the jawline. It is as though the stubble hurts. Now he more clearly remembers being punched—rubbing the injury has helped—and how the sudden, expert blow clicked his head back sharply. That's the moment his cap came off. He has it now. The pain shot through his face and shook his forehead with such force that his cap detached and dropped into the street... where Francine picked it up. Finding her husband's cap but without her husband under it must have unnerved her, surely. It would have been a shock. He's touched that she has bothered to retrieve it, even though she hates the cap—"That filthy thing"—dislikes all hats on men, and has threatened many times to chuck it in the bin. He needs to believe that she was worried for him just a bit. He looks for signs of anxiety on her sleeping face. But there are none. She looks serene and comfortable for once. Perhaps she fell asleep as soon as she sat in the Buzz and hasn't realized that he's been missing for—what? Almost six hours now.

It is tempting to remove the sun cap from her grasp and pull it on. Leonard likes to drive in it, especially to gigs and concerts. His much-repeated tease is that it helps him to concentrate, not only on the driving but also on the music he will play. He has never worn the cap onstage, of course. He knows it isn't cool or hip. Francine has persuaded him of that. It isn't blue. But afterward, when he is signing programs and booklets, he sometimes pulls it on, just for fun; its slogan, QUEUE HERE, seems pertinent and witty. He leaves it, though, in Francine's grasp. He does not want to wake his wife just yet. He is not in a hurry to explain himself to her. He wants to settle himself and unravel his story first, sort out what he has dreamed from what occurred. Besides, the prospect of her waking up naturally only to find him sitting calmly at the wheel is an appealing one. He can play it very cool, he decides. He looks forward to her gasp of pleasure and relief, and then the shock when she sees his injuries.

Leonard succeeds in driving out of Alderbeech through the busy Sunday traffic and almost reaching the motorway before Francine wakes briefly. She puts her hand on his thigh and says "Sweetheart" without even opening her eyes. When he squeezes her fingers, she says "Sweetheart" again, more flatly than before, her voice a little slurred.

"You're whacked," he says. "Don't wake, Frankie. I'll tell you all about it when we're home. You'll be amazed." But she does not respond to the bait. For the moment she would rather sleep than be amazed.

"Who's the dormouse now?" he asks out loud, for his own benefit. He is already a bit annoyed with her. It's time she showed some evidence of anxiety. It's time she saw the state of him, his damaged chin, his blistered, purple mouth, his torn and muddied clothes. "Wow," she'll say. "What happened to your face?" And he will reply, pianissimo and casually, "They beat me up, the police. Three guys. They turned their guns on me. They had me in their sights. I very nearly died. I spent the night in cells." He wants to see her snap awake at what he says and stare wide-eyed at him. He wants to hear her mention pure valiance. Say it, say it, *valiance.*

"I'll tell you all about it when we're home," he says again, though mostly to himself. "Cooked breakfast, or will it be lunch, in bed? How's that sound?" Francine appears to nod but does not make a sound. She rolls across the seat, drawing up her knees, and rests her head on his shoulder. They are that loving couple in a moving car that safety adverts warn against: *Keep Your Distance from the Vehicle in Front; Keep Your Distance from Your Passengers.* Her hair is unusually unkempt and springy on his cheek, he notices. Like it was when they first met. Her breath is spicy and familiar. It is not until he's pulled up at the house and turned the Buzz's engine off that

Francine finally speaks. “Carry me upstairs,” she says, just as she did on Thursday evening, but this time there is no agenda other than her need to sleep a little more. Her eyes are open and she’s looking at his face, but she does not seem to notice how hurt he is. Perhaps he’s not as badly hurt as he would like.

16

LEONARD KNOWS, as soon as he chimes into the house, that there have been uninvited visitors during his absence and ones who have not made much effort to cover their tracks. The first abnormality is that their burglar alarm is not set. It was operating yesterday when he and Francine crept out through the back garden and their neighbor's side gate to drive to the Emmersons' house. It's possible, he supposes, that in their ill-tempered hurry they forgot to turn it on, though that would be a first for him. He is neurotically careful about security. He daren't risk the loss of his customized saxophone. That first cheap instrument stolen from him with punches in the pub car park many years ago still reverberates.

At least Leonard does not have to key in the alarm code before struggling Francine up the stairs and into her bed. She is not light, small though she is, especially when sleeping or only pretending to sleep, as he suspects. She clearly wants to be treated like an exhausted toddler and returned to her own clean bedclothes where, knowing her, she will doze quite happily until midafternoon. Rest comes first, as ever. He cannot hold her like a toddler, though. The stairs are steep and narrow on the turn. He has to tuck his good shoulder into her waist and give her a fireman's lift. His right shoulder tenses, but despite the pain, he manages to tumble her onto the mattress, pull off her shoes, and cover her with the duvet. It's difficult to know if she has offered him a groan of thanks or is merely glad to be in her own bed at last. He considers joining her. He ought to sleep, but he can tell he will not sleep, not while it's light outside.

Their room is still in disarray. She wouldn't let him tidy up before they set off on the drive down. But did they leave the desk lamp on? And were the curtains fully pulled open like that? Leonard has an idea that they weren't. He looks down onto the patio as he snaps off the light and draws the curtains across again. He's half expecting to see shattered window glass, some signs of burglary, his saxophone case abandoned on the lawn. There is no point in looking for evidence in their bedroom. All the drawers have already been pulled out and emptied onto the rugs, the chests and boxes have lost their lids, clothes are shaken from their hangers. A burglar would be hard-pushed to find any valuables. His spectacles are lost in here, Leonard remembers. But with the curtains now shut and Francine breathing evenly, he cannot and had better not hunt for them yet.

The door to their room is a little lower than the others. It has a Tanzanian carving added on—a frieze of drums. Leonard hesitates, as he often does, directly under the lintel and stands on his tiptoes until he feels the touch of timber on his hair. He has not heard anything to alarm him, but in his current apprehensive mood, hearing nothing is disquieting in itself. Usually there is a distant radio or someone trimming hedges or the thrum of a reversing car. At least there should be birdcalls, shouldn't there? This silence seems almost physical, a rippling of hinted sound, something present but unexpressed. What if he and Francine disturbed the burglar or the burglars when they returned, and one of them is still inside the house, holding his breath, holding his knife? Leonard looks for something to defend himself with, but in the half-light of the room can find only a heavy leather belt. He pulls it free from his discarded jeans, wraps the strap twice round his hand, and swings the buckled end in readiness. The floorboards creak as he steps out onto the landing.

He climbs up the attic stairs toward Celandine's room first. It's almost comforting for old times' sake to find it's in a mess, though not as bad a mess as their own bedroom and not even as bad a mess as Celandine might have made herself when she was home. The police have been comparatively restrained. One or two bureau drawers are pulled out. The floor is littered only with a few saved magazines, a towel, some socks. The bed itself has been pulled back, a little overzealously, perhaps—looking for Lucy Katerina Emmerson, fast asleep, he supposes. There is a canvas bag of birthday presents and a few birthday cards hung up on a clothes hook, where Francine must have secreted them last week, which the police, showing some diplomacy, have left unopened. Most of the gifts are decorated playschool-style with Francine's exuberant designs. The number 50 is prominent, of course.

Leonard lifts the bag off its peg and tiptoes with it downstairs to the first-floor landing. Again he detects the glitter of no sound. He pushes open all the doors with his toe, one by one, and, still gripping the belt and the bag of gifts, peers inside: the guest room with Francine's worktable; the bath and shower room; the lavatory; the little laundry room where they overwinter plants. He is most fearful of the door into the narrow side room under the eaves where he composes and practices when his wife is home and demanding quiet. He keeps his chord sheets and his music stand there, and all his instruments: two tenors, an alto that he hardly ever plays ("Too ripe"), Celandine's school flute, the electronic keyboard with which he notates his tunes, and a one-note township saxophone made from beaten tuna cans. He waits on the landing for a moment, listening. There is sound at last, but only Francine breathing. He toes back the door a little more and steps inside, quickly taking stock. More mess. But no one's there. Nothing's missing. Not even the treasured and valuable Mercury citation, or the Carnegie Excellence Medal, or the costly art deco bronze statuette *The Trombonist* that Francine bought for him as a wedding gift and that he keeps on the windowsill, where the light is flattering. Any self-respecting thief would help himself to that.

Leonard is puzzled even more when he goes downstairs again and, still swinging the belt buckle, spots at once what he couldn't see when he got home and Francine was in his arms: that the circulars and papers have been gathered up off the hall floor and tucked neatly into the deep wicker bowl where their post and keys are usually kept. That can't have been his work. The newspapers were delivered only this morning. They won't have picked themselves up off the mat. Nor, come to think of it, would burglars bother being so attentive as to tidy them away. That'd make no sense. It would be inefficient, even. Now he hurries into the kitchen, less nervously and a bit relieved because—of course, it's obvious—he now can guess what must have happened, something more likely than a burglary. He pauses, though. He sniffs. That's the unmistakable odor of tobacco. It cannot be the ghostly residue of Lucy's roll-ups that Leonard washed off on Thursday evening at the sink. Tobacco lingers, certainly. It hangs around, keen to betray its user, always ready to offend. But it doesn't linger that long. There can be no doubt, then, someone has been smoking in their house. Recently. Someone has been drinking coffee too. Stealing coffee. Three used mugs—crockery that neither he nor Francine likes—have been hurriedly rinsed and upended on the draining board. There's gritty sugar spilled on the worktops. The fridge door has not been firmly closed. It's spilling light and cold.

Now Leonard is pretty certain what's happened in their absence. Not a burglary but a bust. The raiding party has returned. Those policemen and the NADA man who spoiled his birthday and turned the house upside-down on Saturday have come back for a second visit. And not long ago, by the looks of it: it was after the newspaper deliveries, that's for sure. Either they knew what he and Francine were up to all along (and that is worrying) or his phone call from

Maven's prompted it. They rang the bell and, getting no response, just let themselves in to snoop around, smoke cigarettes, drink coffee, and create more mess. They won't have taken off their shoes, he's sure of that. It does at least explain why nothing seems to be missing and there is no sign of forced entry. Locks and alarms are meat and drink to trained policemen. They probably set up some means of reentry during their first visit. They might have lifted a window latch or even taken an impression of the front-door key. They must have some device for identifying and unlocking alarm codes. Such chilly arrogance. They should know better, though, than to smoke in someone else's home.

Leonard is offended. He has suppressed his outrage over everything that occurred earlier this morning, before first light, following his final visit to the hostage street. It has not been clear till now what he should feel about it all, the dark disturbances of Alderbeech, or what to do. Now, attached to this uncomplicated principle, the integrity of private households, passive nicotine, all his buried resentment wants to be expressed. He puts down the canvas bag of gifts on the kitchen worktop and pats his pocket for his cell phone. He'll call at once. He will demand an explanation and apologies. Some recompense, perhaps? First he'd better check the other downstairs rooms for further signs of impertinence and damage, before searching for the number stored on his cell from yesterday's call to Agent Rollins. He doesn't suppose that Rollins will be reachable on a Sunday, but that shouldn't stop Leonard from leaving a firm message of complaint about this latest, odorous intrusion. He's pretty sure that it is Rollins himself who broke in this time. What had he said, so icily, on the first visit? "Let's leave it there, *for the moment.*" Leonard should have guessed. A second visit was implied. What were they looking for, what had they found?

There is a fourth used mug and, astoundingly, a greasy plate smeared with sauce and crumbs on the carpet in front of the futon in the teleroom. The screen is switched on, although the sound is muted. "Make yourself at home. Do, please," Leonard mutters peevishly to himself. This room shimmers even more loudly than anywhere else in the house with unexpressed noise. So that is all he's sensed on the upstairs landing, the implied chatter of a silenced telescreen. Now he can relax. He can indulge his anger. He regrets that he hasn't taken the phone number of the woman officer who apologized to him this morning. Someone ought to kick up a fuss among some top brass about this invasion. If the three officers who knocked him to the ground when he was trying to reach Maxie were suspended from duty, the men who broke into his house (in the absence of "the authorizing householder") should expect at least the same. Their actions were literally unwarranted (he smiles at this; he'll use the play on words in his complaint) and are proving to be, in many ways, more upsetting than the rugby tackles and the blows he endured in Alderbeech. He might have brought those on himself. At least in this case nobody can accuse him of being foolhardy. Or inconsiderate. He strikes the futon with the belt.

It is that hair again that catches his attention. Maxie's on the telescreen for an instant, and then almost at once it is replaced by advertisements. Leonard hunts for the console and finds it end-up on the mantel shelf, almost hidden by a vase of teasel heads and dried artichokes. He settles with it on the futon, in his usual place. It's odd to realize that despite the drama of the past few days, he hasn't even glimpsed a television or heard any broadcast news since seeing Lucy's face on the concourse telescreen outside Maven's store on Saturday. He'd better update himself before he phones, see what they're saying about the ending of the siege. He shuffles through some channels and, as it is now almost exactly midday, is showered with a choice of news bulletins. Every one has Maxie. There's no escaping him this morning, or the mug shots of the other two arrested "suspects," all photographed in the NSF custody suite within hours of the freeing of the hostages. Leonard recognizes the decor, though that's a generously inexact description of the cells' stippled gray walls, the canvas investigation screen, and the strips of interrogation lamps. It is a shock for Leonard—and a bit of a lost opportunity—to learn too late that he was so close to Maxie during the early hours. Maybe, stretched out on their banquettes, they were separated only by the thickness of a wall. They could have shouted out. They could have talked.

On *Noonday* on BBC National, Leonard's preferred station, Maxie Lermon is on the left of the picture, his head pushed back against the investigation screen, his features coarsened by the flash of police and agency cameras. He needs a shave and looks exceptionally tired, more hollowed out and cornered than he seemed in the flesh before dawn. Even his hair is lifeless. But—other than some grazing to his face, which Leonard knows was caused by the tarmac in the hostage street—there is no sign of bruising or evidence of beatings. He is expressionless, bored even, as if he's only posing for a passport photograph and has briefly put his features on hold. The face staring from the still-muted screen a meter from Leonard's own face is too remote and stationary to truly care about. Nevertheless, Leonard freezes the image and copies it. He enters his Personal Briefcase, selects Menu, Archive, Album, Austin, and adds this latest image of Maxie and his two comrades to the file of photographs. Again he goes a little closer to the screen and peers at them—the sooner he retrieves his glasses, the better—looking for the romance in their faces, looking for the *valiance*. But the police photographers have done their duty, providing unheroic public images that present the hostage-takers as sullen, dull, defeated. People without feeling.

Leonard sees it now. He cannot help but cry out in astonishment. The screen's a mirror, suddenly. He's looking at himself. A younger self—an old press photo taken on the evening of the Mercury. Then, almost before he has a chance to focus properly, a second image glides across, a close-up portrait not yet nine hours old. He reaches for the console and finds the volume button but is too late to catch the commentary. So he jumps to EuroFox and then to Sky and Five and each time is greeted by the same dramatic still of himself, now with shared agency captions but no name as yet: "Prizewinning jazz musician arrested at hostage site" or "Saxman detained, questioned. Terrorist links." It shows him in compacted profile, his left cheek pressed to the pavement, his shoulder pushed against the curb by a combat boot, the barrel of an automatic weapon pointing at his face, his beach cap trodden into the dirt but still the only touch of brightness—of summer, come to that—in the photograph. He is expressionless, but the image is flattering. As Francine says, he has no sag. His jaw and chin look less than fifty years of age, despite the almost two-day stubble and the blood.

Leonard's hand is trembling now. He drops the belt at last, flexing his aching fingers. It is astounding to discover that while he has not been watching the news, he has become the news, he has been living it. It's too early to know if this is a pleasing or a costly development. A pounding heart can signify both things. He takes a copy of the still, pastes it in the open Austin file, next to the Gruber's photograph. Then, on an impulse, he zooms in on himself in Texas, October 2006, and drags the expanded image across the screen until it sits next to the shot from Alderbeech. Now he can compare. What has become of him?

On the left is Leon Lessing, the nation's most nervous militant, on the evening before AmBush, and only a half hour or so before the restroom beating. He has a decent head of hair but nothing lush. He's not an especially handsome young man, not least because his eyes are small and fearful: fearful of the meat spread out in front of him, fearful of the company, fearful of the day ahead and the undertakings he has given. Leonard has not noticed this before, but the fat man who beat him in the restroom hallway is hazily discernible in the upper background, pictured from the shoulders down, a mist of cloth and flesh. Leonard closes in and sharpens. Now he can just make out some of the darker lettering on the Texan's shirt: "Bar and Grill." It could be the title of a tune.

Leonard restores the Gruber's image to its full dimensions, sending T-shirt Man into the bleary background again, and pans across to the right and the second portrait of himself, the one snatched from this morning's newscasts and Web sites. Here he's fifty years and one day old but, despite the pressure of the combat boot and gun, not betraying any fear, not revealing any of the dread that was his foremost feeling at the time. He seems fierce, and triumphant. His eyes are wide open; his mouth is slightly parted. He doesn't quite resemble himself. The photograph, his photograph, is deceiving, Leonard knows, but it is thrilling too. It looks as arty and theatrical as a cinema still. He is mythologized by it. Already he can imagine the image on a music download file. *Sax Warrior*, perhaps, with Lennie "the Lion" Lessing and the Warrior Quartet. He'll compose some stirring tunes for it. Jazz for Militants. Riffs for Radicals. Improvising for a Better World. He's tapping out a clothy rhythm on his chest.

It is even more thrilling when, a moment later, Leonard finally discovers the video clip. It has only just been cleared and returned to screen after an hour's embargo. As a paste-over explains, the faces of the NSF operatives have been obscured "to comply with security and operational guidelines." Leonard's face has not been touched. Here, in these moving and more expressive images, the resemblance is more accurate. He's recognizable enough to have been named at last. Someone—a jazz nerd, probably, or a neighbor—must have spotted him. He gets down on his knees, hardly comprehending what he's seeing, and studies the screen just within his focus range. He can almost feel the fizzy heat of broadcast on his forehead and cheeks. Certainly his whole body flushes hot with a kind of tumbling displacement, the deepest déjà vu. It is as if his dreams were filmed. He watches it again.

The news video must have been shot, he realizes, from under the entry porch of the press marquee, where he faked such convincing cigarette smoke this morning. The lens is shielded from the weather but the heavy rain is visible nevertheless, smudging the outline of the houses. The wind is flapping canvas, just in the shot. The segment scans across the street and settles on the hostage house for a few seconds before a commotion can be heard off-camera. Several voices shout at once: "Stay where you are," "Get down, arms out," and "On your knees." The framing lurches for a moment—crews and journalists running forward have pushed the cameraman aside—but he steadies quickly and clamps his focus on Leonard again—no mistaking him—moving deliberately but calmly toward the waste ground. Red lights are dancing on his coat. His yellow cap is jaunty on his head. He does not look nervous in the least, just walking catlike from the hips. He manages five steps before three men in combats with pixilated faces burst into the shot, like killers from a wildlife film, like hunting dogs. Their duty sticks are drawn. They pounce on him and knock him to the ground with what seems like redundant violence, exactly as the NSF command knew it would. The camera follows Leonard to the ground. Their feet and arms are going in and out. The spoken commentary mentions something about "suspensions," then Leonard is identified again as "the jazz composer and cult musician"—he's pleased with that—and not displeased and not entirely surprised when it is suggested he is "a known associate of the Final Warning faction." He summons up the Clip Save menu on the screen and sends the video to his Austin file. "Bravissimo," he says.

Leonard is exceptionally tired all of a sudden. It has been a surprising and dramatic Sunday. The drama of it is catching up with him. He stretches, rubs his shoulder, rubs his face—he still hasn't shaved or washed, or changed his clothes—rubs his shoulder again. It hurts even more than usual, but it is less troubling. He welcomes it. Overnight, his rotor cuff disorder has ceased being an older man's condition, a sign of the body losing tone and strength and seizing up in premature rigor mortis. Now it has a stirring narrative. It is a young man's injury, a war wound in a way, his scar of opposition to the Reconciliation Summit, a twin of Mr. Perkiss's shattered, noble arm. He can carry it with pride. It's something that the NSF has done to him: "You must have seen the video." He lifts his right arm as high as he can. Yes, the pain is worse. His movement is more restricted than it has ever been. He turns his ouch of pain into an unexaggerated yawn.

Leonard is still on his knees gazing at the telescreen when Francine calls, leaning over the banister in her clean nightclothes, to let him know that finally she has recovered—and is hungry. Hasn't he promised her a brunch in bed when she wakes up, she asks, or has she dreamed it? He thinks for a moment, incorrectly, that he can hear her coming downstairs, that she will catch him out again, praying at the screen, the surfing serf, that she will see the press photographs and the video before he has a chance to prepare her and explain. "I'm bringing it. Go back to bed," he shouts. She's happy to.

Brunch will be a mushroom omelette and grilled tomatoes with finger toast. He'll halve a grapefruit and loosen the segments with a curved knife. He'll make a pot of tea. He'll take great pains to lay her tray attractively, to decorate the plate, to make it clear that he's taking care of her. He'll carry the bag of gifts and cards upstairs with him and sit on the end of the bed to open them. She's bound to sing "Happy Birthday," as she always does, in that pretty voice with which she entertains and educates her kids. It's been the strangest week, he thinks, adding the smell of eggs to the kitchen's residue of strangers' nicotine. A farce. Too much of a farce, maybe, to justify how smug he feels, how pleased he is with his new public image. Who knows what Francine will make of it? She hasn't got an inkling yet. He will try not to exaggerate in his account. Nothing he has done has really made a difference, after all. She could think that, given what has happened since, he might as well have simply picked up the phone Wednesday night and done his duty as a citizen, a compliant and dreary citizen who's never dreamed of Catalonia.

The omelette is ready and on the plate when Leonard lifts the bag of gifts and looks inside. What he sees is startling. Another Sunday shock. He has to steady himself on the kitchen worktop and look again. No, he has not imagined it: one of the envelopes inside is marked with a single word, written in a familiar hand with one of Francine's blue wax crayons. The word is *Unk.* He pushes back the flap—it isn't sealed—and pulls out the card. She's taken an old family photograph from the album in the living room—a picture of the three of them and Frazzle the terrier, labeled "Norfolk, Summer 2017"—and mounted it on an oblong of thin board. Everyone in it is smiling. Even Frazzle has a phlegmy grin. Leonard turns the card over. She has written on the back in capitals and in the style of texts: "HAPPY 50 BDAY—UNKX. ALL OK—VERY SOZ 2 MISS YOU ALL. GOT YR MESSAGE FROM MY FRIENDSHIP BOX. CAME HOME. MUST GO TODAY." No signature but underneath, and written more conventionally, there is a further message: "I Saw You on the News This Morning. Absolutely Star," and then a name—Swallow—a row of kisses, and a cell phone number.

Leonard goes upstairs as quietly as he can—that's not difficult; he's weightless now—and leaves the brunch tray and the canvas bag on the landing table. He wants to find one extra piece of evidence in Celandine's old room before he breaks the news to her mother. Nothing that has happened in Alderbeech can outbid this. He must be certain, though, that the birthday card is not some mighty hoax. He is almost too nervous to enter. He stands at the door and peers inside. Yes, her room does now seem to have her touch to it, her lack of touch, perhaps, her untidiness and negligence.

He picks up the towel from the attic floor. It's damp. It has been used today. It must be damp from her. He feels the bed, not really expecting any warmth to have endured, though on a day like this nothing is impossible. But when he bends to sniff the sheets, he picks up on her smell at once. He's heard it said that our recollections of smell are the last ones to degrade. They outlast visual memories. They outlive sound. What he has not expected is the sudden weight of tears that smelling Celandine rushes to his eyes. It is still the odor of a sweet and fiery teenager, augmented by the smell of shower gel and pajamas, of being young and coming home a bit shamefaced, the scent of Francine once removed, an overwhelming flood of fragrances. He's crying now for everything, not just for Celandine, not only for her mother either, but also for the strange and bumpy ride he's had all week, and for the shortfalls in his life, and for the children of his own he never had, his mother and his sister and his sister's child; he's crying for Lucy Emmerson and even Maxim Lermontov, and for the music, cool and blue, and for the roads less traveled, and for the waste.

The sobs are brief, too heavy to last long. Leonard is laughing soon, once he's cleared his eyes and settled his breathing. Not burglars, then. Not the return of the raiding party after all. He sees it now, sees the front door opening. Celandine comes home with her house keys and turns off the alarm, glad the code has not been changed. She is both disappointed and relieved that there is no one home to argue with, no one there demanding to be hugged and kissed, no dreadful scene. She's worried, though. She's never seen such a mess and mayhem before, not in this house. It must be burglars, she thinks, or some dreadful fight. She pauses for a moment and she listens. But, as her mother would want her to, she battles to stay calm. Everything will be explained. So she settles into a familiar routine. Can it really be eighteen months since she was here, smoking cigarettes downstairs with the extractor on in the kitchen, the only place that it's allowed? She makes herself some coffee and she fixes a meal, disappointed by the unexciting choices in the freezer. And—this is typical—she sits up into the night and watches television. Mum and Unk will return any minute, she thinks, come back a little tipsy from their birthday treat, to find the mess and then to discover their mislaid Celandine, as large as life, at home. "Don't blame me for the mess," she practices to say. "It's not my fault—for once." But finally she goes upstairs to sleep in her own bed. When she wakes this Sunday morning, she comes downstairs and—as she has done countless times since she was a kid and too frightened of the sloping attic shadows of her own room to stay another second there—waits under the low, carved lintel of her mother's bedroom door, listening for signs of life, waiting for the invitation to climb in. Eventually she looks into the room to find that the bed is empty still. Again she sits downstairs, her stomach in a knot. She is no longer calm. She's learned from Unk that unease is not always inappropriate. She fears the worst while waiting for the local bulletin on the News Channel and, God forbid, reports of car crashes or restaurant fires or shootings. The clatter of the circulars and papers falling on the hall mat lifts her spirits for a moment. They're home at last—except they're not. Her anxiety is deepening. She wishes she'd never come. But seeing Unk in the Alderbeech video provides, once she's adjusted to the shock, some comfort and a kind of explanation. Unk's on the news and he's alive, at least. She's free to go. Or else she's too shaken by her fears to stay. And so she collects her little backpack and is relieved to leave the house again. She's made the first move in the peace process in this small Reconciliation Summit of her own. She's left a contact number in the birthday card. Now it's up to *them* to act on it. She picks up the newspapers from the mat, puts them in the wicker bowl, and, not bothering to set the house alarm, steps outside into the street and her own self-regulating life.

Leonard ought to phone his stepchild straightaway. He suspects he ought to phone before he speaks to Francine, just to make sure that it's really not a dream. It still feels like a dream. Instead, he sends a text to the number Celandine has given. He is not being cowardly (tomorrow, Monday, is a working day, and he can then start finally to be a braver man) but being level-headed. It's hard to resurrect an argument by text. Text's far too slow for angry repartee. It's good for brokering a truce. His message is: "THANX CELANDINE, THANX SWALLOW. AT LAST. ITS BEEN TOO LONG. MUST TALK 2 MUM 2DAY. UNK X.

Leonard backs into the bedroom, self-conscious and attentive with the tray. He knows the omelette must be almost cold. Francine is already sitting up, her table light on, her reading glasses perched appealingly on the tip of her nose.

"You're looking very happy with yourself," she says. "You need a shave, of course. But otherwise . . ."

His smile is loose and unconditional. He can't contain it. "Mushroom omelette, ma'am." He puts the tray across her lap, pulls back the curtains to reveal a brightening sky, but not enough sunlight to slant and cast across the bed. He does not stay to watch her eat or to see her find the envelope and birthday card tucked between her saucer and her cup and weighed flat with a silver spoon. He leaves the room and starts to go downstairs, not hurrying. He plumps his lips and parps a short phrase to himself, a new melodic phrase that he must jot down while he remembers it. He attempts some variations and embellishments, but silently. With every step and every note, he expects to hear his Francine crying out. Then he will go back to the room with his loose smile again. They will embrace and—almost, almost—it will be an end and—nearly, nearly—a beginning. The house is shimmering.

17

LUCY EMMERSON HAS KEPT HER PROMISES. She's sent a music file to Leonard's handset. *Davey Davey, Do It Now,* the Jo Bond song. And she has hacked her hair short, a badger cut. She looks like Maria played by Ingrid Bergman in *For Whom the Bell Tolls,* Leonard thinks. She's boyish and defiant. They sit exactly where they sat before, on the wooden bench behind the Woodsman, below the first-floor room where he and Francine made love on Saturday. She's smoking still, but these are manufactured cigarettes today. They look unwieldy and self-conscious compared to her self-rolled skinnies.

"It was such a hum, you know, to watch it all kick off on the TV," she says. "Didn't you just love the name we chose? SOFA. How radiant was that? I really fooled them, didn't I? I think it made the difference. To Dad, I mean."

"What difference?" Leonard does not mean to sound combative, but for a moment he is tempted to own up. Or is it boast? Perhaps she ought to know he's informed on her. After all, it's only because of his timely betrayal that the police felt confident enough to storm the house, assured that there'd be no costly quid pro quo. But who would benefit from owning up? Not Lucy. She's more than happy to believe that her genius has worked.

"A lot of difference," she says. "No, really. Mighty-mighty major much." Her self-confidence is unassailable.

"Like what? I mean . . . I wanna know, is all." He's talking Texan now.

"So, for a start, like . . ." She hesitates, holds up a hand, and spreads her fingers to count off the differences she's made. "No one was hurt because of him. And that's maybe—well, probably—because he was bearing me in mind."

"Protecting your eye and tooth."

"My dad had hostages, but he didn't fire a shot. Not one. Except, you know, to make a point. A warning shot . . . when they were chasing him. He didn't fire a single shot at any*body*. The family walked out of there unscathed." Leonard raises an eyebrow. *Unscathed* is not a word he always likes to hear. "Yes, yes, I know what you're thinking," she continues. "Only unscathed physically. Really shaken up inside, of course. Did you hear, though? The man said they'd all been treated really well, you know, like it was almost fun, a break from work and school. The woman even put on weight, she reckons."

"All that sitting around, I suppose."

"All those pizzas!"

"And you? What difference has it made to you?"

"To us? To me and Dad?"

He nods. That isn't what he means.

"I'm not sure yet. I'll let you know once I've been and visited. If he'll let me visit him. See what he says. I tell myself he's where he has to be. It's not my fault. It worked out for the best. For everyone."

"And you specifically? You could have ended up inside. Conspiracy. Wasting police time. Wasting taxpayers' money."

"I could have shared a cell with Dad. Back to prison for his gal. I was born inside, you know? I'm quite a lag."

"Be serious. Admit that it was risky, at least."

Now it's her turn to raise an eyebrow. She mimes a yawn. "I'm seventeen! This is the sort of thing that daughters do."

"You might have been fined. You'd not be laughing then."

"Well, I suppose. But yes, it's weird. They only read me the riot act. It wasn't even scary. Mum could've done worse. She *has* done worse."

"And that was it?"

"They issued me with an official police caution. Like a school certificate. Passed with distinction, entrance-level conspiracy. I'm going to frame it and hang it on my wall." Her smile seems to have doubled in width since she cut her hair. "I might kidnap myself again and go for degree-level conspiracy. Disappearing is a piece of cake, and fun. Ask Celandine."

"She's Swallow these days."

"Smart move. Smart girl."

"What now?"

"Want another one of those?" Lucy clicks the side of his glass with a fingernail.

Leonard shakes his head. He's feeling light-headed already. And uncomfortable. The yard is filling up with smokers. He's been pointed out and recognized, he thinks. "Let's move."

"Okay. So what do you say now? Take to the Curb with me?" she suggests. "Let's go and shake our fists at the limousines. For Dad."

Leonard looks up at the sky. It's mild and still. No hint of rain or wind today. Francine will not be home till late; she has taken the afternoon off school and is meeting her daughter, on the neutral ground of a gallery bistro. Their first encounter in the flesh since April 24 last year. Francine has taken a bunch of lilies—a womanly and mature gift, not motherly. He can almost sense their tears, their cautious bickering, their boisterous relief at being back in touch. Their house is empty, left alone to its wedges of light and shadow. The burglar alarm is set. He has no convincing reasons to go home just yet. "Why ever not?" he says; it is the second time that Lucy has occasioned him to use this phrase and take the risk. "Let's Take to the Curb. Yup, Lucy Lucy, do it now."

"It's no big deal."

"You're right. It's no big deal," he says. "But we can't all be big-deal firebrands, can we? Still, I guess we should at least stand on the pavement and boo."

She gets up to take his wrists and pull him from the bench.

It's best to go on foot, even though it is more than two kilometers from the pub yard to the nearest point of contact with the curbside vigil. The first part is eerily familiar. It's been walked before, by both of them. Here's where they first met, just down the road from his parked van, his walking shadow clipping her heels. They have to deviate a bit, dipping down a side road, to take their final look at Alderbeech. There's nothing on the waste ground now except the tire-marked, turmoiled earth, peg holes where the marquees were erected, and an urban construction notice, announcing that in two years' time there will be modern landscaped maisonettes here, "Affordable Family Opportunities."

The street itself is daytime quiet: a pair of cats disputing on a wall; a plumber's van; a bouquet of lost balloons deflating in the clutches of a sorbus tree, now stripped of leaves. There is no longer any interest in the hostage house. The family has sold their stories, and they will even sell the house and move out west when they grow tired of all the fuss. There's not a single moving car for the moment, even though Alderbeech is a twenty-minute walk away from the vigil and traffic could move freely if it wanted to. Starting five hundred meters to the south, the police have closed and coned most of the townways. The route between the airport and the Reconciliation Summit has become a Security Exclusion Zone. The first of the sixteen heads of state should be arriving by now and being collected off the runway by their bulletproofed limousines and the motorcycle outriders. The world is watching, alerted by the arrest of the Final Warning cell to the possibility that there could be a shooting or a bomb.

The pavements grow busier as Leonard and Lucy turn away from Alderbeech. They are not exactly thronged with protesters yet, but there are several groups striding purposefully in the same direction as they are. They give the normally unassuming streets the thrilling kind of rationale that Leonard remembers from his teenage years, when he was always there—part of the gathering, though not at the front—for any demonstration of the left. His walk, then and now, assumes a resolute and cocky swing. It says, Get up off your arse like me, and we will change the world. He takes his sun cap out and pulls it down over his hair. It's not that he feels cold. He has decided that the cap can make him brave. Lucy links her arm round his. "Oh, boy, you look so bloody weird," she says. "Leonard, Leon . . . No, I'm gonna call you Unk, okay?"

The first part of her "genius plan" once Leonard "chickened out," she explains as they approach the comrades at the curb, was to cut her hair. She knew "a scalping" would make her almost unrecognizable. Any photograph they had of her or any description that the police might issue was bound to emphasize her mass of thick and bouncy hair. So before she walked out of her mother's house, she took the scissors to herself and "hacked away," only keeping one thick lock for use in her kidnap communiqué.

"If those boneheads had had the brains to look inside the compost bin, right under their noses in our kitchen, they would have found a wodge of it," she says, pleased with herself and her good luck. Then all she had to do was to take the train to Exeter and call "a really solid friend" who had a flat where she could "throw her stuff—for as long as it takes."

"I told you, didn't I?" she says. "Come on, admit it. I promised three days, three days max. And that's exactly what it was. Friday, Saturday, Sunday. Job done."

"I hear the message. I didn't prove to be your really solid friend, okay? And, yes, yes, yes, you were correct about everything. You're such an unbearable little genius," Leonard says, looking straight ahead. "It wasn't Francine, you know. Not only Francine, anyway. It wasn't just a woman thing. I had my own doubts as well."

"Well, that was obvious."

"It was?"

"I think I frightened you."

"I think you did."

"It didn't matter anyway. At least you didn't let on and spoil it all. Except to Mum. And that was good. I hated seeing her at that press conference where she couldn't even speak and looking, you know, so destroyed . . . You took a risk . . ."

Leonard's smiling now, a touch awkwardly. "What else was I supposed to do? Mothers and daughters. It's . . . umbilical. I know the score, more than anyone."

"But it was absolutely radiant to see you being such a maniac when Dad was marched away. Those guys were terrified of you."

"You think?"

"Took three of them to bring you down. I thought I must be dreaming. I couldn't believe it was you. I played it over and over again, slo-mo, freeze frame. I recognized your little cap."

Leonard taps his head.

"Everybody's watching it. You're the man right now. That bit where you were strolling off as if you couldn't give a damn. They're shouting out. They've got their red sights all over your back. It's Dead Man Walking. And you're, like, *cucumber*. Everybody wants to get your music now. All the downloads have been jammed. Did you know that?"

"I heard."

"You can already buy a poster of that photograph. Under the jackboot. And there's a T-shirt on the Web."

"I heard that too. I won't be getting one."

"You ought to, though. A souvenir. You look like Che. You saw the film? That final photograph."

"Except not dead."

"No, not quite dead. What were you hoping to do?"

"What when?"

"When you were running up to Dad."

I wasn't hoping to do anything, he thinks. I was just hurrying, but hurrying forward for a change, heading for the lights instead of for the shadows. I only wanted to be seen. I wanted to be recognized. By Maxim Lermontov. To show my face to him.

"A bit of solidarity," he says. "No more than that."

"No pastarán."

"Exactly so."

Leonard and Lucy reach the vigil just in time and at a point, in the forty-kilometer route that the premiers and presidents will follow, where it is possible to step up to the very edge of the road. The plan is that at exactly 2 p.m. everybody will link hands and Take to the Curb on only one side of the road to form an unbroken, silent, disapproving line between the airport exit (by the Zone superstores, in fact) and the summit gates. Someone has done the adding-up: if the average span of two arms spread wide is about a meter and a half, completion of the vigil line will require about twenty-seven thousand participants. On a Sunday those numbers might be easily achieved, but on a Tuesday afternoon it is bound to be more difficult. Sympathizers have to work or be at school or be at home. Thank goodness that no rain has been forecast. The weather is being supportive of the cause. Nevertheless, the worry remains that there will be gaps in the line, especially in the long, remote, out-of-town stretches at both ends of the route, where the only guaranteed demonstrators will be those in their own vehicles or those bused in by the cleverly acronymed CARS, or Coalition Against the Reconciliation Summit.

Certainly, though, there are enough demonstrators on the section of road where Leonard and Lucy have finished up. At the moment everyone is hanging back, away from the curb, not wanting to dilute the drama of the link by standing in place before the moment comes. It is pleasing to witness such diversity, in sex and age and race, that is. It's odd too to see so many smiling, self-approving faces. Unlike the usual street throngs, where pedestrians are impatient, rushed, ill at ease, harassed, aggressive, fearful, this crowd seems to have a single expression, a mixture of satisfaction and longing. It is an expression that intensifies, a little before the hour, when the groups of policemen gathered in the central reservation spread out in pairs and take up their stations in the nearside gutters of the road, facing the crowds. A moment later the last civilian vehicles—a couple of slow hybrids and, ironically but to cheers, a World Food delivery truck—pass by and the familiar roar of traffic ends. The route is clear, and there is brief silence until the marshals, counting down the seconds, put their playground whistles to their lips and play their single notes. The hour has arrived for Taking to the Curb.

Lucy and Leonard step forward with the rest. It is a scrum at first, but soon thins out, though not enough, as people jockey for a place. Unk and his very nearly goddaughter grip each other's hand. He takes her left; she takes his right; and then they reach out for their nearest comrades in the line. Leonard finds a man about his own age. They nod and smile at each other, acknowledging the embarrassment and in doing so dispersing it. Lucy's neighbor is a tall, pregnant woman in a blue cord coat and garden boots. Her rings clack with Lucy's bracelet as the two link up. There are too many people. Nobody has to stretch their arms. Their shoulders cannot help but touch, competing for a place in line. Many demonstrators need to turn sideways if they want to poke a toe out into the carriageway.

Slowly, imperceptibly, as the minutes pass and the cavalcades of heads of state progress beyond the airport, the pack of participants around Lucy and Leonard starts to tug apart. The gaps between them widen. Their arms begin to lift. Their chests, which have been cramped, expand. It is as if they're being pulled from both far ends by some force that is as strong and out of sight as gravity. It feels like falling. In all those places on the route where numbers are not so high as here, the CARS supporters are reaching out with their fingertips, dragging their companions after them, in order to close the gaps. And every gap that's closed beyond the town is marked by widened arms in town. At last—it seems to take an age—there is a sudden settling. The pressure's off. The final fingertips have touched. The hands have found a decent grip. No one needs telling that the line is complete, that all forty kilometers are now linked up. Everyone can feel it running through them, the kind of fizzing static that generates a shiver in the spine. Now no one dares or even wants to scratch his nose or reach into his pockets when his cell phone sounds. Leonard does not even mind his shoulder pain. His arms have never stretched this far before. He waits with twenty-seven thousand at his side, all hand in hand and ready for the hum of motorbikes and limousines.

18

FRANCINE IS SLEEPING DEEPLY through the night, no longer waiting to be called, no longer sitting up in bed abruptly woken by a silent phone. She has a daughter now. They talk. They meet. They do their best. Life's not perfect, but it's better than it was. She and Nadia stay in touch once in a while—a birthday card, a text, a scrap of news. Lucy and Swallow exchanged an e-mail each and meant to meet in town when they had the time, but time is short when you are young. It's hard enough to stay in touch with people that you've loved.

And as for Leonard Lessing, he is well. Every dawn renews his hope and courage, he still finds. Each day provides a further chance to love his wife and make love to his saxophone. He leaves his instrument case open on the futon downstairs, ready to resume his long affair with music. He is composing and he is practicing again, determined to recapture any confidence he's lost. "Lennie's back in town," his agent says, amazed to find that his client has attracted so many new, young fans so late in life, and so many offers of work. Next week he's in the studio, recording his latest haul of tunes. He has accepted concert dates. He's doing *Desert Island Discs.* He's working on the sound track for a film.

Tonight he's gigging in Brighton at a pacifist benefit, for free. Back in the Factory once again. It's no big deal, he reminds himself. But it's not nothing either. He drives off early, takes the van down the country route, and arrives with enough spare time to walk along the promenade in the dark and practice embouchures and breaths. It won't be long before he's on the stage, all brass and fingertips and bulging throat. The audience will not know what to make of him. He doesn't care. It's Francine that he's performing for again. He's bound to think of her as she was on the night they met, damp, storm-tossed, and slightly drunk in her red coat, sitting in the third row of the gallery.

It's almost time to play. He turns and heads back to the Factory. The tide is dragging shingle off the beach. The saxman cometh and his head is bursting now with jazz.

With thanks to

Roy Fisher (piano)
Gerard Presencer (horns)
Ryan "Chopper" Fisher (guitar)
and Birmingham Jazz

A NOTE ABOUT THE AUTHOR

JIM CRACE is the author of nine previous novels, including, most recently, *The Pesthouse*. *Being Dead* was short-listed for the 1999 Whitbread Fiction Prize and won the U.S. National Book Critics Circle Award for Fiction in 2000. In 1997, *Quarantine* was named the Whitbread Novel of the Year and was short-listed for the Booker Prize. Jim Crace has also received the Whitbread First Novel Prize, the E. M. Forster Award, and the Guardian Fiction Prize. He lives in Birmingham, England.

A NOTE ABOUT THE TYPE

This book was set in a digital version of Monotype Walbaum. The original typeface was created by Justus Erich Walbaum (1768–1839) in 1810. Before becoming a punch cutter with his own type foundries in Goslar and Weimar, he was apprenticed to a confectioner, where he is said to have taught himself engraving, making his own cookie molds using tools made from sword blades. The letterforms were modeled on the "modern" cuts being made at the time by Giambattista Bodoni and the Didot family.